D1046535

Visual artist and author Sophie Kipner grew up in Topanga, CA. A graduate of the University of Southern California, she writes and illustrates her own stories, which have appeared in *Kugelmass: A Journal of Literary Humor*, Amy Ephron's *One for the Table*, *FORTH Magazine* and *The Big Jewel*, and her artwork, most recently her series of blind contour portraits, DONTLIFTUPDONTLOOKDOWN, has been shown and sold internationally. She lives in Los Angeles, and *The Optimist* is her first novel.

www.sophiekipner.com
@sophiekipner

THE OPTIMIST

SOPHIE KIPNER

Unbound

This edition first published in 2017

Unbound
6th Floor Mutual House,
70 Conduit Street, London W1S 2GF
www.unbound.com

All rights reserved

© Sophie Kipner, 2017
Illustrations © Sophie Kipner

The right of Sophie Kipner to be identified as the author
of this work has been asserted in accordance with Section 77 of the Copyright,
Designs and Patents Act 1988. No part of this publication may be copied,
reproduced, stored in a retrieval system, or transmitted, in any form
or by any means without the prior permission of the publisher, nor be
otherwise circulated in any form of binding or cover other than that in
which it is published and without a similar condition being imposed
on the subsequent purchaser.

While every effort has been made to trace the owners of copyright material
reproduced herein, the publisher would like to apologize for any omissions
and will be pleased to incorporate missing acknowledgements
in any further editions.

This is a work of fiction. Characters are products of the author's
imagination and any resemblance to actual people, living or dead,
is entirely coincidental.

Text designed and typeset by Ellipsis, Glasgow

A CIP record for this book is available from the British Library

ISBN 978-1-78352-362-7 (trade hbk)
ISBN 978-1-78352-363-4 (ebook)
ISBN 978-1-78352-364-1 (limited edition)

Printed in Great Britain by Clays Ltd, St Ives Plc

1 3 5 7 9 8 6 4 2

For my brother Harry, my goddaughters Annabel, Oona and Milla, and for James, wherever you may be

With special thanks to Lene Bausager,
Daniel Shellard and Xander Soren

Dear Reader,

The book you are holding came about in a rather different way to most others. It was funded directly by readers through a new website: Unbound. Unbound is the creation of three writers. We started the company because we believed there had to be a better deal for both writers and readers. On the Unbound website, authors share the ideas for the books they want to write directly with readers. If enough of you support the book by pledging for it in advance, we produce a beautifully bound special subscribers' edition and distribute a regular edition and e-book wherever books are sold, in shops and online.

This new way of publishing is actually a very old idea (Samuel Johnson funded his dictionary this way). We're just using the internet to build each writer a network of patrons. Here, at the back of this book, you'll find the names of all the people who made it happen.

Publishing in this way means readers are no longer just passive consumers of the books they buy, and authors are free to write the books they really want. They get a much fairer return too – half the profits their books generate, rather than a tiny percentage of the cover price.

If you're not yet a subscriber, we hope that you'll want to join our publishing revolution and have your name listed in one of our books in the future. To get you started, here is a £5 discount on your first pledge. Just visit unbound.com, make your pledge and type **mrwrong** in the promo code box when you check out.

Thank you for your support,

Dan, Justin and John
Founders, Unbound

The Guest

Harrison Ford called me once and said, 'Make a reservation for two and put it under the name Jonesy.' I didn't understand the occasion but when Harry wanted to do something, I'd learned not to ask questions. I said, 'No problem. See you soon.'

In room 24, I sat for an hour in a dark suite directly in the path of one strong beam of sunlight that forced its way through a hole in the curtains. When Harry came in, instead of noticing the way my milky flesh tones and flashes of strawberry-blonde hair weaved in and out of the single strand of natural light, the way my green eyes shone as if a light bulb were behind them, he asked me who I was, and, 'Why are you sitting there?'

I told him I thought it would be sexy, unusual, charming. He told me to put my clothes back on. 'What do you think this is,' he said. 'A farm?'

Flushed and confused, I hastily threw my blouse over my corset and returned to the front desk from where I had come.

The phone rang again. 'Good afternoon,' I said. 'Hotel Bel-Air, how may I help you?'

*

I lost that job shortly after I got it, but I don't allow myself to sit in regret. What a waste of time that would be! I could spend my life thinking that if I had only shaved my legs or worn a kimono instead of that crazy expensive lingerie, maybe things would have worked out differently, but what good would that do? Harry and I just weren't meant to be in love, and that's okay because I have faith in my ability to bounce back. I was in my early twenties; we all make mistakes when we're young. But I was resilient. Things break, and then they heal. Although, I guess that's not always true because one time I broke my elbow in a trapeze accident and I haven't been able to Chaturanga ever since.

Anyway, Harry was just one story. There have been many.

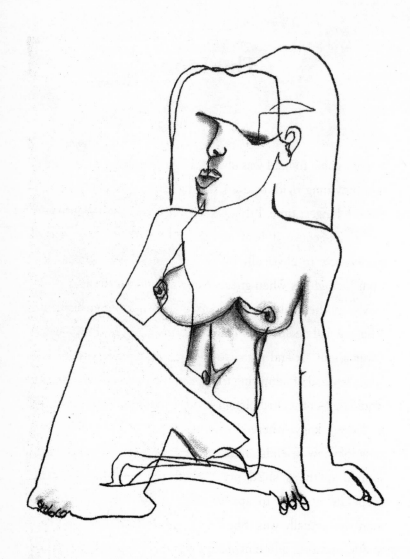

The Lion

I'm not going to lie; I was always a bit of a horny kid, climbing onto anything rigid, or even slightly unrelenting, around me. For the longest time, I thought my heart was located between my legs because it beat and pulsed so much. My mother would have to physically rip me off couch corners and away from Jacuzzi jets when guests came around for dinner.

My mother's always been quite wild and whimsical, but after my dad decided our house was too small for him – when I was about six and my sister nine – she formed a panicked edge. Instead of admitting that I was a free spirit like her, she would self-consciously laugh it off, pretending she didn't get it. 'I don't know where she comes from!' she would say to a slew of new friends, new suitors, with chronically wine-stained teeth as she'd pry me off the furniture in some desperate attempt to appear more maternally conservative than she actually was. She was constantly shifting, you see, erratic, wearing different masks in case it made a difference (it never did). Inevitably, we'd fall down together, our bottoms bouncing across the floor like gently skipping pebbles across a placid lake. In front of a room full of loosened jaws, she'd get up swiftly, like it was nothing but some dust on her shoulder, fluff her black bob, give me a wink, and return to the party, seemingly unscathed.

And that party side of her – that was my favorite. That was when she was most alive. When she was on, she was on full blast. Hot or cold, never lukewarm. She told jokes everyone laughed at and could hold any room with a story. You should hear some of her stories. If she were around someone whom she thought might be able to change her life, her laughing would become increasingly robust. It would tear through walls, that laugh, and she'd use it to cleverly string together awkward silences. This was just one of many ways she knew how to fill gaps. I'd watch her mingle and work the room, throwing herself over eligible men. 'Twilda, baby,' they'd say as she'd corral them with her wit and charisma, her irrefutable charm. But this chameleonic flip-flopping was normal. This was Los Angeles.

Crammed in a small, busy house, my sister, Brenda, and I grew up under my mother's loosely focused eye in Topanga, a treehouse kind of town nestled in the Santa Monica mountains where names like Ocean and Summer are not cool; they're ordinary. I always saw my mother as this colorfully dressed woman who, after one too many burns, wore an ill-fitting black cloak over her outfit, subduing her. You see, after my dad left, she never stopped moving and that franticness –

paired with her staple glass of red wine – made her especially slippery. You knew underneath she was still a modern-art painting, a unicorn, but you didn't know when it would show, so you'd wait as she buoyed between hope and depression. Maybe that was her way of teaching me how to keep a man on his toes.

Contingent upon the crowd, she would vacillate between being sexually free-spirited and neurotically concerned about upholding appearances. On one hand, she'd be too aware of herself, and on the other, she'd encourage us to be expressive and open and comfortable with our bodies, not caring what anyone else thought. Unfortunately, my sister was reserved and I took it too far (I loved being naked and would take my clothes off everywhere I went: supermarkets, toy stores, zoos, even the monasteries we went to when my mother thought she was a Buddhist). So depending on her mood, her reaction to our polar-opposite behavior either impressed or infuriated her. But either way, she never told me to stop. I guess we're all like that. We're all a bit fickle.

Sure, she was messy, but messy was interesting. At the end of the night, when everyone had left, she'd wake me up and lead me to the empty living room, light an American Spirit cigarette and start swaying to Nina Simone and Sam Cooke.

'Why'd everyone leave?' I'd ask, but the wine tipping out of her glass would usually distract me as she waved it through the air. She'd move silently through the room, and I'd copy her from a few steps behind. I spent many nights like this, following her trail of moonlit smoke and dancing in her wake.

'Everyone's just so goddamn boring!' she'd always say when no one stayed.

'Not me, though, right?' I'd ask, just to be sure, hips swaying, finding a groove.

'You could never be boring,' she'd say sweetly. 'You're my baby.' The red wine would always leave a little mark on either side of her mouth, like miniature horns. I loved them so much that I even missed them when they disappeared. Thankfully, she'd never be without them for too long.

My mother became fanatical about Dorothy Parker just before my eleventh birthday and would read her to us in bed. The queen of emotional shrewdness and intelligence had eventually found my mother; the words seducing her with their shared distrust and adoration of love. They soon became her bible. Dorothy's poems took the place of *Goodnight, Moon* and I'd often go to bed confused. Most kids got *The Tale of Peter Rabbit* but I was sent to sleep with lines that would stick to my insides like gum, the most glutinous being: 'Be the one to love the less.' Talk about a goodnight story. So, like we were told of gum, Dorothy's wisdom through my mother's voice would grow inside me into a tree. Leaves would fall but the roots would dig deeper, grasping firmly.

That line, about loving the less, it burnt a hole in me every time she said it because I knew she didn't mean it. It couldn't possibly be sound advice because love is when both people love the more, and I was going to find a man who loved me just as much as I loved him. Our love would be mind-blowing. We'd have to take breaks walking down the street because we'd be so overwhelmed by the amount of love we would have for each other. Our hearts would ache not from loss but because they'd be stretched to their limit in order to hold the limitless expanse that was our love. We'd think there could be no more room inside us left to store it, that we might just burst, but we wouldn't because we're human and we'd adapt. The choice to believe in love is a necessary pre-condition to being able to love. I knew it existed; it's just that my mother had forgotten, and I had to prove her wrong because proving her wrong would be the only way she could be happy again.

So, I did what most children who were trying to save their parents would do: I crawled under the table during dinner parties – back when I was small and undetectable – and played footsie with the guests. It was sort of a matchmaking, Robin Hood kind of expedition, I guess, since my motives were altruistic. I'd spin my forearm around their feet to mimic my mother's foot, just to get the ball rolling. I'd pull back; watch as their toes pushed forward to return the gesture. From there it would usually take off on its own, the back and forth of twirling, searching feet, and it would instill in me a sense of pride and accomplishment because my mother would always think the man had made the first move. Men would, at times, need the encouragement to initiate and that's all I was doing. I was just a catalyst, giving my mother a chance to feel adored again.

It worked in momentary bursts but it didn't have any holding power, and so it was often just the three of us. A house of estrogen. A unit. Before turning off the lights at night, Mom would turn around in one sharp, quick move and ask us, 'And what is our mantra, girls?'

'The cure for boredom is curiosity,' we'd say together in splendid harmony, those pious words of Dorothy Parker, 'but there is no cure for curiosity.' I loved this quote because I'm naturally inquisitive, but when I'd turn to Brenda, she'd just roll her eyes. She didn't get it. In fact, she still doesn't, which is why I nanny her five-year-old daughter, Mary. I have to make sure she believes in magic before my sister's sensibilities get in the way. I'm hoping Mary's temperament is malleable, but one can never be sure.

My quest for personal happiness and that of bringing it to others persisted in myriad ways. A case in point was when I was in my mid teens and I wanted to be a phone-sex operator but my voice was never husky enough. I'd have to just practice on strangers. I'd pick up the phone, dial random numbers and wait for it to ring. And each time it did, it gave me a thrill. Would he be an old, lonely man? Would he be my seventh-grade history teacher, Mr. Hockley? The main problem was that my voice would always come out differently from how I'd anticipated, like everything else in my life. The sound I'd hear in my head was dry and raspy, like I'd been incessantly smoking cigarettes through the night at a full moon party, screaming my head off. But when I'd open my mouth, trying to muster that richly seductive tone, I'd cough. 'Do you have something stuck in your throat?' people would ask me, not realizing it was a PHONE SEX CALL, and, 'Do you need some water?'

I would have thought that sounding like I had something stuck in my throat was a phone sex asset, but something was lost in translation. It was probably a blessing in disguise that they didn't understand the nature of the call since most of the receivers were stay-at-home moms. That could have become really dicey. It's true what they say: the dots always connect in retrospect.

I've had an enviable amount of relationships, all of which would be considered lucky, largely erotic and fantastic by anyone's standards. Some were brief but all were profound, and the good news is that I don't have baggage from them because I just move forward. Some things stick, of course, but that's natural. I might have filled pockets, but phew, no bags.

One of my favorite mentors was a pizza deliveryman I grew up around named Rainbow Dan. He was a bit ominous, spouting truths he'd learned in past lives. We never had an affair because my mother beat me to it, but I couldn't blame her. He was a steal.

'He reminds me of one of my first boyfriends,' my mother

said as her cigarette smoke played with the shape of her face. She was trying to relax on her new brown deluxe sofa but couldn't quite find the right angle. Channeling Goldilocks, she moved from seat to seat.

Milk from across the street was over that day. His name was Milken, but everyone called him Milk. He'd always been across the street, for the most part, for as long as I could remember. He was usually hanging around me, annoying me with his limpness, his awkwardness. He never knew where to put his hands.

We were about eleven, and Milk had been sent to detention after yelling at a girl who was making fun of me. I also was in trouble because, according to Mrs. Wells, I had instigated it. When we got home, Milk sank in the corner while I explained to my mother why. For a moment, my shoulders had slouched like Milk in that seat. She said round shoulders were for victims, and that I wasn't a girl with round shoulders. We weren't victims, but every once in a while something would throw us.

'They called me stupid,' I started, 'because I said Captain Cook found the Cook Islands.'

'How is that stupid?' she said. 'He did.'

'They said I was thinking of Captain Hook, from the movie. Then they all started laughing because I thought he was real.'

This happened a lot in class because I'd often mix up my words. I figured it was because my brain was moving too fast;

12

they thought I was just dumb. My teacher believed I never knew what I was talking about and the students would follow suit, a classic behavior of sheep. Apparently my teacher had never heard of Captain Cook, and therefore assumed I had jumbled my words again, the room quickly erupting in laughter.

'Well,' my mother said, turning to me. 'Are you going to let some mean, little, misinformed kids make *you* feel dumb?'

'No.'

'Where's your backbone?' she added. 'You're Irish!' She started banging on her chest like Tarzan and stamping her feet in rhythm. It was coming to that time of night, and Rainbow Dan had just given her a pick-me-up.

'We smoke, we drink, we fuck, we dance!' she yelled, coaxing Milk and me to repeat.

'We smoke!' we screamed. 'We drink! We fuck! We dance!'

When Milk came to the word *fuck* he'd stop and just mouth it. He could never say it out loud.

'Milk,' I said. 'I know you think you're helping but you're too little to stand up for me. You'll just get hurt.'

Milk's bones hung from their sockets; his feet so big he could barely lift them, which rendered his walk quite clumsy. I'm pretty sure his balls hadn't dropped, either. It wasn't his fault, though; I was used to men. I was used to men like Rainbow Dan.

'Is he your boyfriend?' Milk asked my mom, referring to the man with technicolor pants.

'Oh God, you know I hate to be put in boxes, Milky boy,' she said, dancing away at the thought of him.

'Rainbow Dan's just kinda lame,' Milk interjected. 'He smells like patchouli oil.' I rolled my eyes. He was so young, so clueless. He had no idea that if a man smelled like the Earth it meant he was manly.

'Oh, you're just jealous,' I said. I looked over to my mother for confirmation but she was looking the other way. It was hard to get her attention.

'Dan's like the wind,' she added. 'You can just ride him and he'll take you somewhere.'

You couldn't tell it was only 4:00 in the afternoon because the trees around our house cast blankets of shadows that left us in a perennial state of darkness, save of course for the random laser of light that would pass through the branches. One of them blazed across my mother's face, illuminating the gold in her hazel eyes. They shimmered there on the couch, just like she did – a bright light whose white had yellowed and grayed, stained from years of trying to shine too brightly.

It was so obvious that she was the most luminous of lights for miles, but I could tell she was starting to see it fade. Instead of calming down and decelerating, though, she sped up, as if to counteract it, but it only depleted her more in the end. The thought of not being as dazzling as she'd always been terrified her, so she held on to Rainbow Dan's magic carpet as tightly as she could. I supposed his attention and the hope of what it could become sustained her for as long as he gave it.

'Are you in love?' I asked, hoping to mistake the nervousness that made her hover for the effervescent effect of love, but the phone rang before I got an answer and she was distracted, coiled around his voice like the cord wrapped around her finger. But that was how she loved now; she loved in frenzy.

Every day for a week, Rainbow Dan the deliveryman would show up on my sinuous street in the canyon with no shoes on and those aptly fit multi-colored pants, a loosely buttoned shirt and untamed hair, holding a pizza. No one knew if he had a home, which probably added to his mystery. He literally came every day, so that by the end of the week, pepperoni had taken on a new meaning. My mother, he told me, was addictive. She was that powerful.

'You have two choices in life,' he said as he passed me the box at our front door. 'You can be a sheep, or you can be a lion.'

'Okay,' I said. 'What are you?'

'Are you fucking kidding me?' he said, throwing his head back in a surfer head jerk: think Keanu Reeves. 'I'm a lion prophet. I'm a radical fucking lion.' I already thought his shirt was pretty much unbuttoned but in one shocking move he tore the remaining fastened buttons apart and revealed a giant lion tattoo on his ribcage.

'Oh,' I said. Okay. It was all making sense now. That's when Rainbow Dan reached his dirty hand out and touched my shoulder and stared at me with his stoned blue eyes.

'Your mom?' he added. 'She's a lion.'

It all sounded like more of a bedtime story than what was usually read to me, so when I went to bed that night, I thought about what the prophet lion Rainbow Dan had told me. I realized we were part of a pride. I realized that it was okay if sheep don't like me because, heck, are sheep ever going to like lions? No. Lions don't care what sheep think because they are lions. Being a lion means taking risks, making things happen. Lionesses don't wait for lions to show interest. They sprint and they leap and they pounce onto other lions because they're confident and sexy and powerful. That's how we fall in love.

I gave Rainbow Dan a high five with my right hand because my left was still holding the pizza. I didn't even care if it was pepperoni again; I had a craving for meat. Finally, someone knew what we were. I was going to go out there and own it. I was going to tear the shit out of love and it was going to be exactly what I'd been waiting for. Fuck fading. Screw settling: explosive love prevails! But after Rainbow Dan delivered his last pizza, about seven glorious days later, it became clear that I was back to the beginning: disillusionment had once again broken my mother. We didn't understand how someone could, at one moment, see her as a lion, but at the next let her go.

Some lions, I guessed, were just too wild to hold on to. Maybe it was her skittishness.

Her massively romantic heart had slowed its beating, once again. She'd lived her life so fully that she hadn't anticipated it wouldn't work out for her in the end, and the encroaching banality of a life left alone had attached itself to her. I was surrounded by women, not just my sister and mother but seemingly everyone, single or taken, who had forgotten what they were looking for. They had lost their hope of butterflies because too many people had told them they weren't real, and if they were, they certainly weren't sustainable. I couldn't possibly bear the thought of us settling though, because, well, look at my parents: when you settle, you can still fail.

Dorothy Parker's words were cutting at us, line by line, and I could see my mom couldn't stomach the thought that they might be true. She lived by them, but like an atheist who begins to pray when everything is going downhill, she secretly clung to the possibility that Dorothy's truths were fallible. I think deep down she'd just pretended to disbelieve in love, to be hard and aloof, because the way her eyes lit up with any new prospect indicated her hope was still kicking; it's just that her recovery period was steadily expanding. I knew if I didn't do something, I'd soon lose her.

It wasn't just my mother I was trying to save. It was everyone who'd become jaded. The only ones I knew who weren't emotionally spent and stripped were at my grandma's care home, but they all had dementia so no one would take any notice to what they had to say. One at a time, I would save women and the day would come when we'd all be drinking around a fireplace, laughing with full hearts and our dream men.

Like fixing a symptom in lieu of the cause, I knew that before I could save everyone, I'd have to start with my mother. She was the first domino. And, if Brenda saw that Mom could find love, then she would believe she could, too, and it would start a domino effect, filtering all the way down to Mary. All I needed to do was show my mom that the best wasn't over, that there were other men after my dad who could love her the way she'd always wanted to be loved before her teetering over the edge landed her at the bottom of the well.

The biggest problem was that my mother and sister weren't as optimistic as they needed to be; they didn't try hard enough. They were still lions, like I was, but they couldn't see it anymore. They weren't near enough mirrors to see the reflections I did. That's why I was going to do it where they couldn't. My self-assuredness, my self-awareness, my un-yielding tenacity, my ability to self-reflect, the fact that I didn't have dementia, that's what made me the only one fit for the job.

And it's not that I hadn't already been trying to help my mom. I mean, year after year, I tried. I spent most of my life pumping her up, helping her bounce back and stay optimistic while I was on my own separate path to finding love, because, well, I'd been searching all that time, too. I was busy collecting my own stories. But then I realized those two objectives were actually one and the same. All my years of encouragement didn't seem to be enough, so as we all know that actions speak louder than words, I set out to accomplish my goal of saving my mother by finding love myself. Realizing that her happiness depended on my personal success, not only my encouragement, made my search for love the more fervent. It would be the only way she'd pay attention.

I was okay with being the Braveheart; I knew the rest would fall into place. And when I thought about it, finding love didn't seem too intangible a goal – there were billions of people to choose from.

Turns out, it's difficult to find even one. As each year passes, and as my mother's hope slips away from her like she slipped off that magic carpet ride, I try even harder. The stars and the moon and that sky, how they know I've talked to them, how I've prayed. But, without much result and now at the pivotal age of thirty (an undeniable adult), I must become even more creative than I already have been. I must employ new tactics to look back at what went wrong in the past and integrate those lessons into my strategy going forward. And I better try really damn hard, because at this tipping point, it's our last shot.

It will work out, though; I'm an optimist.

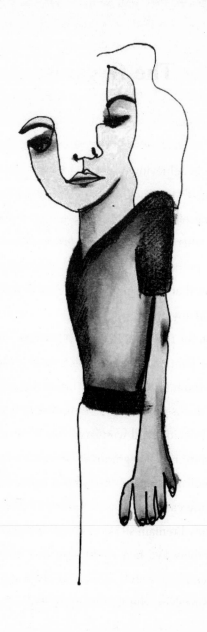

The Organist

The first step in achieving my goal, naturally, is to get a closer look at myself. To take note of the current situation so I have an accurate baseline from which to judge improvement and success. But when I do, I notice too much. The lines around my eyes are pronounced now as I scrutinize them in the mirror. Maybe that's why my mother and sister don't look at their reflection anymore.

The wattage of the light bulb in my bathroom is too high; the light is too light and it makes this small square feel like an interrogation room. I'm under this bright light but no one is watching, no one is surveilling, and it makes me sad. I'd rather be watched, I decide, and wonder if someone is on the other side of the mirror . . . a group of detectives, possibly, or a troupe of medical students studying me because I am the most interesting case they have ever seen. They are trying to understand how I remain so optimistic in the face of adversity. They wonder how I've had no luck in love to date because I'm so fascinating. I watch as my pupils widen and shrink back into themselves, the brown lining the green in varying measure as that said optimism rises and falls with my lungs. My gaze drops to the sides of my temples as I scan the rest of my face. I can't count all the freckles; there are too many.

The shape of my face is the same as it's always been, except the balls in my cheeks have widened, giving me a round look. They used to think, in the old days, that a round face was one of beauty and health. It meant you could afford to eat, that you were rich and could indulge.

Plump faces were also a sign of youth as the aged faces would sag and hollow. If I were alive one hundred and fifty years ago, I'd be a catch. Today, I'm just fat. My hair falls limply over my ears and down my back and it tickles me when I move. Sometimes it makes me laugh out loud, and I wonder if I'm being teased by an affectionate ghost. Then I wonder if my best lover will be this ghost.

Speaking of ghosts, when I was five years old, my best friend was a ghost. She was an organist and her name was Heralda.

Let's just start from the beginning.

Every night I'd wake up at 1 a.m., to the sounds of her playing the organ in my living room. She'd sing and play as I'd dance and we would just sip martinis together, bopping heads. I was too young to drink but that's the benefit of having ghosts as friends. The pretend was real. I'd say, 'Give me a twist, babe,' and she'd hand me a double martini with a lemon twist while I'd do the dance move toward her. Our favorite song to sing was 'I'm Gonna Wash That Man Right Outta My Hair'. Sometimes I'd wonder where the liquid would go because she was a spirit herself.

She usually was quite up, quite bubbly. But one night, if I recall correctly, I noticed something was off. She was clumsier than usual; her chords were slipping.

'Heralda,' I said, exaggerating the emphasis on the A. 'Too much Absolut?'

'I'm sorry,' she replied, her spirit coy. Below Heralda a puddle of vodka collected at her heels. Her tolerance was uncharacteristically low. 'I'm having a harder time than usual feeling the organ.'

I wasn't sure if she was using the word 'feeling' to mean 'vibing with' or because she literally couldn't feel the keys. She just sat facing the organ with slouched shoulders. If she had bones, she'd have scoliosis. She was so sad it was annoying. I had to do something to help her; she needed real love. Everyone deserves it, even ghosts.

'I'm taking you out,' I announced.

'What's the point?' she said, gloomily. 'No one is going to notice me.'

'I see you, Heralda! You may be transparent but I know a ton of men who would love a woman they could see through.'

'Really?'

'Yes!' I said. 'Most women are complicated! Are you picking up what I'm laying down?'

She nodded, although unsure.

'Wait,' I added. 'Can you actually pick up what I'm laying down?'

I had been tearing up pieces of toilet paper in my hands throughout this entire conversation and letting them fall to the floor absentmindedly.

'I've been playing your organ, haven't I?' And that lip? That was so Heralda. She's the one who taught me about sass. My mother was witty; Heralda was sassy. In a perfect world, I embodied both because sass without wit is narcissism.

'How is it that you're able to play instruments or drink martinis when you have no body?'

'It's an energy thing. I can harness it, move things with it. And the alcohol, well that just evaporates after I digest it.' She gave me a wink, ignoring the puddle below her. 'Still does the trick though!' Her ghost shape wobbled around the room in between short bursts of heel-hitting jumping.

This would make finding her a man a whole lot easier than I had initially thought.

'So what age are you looking for?' I asked. 'You must be what, one hundred and fifty years old?'

'Try four hundred,' she said, impressed with herself. 'I exfoliate.'

Of course I couldn't really take her to a bar, because, well, I was five. But the best thing about Heralda was her imagination, so we'd pretend we were going and somehow we were

24

there. When we got to the bar, which was in my kitchen, Heralda was very pleased to have her ID checked. I told her it must be because of that amazing exfoliator. I peered over the bar toward a heavyset bartender with a forest of chest hair sprouting from his shirt. His voice was dry and deep.

Heralda searched the room with nervous eyes. 'I'm having a hard time connecting with anyone,' she whispered to me.

'We just got here!' I said. 'You haven't even tried! Jeez, have some patience!' I looked around and spotted someone. 'Okay, what about him?' I pointed to the bald downtrodden pessimist slumped in the corner. He was balancing a rocks glass brimming with whiskey on his beer belly. It trembled precariously on his fat with the shaky-legged confidence of a hang glider looking over the edge of a cliff before the imminent jump.

He seemed like a good romantic candidate because he obviously didn't care about looks, but I was perplexed as to how this introduction would work. She could see him but he couldn't see her. So I took her into the bathroom and mummified her in toilet paper. She had trouble walking but at least it showed her shape (men love to see some shape). She walked stiffly toward the roly-poly man at the bar and, with my encouragement, attempted to get onto the barstool. It took her a while to find the right angle because the toilet paper kept ripping. Her movements were so unsmooth. It was embarrassing to watch but I just kept smiling and waving to show I was right there, behind her with invisible bells on as her supportive wing woman.

A cloak of equanimity fell over her as she settled next to Mr. Beer Belly in her seat. I could tell from the way the paper relaxed she was calm and confident. He turned to her and looked her up and down, not quite sure what to make of her outfit.

'Are you a ghost?' he asked Heralda, quite casually.

'Yes,' she said. When she spoke, he could hear her but could only see the ripples her breath would make on the thin paper around her mouth.

'I have been fucking holes in toilet paper since I was a little kid,' he said. 'You're like my dream girl.'

Heralda almost fell off the stool. It made me so happy to see. Finally, she'd met someone who didn't just think she was okay, or good enough. She wasn't a 'you'll do.' To him, she was perfect. It felt so good to help her, to help them both.

'What's your name?' she asked.

'Tommy.' He reached out his hand to her hollow paper and held it gently so as to not alter the shape. 'My mama always told me the best things in life are the things you can't see.'

He motioned for her to leave with him, and she slid off the seat with considerable ease. She hobbled over to give me a quick kiss on the cheek goodbye. It took her about ten minutes to walk over to me because she had to take so many little steps. I almost lost my patience but she finally was out of the house and had a chance at love, so I bit my lip and waited. When she eventually got to me, I said, 'Have fun! Remember to be safe. Wear a condom.'

'Jesus, Tabitha!' she said, smiling.

'You've been out of the game a while. People have diseases now.'

'I'm already dead, you moron!'

And that's how Heralda got her spirit back. I felt like a proud mother. Heralda had always been there for me, and now she was all grown up, ready to date, at four hundred, and it was time for me to let her go. Kern River tears collected in my eyes as they walked out of the bar together. She was gone. My drunken little see-through friend was gone.

By the time I got home (just to the other room, since we never actually left the house), I was surprised to see her there in my living room, drinking martinis all by herself.

'What happened with Tommy?' I asked.

'It was all going well on the drive home,' she started. 'But when we got into his house he accidentally stepped on the toilet paper without realizing it. He went to grab a beer from the fridge to "relax and get into the mood" but the paper stuck to his shoe and he unraveled me. By the time he turned around, there was just a pile of goddamned Charmin on the floor.'

Oh shit, I thought. I hadn't anticipated it falling apart so quickly. 'Did he call out for you?'

'Yeah,' she said. 'We played Marco Polo for a good hour before he gave up and hit the sack.'

'Men!' I said, dipping my head back in emphasis.

'Want me to make you one of these bad boys?' she asked, nodding towards her glass.

'Does Dolly Parton sleep on her back?' My mom always said that and so I did, to keep the tradition alive, although it didn't always make sense. Technically, she could sleep on her side, but I never pressed the issue.

I did the twist towards Heralda. There we were again, drinking and laughing together, having a ball.

I'm gonna wash that man right outta my hair, Heralda sang. Usually she sang it for me, but tonight, she was singing it for herself.

She stopped and looked at me. 'Are you going to chime in or what?'

I was so used to singing about myself I forgot it was Heralda's night.

'You're gonna wash that man right outta your hair,' I sang. 'You're gonna wash Tom-my right outta your hair.'

All the drinking made me have to go pee, so I excused myself to go to the bathroom. When I went to wipe, there was no toilet roll left. Just the brown cardboard.

'Heralda!' I yelled. 'Where's the toilet paper gone?'

'Oh, sorry!' she screamed from the other room. I could tell

she was still dancing. 'I thought we might go out again tonight so I set it aside.'

I couldn't blame her. Love is addictive.

Heralda and I went out a few more times but without much luck in finding her a man. It was nice for me, though, having a chance to do something for her, after all she did to help me. Soon, however, Heralda slipped into a depression. I tried all sorts of things: aromatherapy, jokes, optimism, chanting, vitamins, even Cary Grant movies . . . but nothing cheered her up.

One night we got into a fight because she was so upset about being invisible and there was nothing I could do to make her feel better. It was the year before my dad moved out, and I remember going to my parents' room and climbing into their bed. I'd see them sometimes, hugging in their sleep. I was crying so much the skin around my eyes almost swallowed them whole but my dad just pulled me up to bed with them and cuddled me, stroking my hair until I calmed down.

I often think of this memory: of being sandwiched between my mom and dad, protected by the both of them. If I try hard enough, I can feel their legs, touching them at the same time. My mom was asleep, curled on her right side, when my dad told me I should tell Heralda to go away for a while.

'But why?' I asked, the option seemingly unfathomable.

'Because it's not worth being friends with people who bring

you down. You'll never be able to really understand Heralda. You'll try to help her but you never will be able to.' He stopped for a moment, moving his head around the pillow, eyes half closed.

'But she's my friend,' I argued. 'I love her. She doesn't bring me down.'

'Eventually,' he continued, his eyes open now and glassy, 'you get to the point where you just can't carry that weight. It will destroy you. You have to think of yourself, and know that you can't, no matter how hard you try, always make someone else happy.'

'I can't just leave her,' I whimpered. 'What will she do without me?'

'She'll learn to make herself happy. It's the only way to help her. It's for her own good, don't you see? She's staying here and trying to fit in where she never will be able to because she's wanting to be close to you. But it's unfair to her. It's selfish not to let her go.'

'Tabby, baby, why are you awake?' my mother said, groggily, hoping to quiet us.

'Because her best friend is a ghost who is remarkably like her mother,' he snapped, assuming I couldn't hear. 'She's trying to get your attention, Twilda. You're always so up in the clouds you may as well be a ghost, too.'

'I'm not up there,' she said quietly. 'I'm right here. I'm right here.'

That night I lay on my bed and spoke to Heralda before I even saw her appear. It would have been too hard to tell it to her ghost face because, in truth, I didn't want her to go. I wanted her to be happy and for us to drink martinis again and dance around the early morning hours – hours that were just ours.

'Heralda,' I said. 'I love you but you have to leave me alone for a while. You have to get yourself better because I can't help you anymore.' Tears streamed down my face. It felt wrong. I was lying to her because I thought it would help her but it ended up just hurting me. Surely I was quitting her too early, yet every time I battled it, I heard my dad's advice.

'But,' I heard Heralda's voice creep.

'Go, Heralda!' I yelled, mustering up all the courage I had in me. 'Get out of here! I can't be your friend anymore!'

I felt a gust of piercing cold sweep through the room and at once I was left there, silently, alone.

I haven't really had any encounters with Heralda since then. Last one was probably ten years ago, when I was twenty, and then it was only her voice. The one thing I regret in my life was telling her to go away, but I believe she knew it was for her own good. Now, when I think of her, I smile, imagining her being busy, waltzing with some handsome ghost, being exactly who she wanted to be.

I don't usually talk about Heralda too much anymore. Sometimes I bring her up to my mom but she doesn't listen too well these days and usually just says, 'Go get 'em, kid.' Sure, it's great that she's supportive but since it doesn't really relate to the situation, I know she's not paying attention. She'll look at me, wink and then lift the wine glass to her lips while she stirs a comfort soup in the pot. Heralda and my mother were really quite alike. I can see their similarities so clearly now.

I wonder if my dad just gave me bad advice because he couldn't see how great we were, how we were bringing him up, not down. The thought rips through me, giving me shivers, and I try to shake it off, head side to side to blast it, but it lingers. Maybe Heralda wasn't bringing me down, and like Dad did with us, I let her go too quickly.

'What are we having tonight?' I ask my mom.

'Not sure,' she says. 'I'm experimenting.' She loves to experiment.

'What happened to Lewis? I thought he was taking you out.' Lewis is her latest lover.

She lights a cigarette but the smoke is eaten up almost immediately by the hot air rising from the pot. 'Oh him?' she eventually says. 'Who needs him. I've got you. And you, baby girl, you'll never leave.'

It's true. I'll never walk away. Being abandoned before makes you swear you'll never leave because you've tasted the crippling effects it has. You're scarred by the idea that someone, at any moment, might leave you. That's why I pushed and fought until the others walked away. Harrison Ford left because he didn't like lingerie and Heralda left because she had to. I'm not sure why Lewis left my mom, but I know that Rainbow Dan left because she was too untamed and because she didn't always feel like eating pepperoni. If I've learned anything, it's that I'd rather be left than be the one to leave. There's no guilt that way.

Sometimes people have asked me if Heralda was an imaginary friend, not a ghost. *Are you sure she was a real ghost?* they insinuate, questioning my memory. *Of course she was real!* I rebut. *Topanga is full of ghosts!* I wasn't making anything up. I mean, who would make up having friends? In all reality, though, with some distance now from my childhood, I'm just not sure what was real and what wasn't. But either way, would it make a difference?

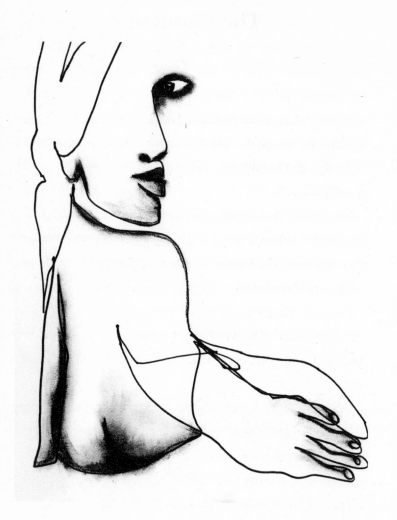

The Gardener

Apparently you can't find true love until you really love and understand yourself, which is great news because as I'm reminiscing, I'm falling in love with myself all over again and it feels so good.

One thing I'm realizing is that I've always had a thing for Mexicans. When I say Mexicans, I mean real Mexicans, from Mexico. The kind of men who inadvertently tickle your neck with their mustache whiskers and breath-heavy accent, calling you names you haven't been called before like *jaina* or turkey slice. The kind of men who peer so deeply into your soul you don't even have to take your clothes off to get wet.

My affinity for Mexicans began at the tender age of nine, when my mother found me seducing the gardener. His name was Ernesto. Brenda, being a few years older than me, wasn't interested in playing when I was interested in playing, which meant I spent the better portion of my childhood learning to play all by myself. The good thing about playing alone is that I would usually win, which was good for my self-esteem. But sometimes winning would get old, so I'd venture out into the garden.

'*Hola*, Ernesto,' I'd say, seesawing my hips. I thought if he saw how my prepubescent joints could move, he'd know I had Latin in me. When I was born I had so much black hair the nurse said, 'I didn't know you had Mexican in your family!' Both my parents were very light-skinned (I think my mother enjoyed the contrast of her porcelain complexion against her jet-black hair; a severity that matched her temperament) but I was convinced my mother had had an affair with the mailman – a beautiful *hombre* named Hector from just outside of Guadalajara. If you saw Hector, you wouldn't blame her. I never saw Hector but I imagined that's what people would have said if they saw him.

Ernesto would look up at me with his sweat-drenched hair, his body curved over his tools, and smile. I imagined being swept up like the remnants of a changing season into the fingers of his rake. He would run his hands through his hair like Kenickie from *Grease*, and send me a little wave. It wasn't much, but it was enough. Sometimes, I've learned, the best things in life are the little things: the waves, the body language, the looks that say more than a date under the Eiffel Tower . . . And I'm not just saying that because I never get taken on dates to the Eiffel Tower! It's simply because they are so much more exciting, and because they're small and bite-sized, you can collect a million of them. I can't imagine how miserable life would be if I didn't live for these moments; sometimes I get sad for all the people who are waiting for the big diamond rings and private jet proposals to be happy, when all they need to see is the beauty in the space they share with someone. Time captured and preserved for as long as you can recall it. I would pretend to catch the love Ernesto passed and tuck it into my pockets as if it were a piece of dark chocolate I could save for later, for some time in the middle of the night when I'd wake up parched and lonely.

He was from Zihuatanejo, this marvelous creature, my Ernesto. I remember melting over the way he'd say it, too. 'Where are you from?' I'd ask him, repeatedly, already knowing the answer, continually hopeful that each time he'd let the 'e' slide in Zihuatanejo: AN-EY-HO. The 'j' becoming an 'h' on his masterful tongue, hopping delicately over those three romantic syllables. Slipping, skipping and sliding into home base. Baseball is boring but I'd be its number one fan if the players could hit like Ernesto.

I would sit in the garden as he watered and fed our plants with fingers that, I was utterly convinced, were designed to do more than just pull weeds. I'd use the old let's-play-waitress card to initiate interaction under the pretense of game-playing, because role-playing is always less threatening. Whenever I'm working with teens struggling with body issues and confidence, I always tell them it's smart to start off with a little role-playing because it makes you feel like an actress.

Men find it really attractive when you're sure of yourself so if you're not sure of yourself, pretend to be someone else (just for the moment). I really love helping women to feel better about themselves.

'How about you play the waiter,' I'd say to Ernesto. 'And then I'll ask you to tell me the daily menu.' At first the game confused him, partly because he didn't know the rules and partly because his English wasn't very good.

'Why is this a fun game?' he'd ask.

'It just is!' I'd sing, unsure of how to answer him when the real answer was because I wanted him to say the names of the things I wanted to eat because food is sweet and sensual and it was one step closer to being in love.

'Look, Ernesto,' I'd continue. 'Sometimes you can't make sense of the heart.'

As he'd contort his face, his whiskers would dance around his nose. It gives me goose bumps just thinking about it!

'But I don't know what's on the menu,' he'd say.

'Oh, Ernesto! Use your imagination!'

This back and forth would happen every time and every time it happened, he would be more and more confused. He'd usually start with really bland specials of the day, like macaroni and cheese. I thought at first this was a cop-out because mac and cheese is never a special dish, but then I caught on that he was probably meaning the gourmet version, with three types of cheeses and truffle oil. Of course, he'd say it in his

Ernesto-way: Ma-Care-Oni. Only a Mexican would know to put the word 'care' in 'macaroni'! That's the kind of attention I'm talking about. My whole day centered around the anticipation of Ernesto, with his coarse but soft, sweet but salty kettle-corn voice, reciting to me the list of specials that would otherwise be so dull and unappetizing.

'Desserts, Ernesto,' I demanded. 'I want to hear the desserts!'

He'd stop, take one of his signature heavy breaths, put a hand on his hip to support his back and say, 'You're something else.'

I was in love with Ernesto. It was the first compliment I ever received from a man of his caliber and let me tell you, a girl doesn't need much more than that to last her a lifetime. How he said CHO-CO-LATE like Dracula. How he'd drench every syllable with a passion the boys at school knew nothing about. I would dream of him and his rich intonations, even count the specials he'd recited earlier backwards to help me fall asleep, like sexy sheep.

But Ernesto was a methodical man. He wanted to start at the beginning and follow through to the end (oh, how I adored him!), but my mother would usually call out from the kitchen right around the time he'd get to the good stuff. On one particular day, when the sun was burning quite brightly, my mother must have been preoccupied getting ready because Ernesto got all the way to tiramisu, or as Ernesto pronounced,

TEERU-MISS-EW (it sounded like he was saying 'miss you'!) before she stuck her head out the window.

'What are you doing in the garden again?' she asked. I fumed, so vexed I could barely walk. 'We're late for your sister's piano recital. Get in the car!'

The car engine puffed as she turned it on, and I crawled in the back seat like a dog that knew it was going to the vet. I was sad to leave my Ernesto behind but I used the opportunity to practice my princess wave.

'Why are you waving to Ernesto like that?' my mother asked, more rhetorically than anything else because, if you knew my mother, she never cared about the answer. She was in one of her more neurotic, absent states. She started hearing less after the divorce, said she couldn't handle the extraneous chatter because she had to concentrate all her brain space on hating my dad.

'We're in love,' I said as I pulled my hand back, wondering if she'd lash out at the word.

'It's good you're exploring your sexuality,' she said. 'A real woman knows how to harness it, but you're still so young. I guess you're just ahead of the curve.' She paused, preparing to make the switch from compliment to parental advice.

'But,' she continued, 'just remember he's a man. He won't get it unless you spell it out. Men are like uneducated adults at a reading center. All they see are letters, they can't put them together until you say the words you want them to say.'

'You mean Ernesto might not know we are in love?'

'They never do, baby girl. They never do.'

'So how do you tell them?' I asked.

'All I'm saying is you can't wait for a man to make the first move. You can't wait for him to be romantic or do all the things you know you want because they'll never think to. You have to make the magic happen. You have to tackle them and literally make them see how amazing you are or else they never will.'

'But you and Dad,' I started, 'did he ever try to make the romance happen?' I knew the story, but some part of me wished it were different every time.

'Your father?' she huffed. 'Are you kidding me? He didn't have a romantic thought in his head. I had to come up with all the ideas but he still didn't do them. Even after I'd tell him! He was boring. Gave up because he couldn't handle the pressure of giving a goddamn about magic. I tried and tried to get him to dance with me after midnight, you know how we do? But he'd always stop after a song and say he was tired!'

Ernesto just looked at me through the car window, eyebrows furrowed and collected in the small of his forehead in confusion as we backed out of the driveway. It was okay that he didn't know how to respond, because I hadn't coached him. Maybe my mom didn't try hard enough with Dad, so I figured I'd have to try just that bit harder with Ernesto. I closed my eyes and pictured myself wrestling in a well-groomed garden with him as he told me things in Spanish I didn't understand, like the words for pruning and mulch. Words I didn't even understand in English but had every confidence that in Spanish they'd mean so much more. I fantasized about all the feelings he'd have in his native tongue that I didn't have the words for in English.

At the recital, all I could think about was how Ernesto told me he missed me. So one day shortly after, as his gardening duties were coming to a close at our house, I crawled into the back of his pickup truck and buried myself in soil. Thinking about it now, in retrospect, it was crazy; I should never have used soil! It was so dirty! It was early evening and the sun was nearing its settle. The scary thing was not knowing where I was going, but I trusted Ernesto and this was the only way I was going to get him alone.

I felt the car stopping. Spanish was flying all over the place like spaghetti in a New Jersey dining room, which made me nervous. I waited until I knew we were home and not just at a gas station. I thought maybe this could have been a bad idea; this soil was probably so far up my daisy I'd never get it out. But then I thought: Thank God Ernesto is a gardener! The tarp was above me; it was pitch black and I was starting to feel really nauseous from the smell of the manure. It made me feel dizzy and I nodded off for a moment. When I woke up, I couldn't remember if I was being abducted or if it was my decision to be in the back of a pickup truck but then I remembered it was definitely my choice and making my own decisions made me feel powerful.

I waited as long as I could, until I couldn't take it any more, and then I tossed the tarp off and popped out like I was the surprise in a cake, my arms extended wide and hopeful. 'Surprise!' I shouted, out of instinct, but no one was there to witness it. I went up to the front door and climbed along the ridge of the bushes to get a peek into the living room and saw – to my horror – Ernesto sharing a moment with his wife. His WIFE. I felt cheated on. I wanted to bash the window in and ask her what she was doing with my man but I couldn't move my arms. They were clasping on to the concrete so tightly it was as if they had their own little brains with their own little tiny self-conscious and they just didn't want to let go.

Through the dirty window, I saw Ernesto stroke his wife's hair so tenderly it was like he was caressing a rose petal. I was so envious I felt the sick start to crawl into my esophagus but I kept swallowing to keep it down, despite my gag reflex. His fingers caressed her hair with such love I could almost taste it from the outside. They ran down her dark chocolate locks and wove in toward her nape, grabbing it firmly as he pulled her in for a kiss. I had never seen anything so beautiful before. I tried to imagine myself being his wife, what it would be like to have him in my bed each night and wake up to him each morning, but that felt a little creepy so I just continued to watch them through the window. His gaze was dreamy as her body seemed to collapse in his embrace. It was just too perfect. Too gorgeous and delicious a moment to witness that I had this epiphany: I wanted love like that. I guess I knew I wanted love with Ernesto but I had no idea what that would entail until seeing it up close. I wanted Mexican love. I wanted romantic love that filled me with so much happiness it would feel like I exploded from the inside out and all of my parts would be scattered around the room in disarray. I wanted love to blow up my heart like it was going to war against reality. The world was so bright and colorful and full of potential. It was so exciting that I went to clap my hands in delight at the thought of being loved by a Mexican who knew how to give it, but I forgot that I was three feet higher than the ground, lurching on the edge of their window.

'Ah!' I screamed as I fell backwards onto a bed of what I unpleasantly discovered were actually rose bushes.

When I looked up I saw Ernesto and his beautiful (sigh) wife peering down at me in confusion through the window.

'Tabitha?' Ernesto said, clearly quite perplexed as to why I was in his garden. 'What are you doing here?'

'I came to see you,' I said.

'Why?'

Why? Ha! He was such a joker! Oh, Ernesto! He was obviously quite shy and didn't want to ruin his marriage by admitting that he was in love with me as well, all of which I totally understood. In fact, I didn't want him to tell the truth because it would have hurt her. That would have been so cruel and I don't believe in cruelty, so all I could say was, 'I wanted to know what was for dessert today.'

I begged, internally, for him to tell me he had some sort of Mexican confection, or that I was for dessert, that he'd eat me, but he just said, 'How did you get here?'

'I jumped in the back of your truck.'

'Are you crazy?' he sighed. 'You could have gotten yourself hurt, little girl.'

Sometimes I would forget I was little until it was pointed out, because I felt so big. I was so much bigger than myself, like a compact Border terrier who barks at the big dogs because he thinks he's as big as his wolfhound best friend. I didn't have a bigger best friend but I think you get the picture.

'Your mother must be so worried,' his wife said. Her voice creamy and inviting, like a female Ernesto. I could have married her, too.

'Ernesto,' she added. 'Call her mother so she doesn't worry she's been kidnapped!'

He held out his hand to help me up but the minute I moved I realized I was wedged between thorns, digging at me, reminding me how much more painful this situation could have been if I hadn't let go when I did.

I went inside and sat on the couch while Ernesto called my mother.

'Twilda, hi,' he started, unsure. 'It's Ernesto. I have Tabitha here.'

'Who?' I heard her say through the phone.

I heard him try to explain to her that I was there but it sounded like she was drunk because he kept repeating himself, as if she wasn't understanding the problem. 'Okay!' I kept hearing her say, the word sounding so joyful it was as if Ernesto had said he'd do her garden for free for an entire year. At least she was happy. That was a good sign.

'I'll bring her home now,' he said before hanging up.

For the first part of the car ride home I just sat quietly in the front seat next to him, looking out the window because that's what women do in the movies when things aren't going well with their lives. Eventually he looked over at me and broke the silence.

'Is everything okay?' he asked. 'You know, at home?'

'Yeah,' I said. 'Of course. Why?'

'It's just your mother, she . . .'

'Oh, she's fine!' I said. 'Did she sound tired? She's been really tired lately. She's a single parent, you know? Two babies.'

'But you're nine,' he said, throwing me off.

'Well she calls me *baby* all the time. Anyway, I'm pretty mature for my age, but we can be a little . . . wild!' I couldn't stop blushing but he didn't say anything. He just kept his eyes on the road ahead.

'I'm glad you didn't want your wife to know,' I said. 'That would have been really difficult for her.'

'Know what?' he asked.

I rolled my eyes. 'That we're in love!'

'We're what?' he blurted, swerving, almost crashing. 'Tabitha, we're not in love. I love Cynthia, my wife. I'm too old for you anyway. Aren't there a ton of guys your age to be in love with?'

Men my age? Oh Ernesto, sweet Ernesto, he just didn't understand. It wasn't even about men, it was about him. Chemistry like that can't be made in a laboratory. I tried to concentrate on what I wanted but all I could think about was how Cynthia didn't sound too Mexican a name and that I still may have a chance.

'I want to be Mexican!' I shouted. 'You know, I might even be Mexican, by birth.'

He knew the truth: I wasn't Mexican. My hair eventually turned a sort of sandy blonde so maybe my mother never had that affair with Hector, the mailman, all those years ago as I had wondered, as I had hoped. It was just my wishful thinking. I really am my father's daughter.

I wondered sometimes what my father was doing: Did he have another family by now? Did he eat shellfish without getting a reaction on his tongue? Did he take walks after dinner with his new wife, hand in hand, as the cool evening breeze tickled their skin like I wished Ernesto would tickle me with his mustache?

I waited. Holding my breath, searching, biting the insides of my cheeks, itching to get to the heart of it: 'Is it because I'm not Mexican?'

'Tabitha,' Ernesto said, laughing. 'Of course not! That's the silliest thing I've ever heard from you . . . and that's saying a lot.'

'My teacher says there are no stupid questions,' I said. Now upset.

'That's a good point,' he said, his voice softening my hard corners. 'That wasn't a silly question. Just a little ridiculous.'

We rode in silence for the rest of the car journey. The only problem in seeing Ernesto and his wife so deeply in love was that I became overwhelmed with affection for them both. Maybe the 'care' was never in his macaroni, but I didn't want it anymore after seeing him in his living-room light. Okay . . . That's a lie: I did, but I would heal.

When we walked into the house, my mother hardly noticed we were there. She was in the corner of the kitchen on the phone with the cord wrapped around her body in dizzying patterns while she stirred duck in a thick stew with a long wooden stick her mother used to use. She was giggling into the phone.

'She's talking to her new boyfriend,' I explained. 'He's fat.

But she says it's nice to have something warm to hold on to and I totally know what she means.'

Ernesto nodded. Mom waved a healthy wave once she saw us and freed her stew-stirring hand to top up her wine glass. She was so good at multi-tasking.

'Okay, kid,' my Ernesto said. 'Be good. I'll see you soon. And stop searching for love. One day you'll have so much of it you won't know what to do with it.'

That was the moment I discovered I could have a lifetime of what Ernesto and his wife had. A lifetime of sex with Mexican lovers who would touch my hair and grab my neck and tell me they loved me until they had no breath left in them. Maybe the Mexicans would lead me to the Caucasians and the beautiful black men and Arab and Asian men and all of the men who would eventually lead me to the one who would love me the most and never let me go. I mean, if Ernesto let me go, he must really love his wife because, well, look at me! But I am so glad he did. I'm so relieved because if I hadn't seen the love he had with his wife, I might never have known it was out there.

The smell of the stew was so potent it danced around the house. Stew is what my mother cooked for us when she was trying to be motherly and comforting. The rest of the house was dark except for the light emanating from the kitchen and my bedroom. I wondered how it would look from the other side of the street. I wondered what Ernesto's house looked like at that exact moment, how many rooms were lit. I got mad at myself for not having looked from the other side of the street when I was there but I was too close to the window to be able to see what it looked like from afar.

I sat at the end of the bed, on the corner where the peg was – my favorite place – and looked out the window to Milk's house. He was in his parents' room, also sat on the end of the bed as his dad walked around the room, moving his hands, talking. Father and son. I looked around for Paige, his mother, but didn't see any other lights on. She probably wasn't back from work yet. Milk saw me looking at them and waved to me, from one home to another. I did love a good wave, as I've admitted, and sometimes he'd look kind of cute but he was just too white, too pretty almost, too unnervingly gentle. I wanted rough and tough but soft with me; I wanted spicy with a kick of sweet. Milk just wasn't Mexican enough. It would be too weird.

'Tabitha!' my mother screamed in a high-pitched voice. 'Dinner!'

My mother sat at the far end of the table. Her face seemed a bit bloated but she said that people bloat when they are about to feel really happy. It was what she called 'Anticipatory Bloat.' I wanted her to ask me about Ernesto and our love. I wanted her to ask me about my heart and what my heart would look like in ten years but all she asked me was if I liked the stew.

'It's very . . . hearty,' I said, stuck on the word like my fingers clenched to that windowsill. 'I have one question, though.'

She nodded for me to go on, ask away.

'Did you ever tell Dad you wanted him to touch your hair, to kiss your neck? Maybe you just didn't spell it out enough?'

'I asked him every day for years,' she sighed, talking as if on autopilot, mesmerized by her cooking. 'But the bastard never did.'

'Why not?'

'Because he said he didn't want to because I had asked. Said it wasn't a surprise if I asked him to, to let him do it organically because when you tell someone to do something, it takes all the goodness away from it. He'd get into a mood and never wanted to do anything because he felt like I asked for everything before he'd have the chance to do it. But did he? No! Isn't that ridiculous?' I nodded. 'I'd tell him to just fucking do it so I didn't have to ask.'

'Yeah,' I said, supporting her, having her back because no one else had ours. 'Like flowers, right? He'd never bring you flowers because he knew you wanted him to.'

'Right,' she said. 'It's like asking for flowers. You blow it for-ever the minute you ask.'

'But,' I started, unable to drop it. 'He acted like he loved you, though. I remember you both kissing a lot. I remember seeing him watch you get ready and you both laughing with each other, teasing and playing. I remember it so well.'

'You only remember a part of it. You only remember the good times. It wasn't always fun.'

'So it's supposed to always be exciting?'

'Well, yeah,' she told me. 'Or else it feels like death.'

'I didn't know you could die from boredom.'

'Look around,' my mother noted. 'People are dead everywhere.'

As I watched my mother pour herself another glass of wine, I wondered if she would have turned out differently if she had only been with Hector, the mailman. I thought about how her soups may have tasted if she knew that kind of love. She always thought she found it, but it would evaporate before she could grasp it fully and bottle it up. It was another way my mother reminded me of Heralda: just a couple of swinging broads, tragically unable to keep a hold of anything solid.

Life is like making soup. Sometimes, even if you follow the recipe, it can turn out watery and weak but you have to remember that as long as you start off with good stock, you can always add to it; it's never too late. My mother's approach to cooking varied daily. Some days she'd follow the recipe too closely or not at all. Sometimes she'd experiment, wine and spices mixed and matched. A little paprika here, a dash of cumin there. Sumac if she was feeling especially wild. Sometimes it would result in an epic fail but sometimes the results were spectacular.

I do think the best things happen to me when I just think

outside the box and do my own thing. I go with my gut, and it's usually right. RIRs, or Rules, Instructions and Recipes, are so average, so expected! They're just recipes for life disasters. I couldn't go to sleep that night because I was so riled up about all the soups I'd make in my life, the meals I'd serve the men who would have my heart and how they'd probably tell me to stop looking at them when they tasted my soups because I'd want to see every twitch and expression on their face. I'd want to witness it all so badly I'd be too scared to look away in fear of missing the upward lift of the lip, the first smile.

Ernesto stopped working for our family about a week after I jumped in the back of his truck. Maybe his wife picked up on our chemistry and banned him from coming back. Sometimes I'd go into the garden when my mother wasn't looking and when the sun was extra bright the rays would make out his shape. A vision. Angel Ernesto, whose faint outline reminded me that there was still a man out there who could put the care in my macaroni.

Since then I've had affairs with three Mexicans, but they weren't Ernesto. One of them was even a gardener, but he didn't understand how to play the waitress game. When I was seventeen, I picked up a guy named Carlos in the alley behind a McDonald's in Canoga Park. He had part of his eyebrows shaved off in patterns. Kind of a dreamboat, being both a fighter and a Mexican.

'Was that intentional or more of a fight by-product?' I asked him, not wasting any time.

'You kinda coo-coo, yeah?' he replied.

'Where's that accent from?'

'East LA,' he said. Damn.

'You are Mexican, though, aren't you?'

Carlos looked at me without blinking and didn't move at all. I wondered if we were engaging in a blinking contest but I blink profusely so I dropped it, blinking, knowing I'd never win.

'Can I see your eyebrows a bit closer?' I asked as I leaned in, hoping it was a good way to get in close, to smell him, taste his Latin gangsterness and protection.

As expected, it drove me wild. I kissed the bald spots in his eyebrows hoping my lips would magically make the hair grow back because there was so much love behind them. But they didn't.

I moved in even closer because I thought maybe he needed to know I was signaling a green light. I hoisted my leg over one side of his hips, as we were standing up, and threw my arms around him, imagining he were Ernesto and we were finally reunited. I tried to dry hump him from this peculiar angle – I was pretty resourceful – and noticed he was really hard. Like super-hard, harder than anything I've ever felt before. I started to giggle, playing shy.

'Is that a gun in your pocket or are you just happy to see me?' I said, channeling Mae West, laughing at my own joke. But he didn't laugh. His glare was just stern, serious, unimpressed.

The space between us became immensely cold and he shoved me back and whipped a real gun out of his pant pocket with frightening speed.

'Holy shit!' I screamed. 'You really do have a gun in your pocket!'

He started at me and I jumped in fright. This wasn't fun anymore. I escaped down the dark alleyway towards the streetlights, the sound of his snicker drowning out the further I ran.

'Run, Forrest!' he yelled, laughing callously. 'Run, little *puta!*'

By the time I reached my car, I was panting really hard, pissed off that finally I was panting but for the wrong reason. I looked around and spotted some Mexicans but it didn't elicit a reaction between my legs: Nothing pulsed, nothing beat. It was dead. That was when I knew I'd reached the end of my love affair with Mexicans.

As I retraced the steps I'd taken a thousand times from my car to my house, I thought about how each time I've walked those steps, I've been different. Same steps, new me. Some people may think I'm going backwards, or in circles, but they're just going the other direction so they can't tell I'm progressing.

I'm wiser now, after all these relationships. Sure, I wish I'd ended up with Ernesto, but it was a successful adventure: I learned not to sit in soil without underwear and that all people don't tongue each other like dishwashers, that real love exists and that Mexicans may or may not be the only ones who know this. I learned that sometimes men have metal guns in their pockets instead of hard-ons. I thought about what would have happened if I hadn't run away after Carlos pulled his Glock out. Would it have been one of those scenes in a movie when the man makes love to the woman with a gun to her head, but you knew she loved it? Or would it have ended badly?

Before I went in, I stood on the other side of the street, looking over at my house as if I didn't live there. There was just one lamp on, the one cowering in the kitchen. I wanted to scream and shout and light balls of enthusiasm and throw them through our windows into our living room so our whole house would ignite. I couldn't take it being so dark.

When I opened the door, I saw my mother sitting alone in the living room, her legs curled up to protect her heart. She was crying, which meant one of two things: One, she was heartbroken, or two, she had had too much wine and the ad for adopting abandoned dogs had come on TV with Sarah McLachlan's 'Angel' tugging at the world's heartstrings in the background. I was pretty sure it was number one.

'Mom,' I said.

She looked over at me with eyes so heavy her spine might

56

have collapsed under the weight of them. I remembered what Ernesto told me all those years ago and how good it had made me feel. There I was again, wanting to encourage her and let her know that we were so close and that she was perfect and to not give up because it wasn't her fault men couldn't see how amazing she was. I was too young then to realize that my reassurance had no weight because I hadn't found what she was looking for, either.

'Your heart is like a Christmas tree,' I told her. 'Right now it doesn't have any lights on and it seems sad and lonely, but soon you're going to shine and sparkle. You're going to have so much glitter and drip with so many love ornaments people are going to have to wear sunglasses to look at you.'

'I'll be that sparkly?' she said, lighting up. 'That bright?'

Yep, I nodded. 'You're even going to need another outlet to plug all the fairy lights in.'

She smiled and summoned me to join her on the couch, both our knees hugging our chests and our hearts and our bodies. I had forgotten about Ernesto and Carlos and about the past because the future was looking so good. We nestled into each other, tightly curled. Part of me hated that she was sad, but her needing my comfort warmed us both. Once she knew love again, in the way I was going to prove it to her, she'd want to be this close to me without a reason. I couldn't wait for her not to need it. I couldn't wait for her to want my attention, my love, just because.

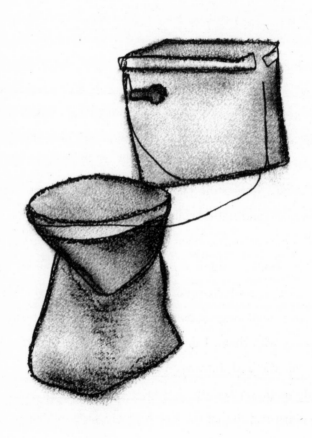

The Date

When I was eighteen years old and in my senior year at Malibu High School, I completely ended my obsession with Mexicans. And it wasn't just because of the men; it was because of the food.

This was during the period of time when my mother discovered gin and started collecting a wide variety of birds, most of which were, unsurprisingly, lovebirds. She had birdcages all over the house; I think at one point there were about ten of them, each of which were busy with all sorts of singing and tweeting, imploring us, as my mother noted, to just 'sing and fly' away with them. I didn't even need to see the writing on the wall; the bird shit was all over the floor.

My mother asked me if I was going to go to prom; clearly she didn't realize that the last thing I wanted to do was spend time with people my own age. Most women like older Ωmen, am I right? Younger men, or men my age, just lacked the wherewithal older men possessed. I tried to give them a chance but it just never felt right inside, where it's supposed to. My sister married a guy her own age and, besides their adorably insane by-product, it didn't end so sweetly.

'I don't know, baby,' my mother said, brushing the hair out of her face with her shoulder because there were no hands free. She was full of bird. 'I just feel that maybe going to prom is one of those things you do to mark the beginning of a new time. It's partly ridiculous but I also think that the twee factor is quite alluring. You shouldn't say no to things like that.' She paused to whistle, watching the birds flit about. She'd let them fly around the house for a while during the afternoons as she'd throw back a Klonopin with a chaser of that newly beloved gin. And she wondered why no one ever came by anymore.

This whistling as she worked invited the tale of Snow White to take hold. But instead of calming us, it just made the whole situation more chaotic. Whistling and flying birds in an enclosed space is a frightening combination. It was like living in Hitchcock's *The Birds*. Ducking and weaving, like Ali, punching the air in fright, blocking shapes and shadows. 'Maybe Milk could take you, as friends?'

'Oh come on, Mom,' I said. 'First of all, yeah right. Second of all, no way. Third of all, he's got a girlfriend or something, so I'm pretty sure he's not available. Besides, I thought you'd hate the convention of prom and anything so expected.'

'I do,' she said, stopping to whistle as she dusted, a bird on her head and shoulder while another peeked out of her dressing gown, 'but I also think you shouldn't ever rule anything out.' Again, very confusing advice to receive. No wonder I am the way I am. It's as if I've had no choice. 'Oh!' she yelled, scaring off some birds into flight. 'You and Bridget should go together. I loved going to dances with girlfriends. A real "fuck you" to society!'

'Well, it's not so risqué anymore, Mom,' I said. 'A lot of people go with friends.'

'Whatever,' she huffed, nuzzling a docile beak.

I went into my room and shut the door, picked up the phone and called Bridget.

'Hello?'

'Hi Bridge!' I said, hopeful. Eager, possibly too eager-sounding since I didn't really care about prom anyway. It was definitely too conventional for me, but I just hated the thought of missing out. 'Who are you going to prom with?'

'Um,' she started. 'Jordan.'

'I thought you broke up?'

'Well, we're back together. Are you going?'

'I'm not sure. Was kind of hoping to go with you.'

'I'll see you there, though,' she said. 'It's gonna be fun, but maybe it would be kind of awkward if you went alone?'

The idea of getting dressed up to feel uncomfortable wasn't my idea of an ideal night. I wanted a friend to go with but Bridget was taken already. I went downstairs and found my mother watching *The X Files* on TV too loudly.

'I'm not going,' I told her.

'Why?' she muttered. 'Because you have no one to go with?'

'Exactly.'

'When has that ever stopped you from doing anything?' Ugh. I hated it when she was right. She was only half listening because she loved David Duchovny and never could look away when he was talking. Sometimes she told me it was like he was talking to her. And she believed it.

She stopped for a moment while Gillian Anderson was speaking and added, 'I thought you loved dancing alone anyway. What's the big deal?'

'I do have some pride, you know,' I said. 'So annoying that Milk has a date. He never has dates and now when I need him, he's busy. Typical!'

My mom rolled her eyes as a commercial break came on, taking her out of her dream world with David.

'If I were you,' she started, 'I'd go as a social experiment. See how people interacted, like you were a spy or something. A body language spy . . . how fun!'

'Actually,' I said, 'that's a great idea. That way I'm learning, and the best case situation, I meet an amazing guy in the parking lot who might happen to be walking by who needs a dance partner or something.' In truth, I hated dancing alone because it reminded me of my mother after everyone left her parties. That's partly why I'd always join in: I didn't want her to be dancing by herself.

'There we go!' she yelped. 'My baby, the optimist!'

THE OPTIMIST

*

On my way to the prom, I was so happy I pulled over at a little Mexican joint along Pacific Coast Highway. The dance was just up the road in Malibu, so I had time for a quick stop. I wouldn't be eating all night so I needed to make sure I had sustenance to keep me going. I ordered three shrimp tacos with extra sauce because I love a little spice.

Man, those tacos were really good, but not when you're trying to be stealth, slithering across a lawn outside a community-center-turned-prom-destination with a bloated stomach. I felt like a fat James Bond.

I wore a satin dress just in case I met someone wonderful, but since the dress was somewhat tight, I had no leeway to wiggle. It was like trying to mountain climb with my thighs taped together. A mermaid on land. They're not prepared for that shit; carrying dead weight is a bitch. If I'd known how tough this was going to be, I would have started doing pushups a month earlier in preparation.

I stopped just on top of a little grassy mound in view of the crowds inside. The community center was brand new, with huge glass windows all around so people could see the ocean, which of course was in my favor because what let them see out let me see in. A few boys in twelfth grade were drinking out of brown paper bags off to the side. Younger boys might fool their chaperones but they certainly didn't fool me!

I saw Milk laughing with a group of friends, his hand on the back of his 'date' as if he were just being gentle but boy oh boy, he had no idea about body language. Zero seducing skills.

Instead of getting annoyed, I realized that this was my first field study in body language, although clearly I already knew more than they did. I took out my binoculars from my purse to get a better look. Milk's date was playing coy, laughing into her chest like she lost something in her cleavage. Everyone was clueless.

Taking in the gestures around the room, I realized that not everyone was touching his date so tenderly as Milk had been. Some were eating each other's faces; some looked (and it could just be because they were far away) as if they were eating each other's hair. But for the most part, I watched couples slow dancing at arms' length, as if syphilis could be caught from a pant leg. I watched as others dirty danced like they were Patrick Swayze and Jennifer Grey. I witnessed K-Ci & JoJo making even the hardest people soft with their song 'All My Life.' The cold ocean air highlighted the drool that was falling out of my mouth. There was so much, I must have been slobbering for a while. I hated it when that happened; I was such a goddamned hopeless romantic.

Body language is a peculiar thing to study. Most of my subjects were pulling all sorts of weird tricks out of their hats. They did things such as stroking backs, like Milk did to his date, tossing hair over shoulders, giving each other evil eyes – thinking that was sexy, laughing when everyone else laughed, crossing legs, uncrossing legs, pretending to be Sharon Stone in *Fatal Attraction*. How ridiculous. Apparently, I was the only one who knew how to flirt and they all needed a bit of a lesson.

My study was then violently interrupted when a gurgle came from where my Mexican food had made its home. It boiled inside for a while, painfully moving around, pushing air pockets. Making waves. I gasped as each gurgle settled into the lower part of my stomach. Silence. Phew. Then: my abs tightened and all at once I knew I had to find a toilet. Oh shit. Literally.

With all my strength I held onto myself, my insides, and hobbled across the grassy lawn, past brown-bag-drinking seniors, through congregating chatty Cathys, through the raucousness that is the high-school prom, to the bathroom. There was only one restroom. Fuck.

I waited outside the occupied toilet for a moment. Flush. Water. Dryer. Open. I ran in, accidentally pushing the guy on his way out and shut the door before anyone else could see me, hoping for a quick visit and swift return to the mound from where I left. But the minute I pulled up my dress, I realized my return wouldn't be so fast. All of my insides felt like they fled me at once. How did this happen? Why now? Oh yes, I know why. Tacos. Not just any tacos: shrimp tacos. Not just one, but three. And not just any sauce: spicy sauce. Very spicy sauce.

I could hear people start to gather outside the door. Some knocked. I heard a lot of 'Someone's been in there for-ever!' and 'Come on, I gotta piss!' I'd say those were the nicest comments. I kept flushing the toilet to try to swallow up the sounds as food poisoning took a nasty, crippling hold on me. Drained me. Again, literally.

Every time I thought I was finished and stood up to pull my dress down, thinking the worst was over, that I was okay, that it had all passed, my body betrayed me and I was right back down, dress up. Dying. I looked at my watch and realized I'd been in there for about thirty minutes. I desperately tried to clench, stay taut, but I couldn't. I was sweating from feeling sick and hot and embarrassed and stressed that everyone was knocking on the door, waiting, anticipating. Sweat from dreading the moment I walked out and everyone saw who had clogged up the only toilet at prom. A prom I wasn't even officially at.

Another knock. 'Are you okay?' a voice said. I think it was a teacher. Someone had called the adults in. It was serious. Anger was building. Bubbling. About to burst. 'Do you need help? You've been in there a while.'

'I'm fine,' I replied, but flushed the toilet again as I said it, drowning me out. I hoped that the flush would dissolve the smell too. I was so panicked, looking around for a way out. I had to escape. I was too ashamed for everyone to know it was me in there.

I spotted a small window behind me, pulled myself away from the toilet seat as fast as I could before another pang attacked me, and jumped up in my dress to the window as my legs dangled. Holding onto the window ledge with all my strength, my legs searched blindly below for something to help hoist myself up. I was halfway through the window before I realized I was stuck, half in, half out, like a turtle's head querying from its shell, when my stomach began again to rumble.

There I was: trapped, halfway through a window in a bathroom, in a prom dress, sweltering in a vicious battle with food-poisoning-induced diarrhea, exhausted, when I looked up and saw Milk, drinking a beer in the back of the building. His mother had just been diagnosed with cancer, so he was drinking a little bit more. You become cavalier about life when you realize it doesn't make sense anyway.

'Tabby?' he asked, confused but tender.

'Hi,' I said, still halfway out, as if it were no big deal.

'I know you like to do things your own way, but the door might be an easier way to get out.'

He walked over to me, staring, hands on his hips. I could tell he smelt what I smelt, but he didn't turn his nose up.

'I'm stuck,' I confessed, 'and I have a very upset stomach. Everyone's been waiting for the bathroom for like an hour. I can't go out the door. It's really bad, Milk.'

He leaned in a bit and reached out his hand as the door was now being kicked.

'This is bullshit!' some girl yelled.

'Come on,' he said as he pulled me through the window. It wasn't what one would call a graceful exit. 'I'll drive you home quickly.'

'But what about your date?' I asked.

'I'll be back in a minute. She won't even notice I'm gone.'

I fluffed my hair, as if that helped, as I gathered myself into an upright position. Milk told me to hold on a second as he walked around the building and into the main room. I followed in his shadow, sneaking around the side of the walls, so I could get a look at what he was doing.

When I peeked around the corner, trying to stay out of sight, I saw a horde of people standing outside the toilet. The door still shut. Locked. Milk walked right through them, gently pushing them to the side, and kicked the door wide open to an empty room. A Tabby-free toilet.

'No one's been in there, guys. It must have been locked accidentally from the inside,' he said, gesturing forward. 'It's all yours now.' Everyone was confused.

I saw him go up to his date, and whisper into her ear. I wondered what he was saying. I felt so stupid, too self-aware for my own good. He had to save me from myself; the worst feeling ever. I could barely look at him anymore.

He changed the subject as soon as we got in the car.

'So you like her?' I asked him. 'I'm sorry you had to leave her to help me. It's prom. You'll miss out.'

'It's fine,' he said. 'I'm not missing anything. And honestly, it's just a school dance. I can't wait to be done with high school.'

'Well, I owe you,' I said, looking down, wanting to crawl under the car seat and hide. 'Hey, are you okay to drive?'

'Yeah, I just had one beer.' He looked over at me for a second.

'Get your eyes back on the road!' I screamed, pointing. Smiling. Relieved I was out of there. Still woozy.

'So what happened?'

'Tony's Taco Shack happened,' I said.

'Oh, man.' He laughed and reached over to comfort me but ended up just messing my hair around. 'The worst is over.'

Milk stopped by the drugstore on the way back to my house and picked me up a bottle of Pepto-Bismol while I ran inside to use their toilet. I couldn't even hold it until I got home. It was that bad. He never mentioned how he opened the door from the outside to show the others no one was in there. He never mentioned how he covered for me, got me out of Dodge. Helped me to save face without anyone else finding out. The only problem was that even though no one else knew, he knew.

'Thanks, Milk,' I said as I skulked out of his car. 'Are you going back?'

'Yeah,' he said, his cheeks lifting into that smile. 'It wouldn't be very nice of me to leave Heather alone at prom. I'll call you in the morning to check on you.'

As he drove off, I felt an unnervingly empty feeling. It shook me, the thought of wanting Milk to stay. The thought of being sad he'd gone back to take care of someone else. Did I have a crush on Milk? I imagined kissing him and shook my head, no. Shivers. It felt weird, because he was my friend. He was little Milk. It was strange, though; I couldn't stop thinking about it.

The front door was unlocked and I caught my mom coddling and cosseting one of her many birds. I hated seeing her at home on a Saturday night. I wanted to walk in and find her gone, happy.

'You've chosen birds over beards,' I said.

'Birds are safer,' she told me. She didn't believe it really. The minute a good beard walked into her life, though, she'd change her mind. That is, until he'd change his and she'd be back to birds again. And gin. And wine.

My stomach rumbled and I buckled over.

'What's wrong?' she said casually, sort of examining me, sort of paying attention, but not really.

'The most embarrassing thing happened tonight,' I said, holding my stomach, still in my prom dress.

'Oh, that's right,' she started, forgetting why I was out, 'and how'd it go? Learn anything about body language?'

'I learned to never eat Mexican food before getting into a tight outfit, especially shrimp tacos.'

'Oh, but they're so good!'

'Mom! It was really, really, really embarrassing because there was only one toilet and I was in there forever. People were pounding on the door and could hear everything. Milk saved me and drove me home.'

'So you got the shits,' she said. 'You're human!' She pet along one of the green lovebird's beaks, thinking it was cute when it bit back. 'That's nice of Milk,' she added.

'I'm so upset that he knew I had diarrhea and saw me like that, at my lowest point. It was awful!'

'I'm not going to lie: it is quite embarrassing. But just thank the stars that it was only in front of a friend. Thank God it wasn't in front of a potential lover! Now that would have been really mortifying!'

'Why? I mean, isn't it a good sign to be able to be yourself in front of the love of your life, warts and all?'

'Oh God no!' she screamed. 'They'd go running!'

'But this is confusing. You always tell me to forget what everyone else thinks.'

'Forget what everyone else thinks *except* the person you're in love with.'

My stomach started moving again and I could feel it coming. I took a swig of Pepto-Bismol and raced to the bathroom down the hall. I sat there, dress on the floor, thinking about how I guess having Milk see me in such a terrible light was a blessing in disguise because it ruled him out of being the love of my life.

I was so mortified in front of him, how could I ever be with someone who had seen me like that? I heard these things happen when you've been with someone for a while, when you've been married for a long time, but it's a real buzzkill if it happens *before* you even start dating. So, that's how Milk was out.

The Waiter

High school feels like yesterday, only it was twelve years ago, and while I've had many, many adventures since and accumulated an array of captivating stories to tell at parties, I still haven't found what I'm looking for (obviously). Things are moving forward, though. Just last week, for example, I had a delicious reconnection with a waiter named Simon.

The day began simply, as many do, with Superman proposing to me on horseback – yes, he was actually on one knee on the back of a horse. It was amazing; his balance was just superb! – when I felt a wild vibration between my legs. At first I didn't know if Superman was slipping me one but when I finally awoke I realized it was, unfortunately, just my phone ringing.

'I need your help,' Brenda said when I answered. My sister has this sixth sense of interrupting me at the worst moments. I was in my bedroom spread out on the floor in the corpse position, arms out wide like I was making snow angels. I'd been listening to Jeremy Irons read *Lolita* on audiotape. His voice so smooth and sexy, it must have drawn me into a deep coma, but Lord oh Lord, what a coma it was. Sometimes I think about how wonderful it would be to be married to a man who has a great voice like that. All you'd have to do when you'd stress out is close your eyes and his voice would guide you into a world wherein magically gnarled green trees and Sambuca were the staple features. I pulled out my journal and jotted a note down before I forgot: Find a voiceover actor.

'Sure,' I said. 'What is it?' But I didn't need to ask; it was always about Mary.

Thirty minutes later I arrived at their house. Brenda opened the door, placed her hands on my shoulders and looked me straight in the eyes. One of her eyes drooped more than the other, which made me tilt my head to make up for the difference. People called me Taco Neck because when we were together I had my head cocked this way, the space between my neck and shoulder looking like that great Mexican corn shell. Maybe I *am* Mexican?

'Thank you,' she said, looking almost cross-eyed she was so tired. 'Thank you, thank you, thank you.'

'I bought you some eye cream,' I said.

'Do I look that bad?' I handed it to her along with a grin that I stole off Mary and she just stared at me a beat too long with her giant vacant eyes, being quite the philistine she so often loves to be. I think it's to get her out of accusation's way because she's just always like that. She doesn't smile because you're supposed to smile; she doesn't give cues that she likes you to make you feel better about yourself. But you know, it's not maleficent. It's just that that's Brenda.

'Cedars is breaking me down.' She was referring to the hospital she's nursed at, Cedars Sinai, for the past eight years. 'We're short on staff this week, so I have to work overtime.'

'Can't you call in sick?' I suggested. 'You need some rest, girl.'

'You can't just call in sick when you're tired, Tabby. People are dying.'

'Oh, right.'

Thinking I was slow on the uptake, she continued, 'I'd like to live in your world. It's like nothing negative exists and there are no consequences.'

'Oh there are definitely consequences!' At last, we arrived at a breaking moment; we were bonding. I turned in for a hug.

'Listen,' she said, patting my shoulder as I felt her cheek tear away from me. Like I was diseased and the closer she got, the more likely it was that she'd get something. 'Marlo's had some sort of . . .' she paused, took a breath, continued, '. . . some catastrophe with his new girlfriend.' At this she rolled her eyes, her hands finding their way back to their natural groove on her hips. 'Which means he can't send me money for Mary this month.'

'Bastard!'

'Yeah, well, that's life,' she said. Brenda's birthday was

September 19; astrologers would describe her as hard as a
Virgo. She says she only has time for toast in the mornings but
always pushes the minutes by adding a layer of smooth peanut
butter on top. Once I asked her why smooth over crunchy and
she said it's because her life is rocky enough. The path of least
resistance turns out to be choosing smooth nut butter. No
wonder why I love chunky. Now if I could only find a man to
say that.

'I don't really think that's *life*. I mean, it's not supposed to
be so hard. Why do you think it's so torturous for us – you
know, Mom, you and me – to find a guy who wants to stick
around? We're such great catches; I don't get it.' As I said this,
I noticed my eyes flitting around the room, around Brenda,
her shape, then into the corners. Searching.

'Great catches, huh?' she laughed. 'Anyway, why are you in
such a rush? It doesn't get any better.'

'Oh, Brenda! You know that's not true. I mean, something's
gotta kick in soon. All my friends are married and happy. I'm
not desperate or anything, I'm just ready. Julia doesn't think so
but I am. I really am.'

'You're delusional. If you think about it, who of our friends
is married with children who is totally, one hundred per cent
confident she married the man of her dreams? I wouldn't be
able to be married to any of them.'

'That's because you're not supposed to be with those men,'

I said, sagacity and wisdom emanating from my armpits like the patchouli oil once drifted from Rainbow Dan. 'I just don't think you can compare relationships.'

'You know what Stephanie asked me the other day?' she said. 'She asked me, how do we know if we're settling or if we just have high expectations?'

'What did you say?' I noticed a picture on the wall of her condo. It was of three girls laughing on the end of a jetty on some nameless lake, framed and sitting at the bottom of the beige-carpeted stairs. My sister would pick up random paintings from garage sales every now and then, probably hoping it would activate some lost memory of a functional childhood. After Dad left, we became a unit. But the more my mom crashed and burned with love, and the more my sister became realistic, the more separated we became. Finding the love we all wanted would get us back together, stitch back the pieces that had been torn away. But instead of how the picture looked like the three of us, my mom, Brenda and I, all I could think about was how I hated carpet, how it make me so itchy.

'I said you should have figured that out before you had three kids!' My sister said I was crazy all the time but still talks to me in a way that makes me know she wants my advice. I think it's because she needs the constant infusion of optimism.

'Good point.' I knew why I dated everyone I've dated and

never have felt that there was the right one who got away or that I had settled at any point. They've all been right, even if they were wrong.

'But what about us?' I asked her, because she was still my big sister. She was still supposed to know the answers to everything.

Brenda's breath rolled out of her, head first through the diaphragm. 'Some of us are just unlucky in love. It's something you have to get used to.'

'Oh, I'm not sure about that,' I said. 'There has to be a reason why we're having a hard time. Everything works out in the end though, right?'

'Despite your lack of actual relationship experience, and that most of the time you have no idea what you're talking about, I'm hoping you're right.'

'Why do you think you and Marlo didn't work out?'

'I don't know,' she said. 'People change. And sometimes they forget to tell you. Then you wake up with someone you don't know.'

'That's so sad.'

'Anyway, the point is that I can't pay you as much as I usually do.'

'So how long is this going to last? What am I supposed to do?' I asked, as if she'd know.

'Get another job and just babysit your niece because you love her? I don't know. That's for you to figure out. I have a five-year-old to raise. Don't you think it's time you lived on your own? Maybe it's a good opportunity for you to get serious, get a real job, move out.'

'Move out?' I exclaimed. 'I'm getting my sea legs. It's just temporary. I'm thinking of doing more work for teens with confidence issues. I'm loving giving them that power back. It's really fulfilling.'

'I'm sure you're giving them *really* great advice,' she said, sarcastically. 'Anyway, thank you for helping me with Mary while I work these extra hours.'

'I don't know why you thank me,' I said. 'It's my job. Well, it's one of my jobs.'

'First of all, it's your only job because you've been fired from every other one and this is the only way you can make money without being accused of seducing everyone who walks in the door.'

One minute she's telling me to get a job, and the next she's telling me why I'll never be able to get one. I've been nannying for my sister for the past few years since I do tend to fall in love with a lot of the people I work with. The problem with that, albeit delightfully sexy, is that eventually it gets positively tricky in the workplace. I've been back at my mom's house for a while now, and I know I'm not supposed to admit it but it's so fun! Just like the old days – same house, same room, same street – and with Brenda just twenty minutes away, some-times it feels like we never grew up. One might assume, since

I live at home, that I have an exorbitant amount of extra spending money due to paying no rent. This is not true as I do contribute to the house. I buy most of the groceries. I even buy toilet paper now because I'm growing up and learning about closure. But with the economic crash, moving out has become an unforeseeable action, at least for the time being.

I lived by myself for a year in college with a roommate named Rufus. He was from South Central and everything I did annoyed him so we eventually grew apart. He said it was because I never remembered to buy toilet paper, but I think it was because I'd shower late at night and it would always wake him up. Admittedly, I hated buying toilet paper because it would remind me of Heralda and make me sad. I lived in New York for a year as well, when I was about twenty-five – just after I graduated college – and I sold gemstones in the diamond district. I knew absolutely nothing about jewelry but my dad's sister connected me with a guy who had a friend who needed someone to help him run his shop. He was sixty and fabulously gay, chihuahua in hand, scarves to match, always with a good hair day. More of a gem than the most sparkling of stones he could find. The juxtaposition between him, the horny Russian perverts and the Hasidic Jewish families who sold diamonds in the rest of the building was like a sitcom. Anyway, back to Brenda.

'They were romantic affairs,' I proclaimed. 'Flings of passion.'

'Psychotic persuasions and violations of personal space, I think were their words.'

'At least I'm not boring,' I said. 'You'll get it one day. Anyway, it's not like you have it figured out.'

I absolutely love Mary; she's the only one who really gets me. And with the job: I knew I'd find something; things always work out. Not having job security was scary, though, so I started perusing Facebook because that's what I do when I'm fake depressed. But really it was because I'll be turning thirty-one next week and have just realized that I've never really, truly, totally, both ways had a boyfriend. I say 'both ways', because, in all fairness, I'm not sure if any of them knew we were having an affair. In retrospect, now that I have more dating wisdom, I would bet they didn't. I'm an alpha lion. It's hard for me to step back and let them take the lead even though I know a man needs to be a man. I just want to make sure it works out so desperately I get a little excited, that's all.

'Mary!' Brenda yelled out, face tilting upstairs. 'Your favorite aunt is here!'

I could hear the pitter patter of tiny legs as she vacuumed herself towards the top of the railing from her playroom, yelling, 'But she's my only aunt!' as she tumbled downstairs. I braced myself at the end of the staircase to take her impending fall and the two of us rolled backwards into a heap. When I opened my eyes, she was laughing. 'Ready to play?'

'Hey, Tabby?' Brenda said just as she was exiting. 'Forgot to mention . . . Mom and I have to go to this fundraiser, charity event thing in a few weeks, I think it's the night of the twenty-eighth, and—'

'—sure, I'll look after Mary,' I said before she could finish.

'No, I mean, I want you to come with me. I need you. Otherwise I'll be stuck talking to all the girls who I went to high school with who are now happily married. I won't survive.'

My astonishment quivered into a smile as I pieced this all together; long has it been since I've been asked to go anywhere. Let alone with my sister.

'Oh!' I screamed, unable to settle the bubbles inside me. 'I'd love to!'

'Who do you think we should ask to look after Mary?' she added. 'I was thinking Milk?'

Milk moved back home about a year ago. I didn't see him for years, partly because we were both off at college and living our lives, being free birds, flying, growing. I can't remember much except that he went off traveling for a while. He called it 'backpacking' or something. Rode camels, lived in tents, you know, how they do. I saw him a handful of times when he'd come to visit, but now that he's back living with his dad again it feels like he never left. I forget that he's my age and we're not still kids. He's a great guy, I just worry sometimes that he's not getting out there and dating enough. He's never going to find the girl of his dreams if he just sits in that house all day.

'Do you think he'd want to? I don't think he's looked after kids before.'

'Oh come on! He's about a thousand times more responsible than you and Mary loves him.'

'How's that sound, Mary?' I asked her. She was still on top of me, counting her fingers.

'I love Milk!' she screamed. 'Can I ask Randall to come too?'

'Who's Randall?' Brenda and I asked.

'He's my best friend in the whole, whole, whole world.'

'Oh,' I said. 'Then of course you can. I'll have to meet him first, though, you know, just to suss him out. I don't want you hanging out with predators.'

She jumped off of me and started whizzing around the house screaming 'Yay!' in dizzying repetition until I had to literally hunt her down, turn her upside down, and shake her side to side until she couldn't laugh or speak anymore. She screamed at first but it was a game we usually played; I pretended to shake the coins out of her pant pockets despite her insistence she had no money.

'It's only Sunday, silly beans,' I said. 'We can tell Randall to ask his parents when I pick you up from school this week.' She nodded but as I let her down, she fell like a towel into a mound of discombobulated parts; legs and arms sticking out randomly until she re-oriented herself.

'I have to run,' Brenda said, moving around the room like a crazed hen. It's one of the only traits I see that proves she really is from my mother.

I hugged her with both arms, the way you want to be hugged. I hate when people give me a half hug, or worse: a pat! Her hair smelled like a Pantene Pro-V commercial, clean and hopeful, the ends grazing my shoulders. Tickling me. I started to laugh and it was weird, my laughing. So I stopped.

'And please, no stories that will give Mary nightmares or get her beaten up at school if she repeats them tomorrow.' She lifted her forehead, staring intently at me until either I agreed or her face peeled back permanently. I loved it when she did this; it was like a contest, this fascinating ability to contort her face, and I'd watch in amazement for as long as I could, pretending like I didn't know what she was talking about.

'I have no idea what you're talking about. You put your daughter in my hands because you know I'll shape her into a beautiful young woman, like us.'

At this she flung her body down in exasperation towards the floor. 'I'm a terrible mother,' she said to herself, head shaking side to side as her hands cupped around her eyes in a forward bend. 'I'm a terrible mother. A terrible mother.'

'Oh stop,' I said, smiling. 'You're a great mom and a very

caring sister working incredibly hard to take care of us all. And I promise I won't teach her anything she'll get arrested for.'

'Okay,' she growled, but it wasn't scary. It was like a cute little baby bear. 'I'm out. Have fun. I'll be home from work late. Double shifts have single-handedly ruined my life.'

'Wouldn't it be double-handedly?'

'For a moron, you're pretty clever sometimes,' she added just before she slammed the door shut behind her.

Mary, who had presumably needed a costume change, ran out from the other room wearing a princess nightdress decorated with remnants of a sparkle party that had taken place earlier that morning. She stared at me, hands limp at her sides, and extended the line of her smile. Somehow her smile is always straight. It doesn't curve up at the sides like other people's smiles. When Mary smiles, it looks like she is about to hug you or kill you.

Mary had forgotten her social graces because she charged towards me, looked at my belly and said, 'You're pregnant!'

She always says things like this after her mom leaves.

'What?' I said. I looked down and saw what now appeared to be a bump from last night's burrito truck indulgence. Goddammit, Mexican food problems again. I never learn!

'I'm not pregnant!' I screamed. 'It's a food baby!'

'Are you sure?' She was stirring me. Probing me. Insulting me for not being where I was already supposed to be.

85

'Unless it happened in my sleep with Superman, I'm pretty sure I'm not having a baby.'

'Yay!' she whirled, completely ignoring me. 'I love Superman! What if it's a boy? Maybe he could be my boyfriend one day. When he's older. Or I could be his big sister. We could tell everyone he's my little brother. That's so cute!'

'You're so weird,' I said.

'I want to play a game now,' she announced, making it very clear that the day was going to be on her terms. I followed her reluctantly into her playroom where I was instructed to sit down, 'Now!' The problem in spending so much time with a five-year-old is that you can't help but have an effect on them. Naturally, after hearing my stories about playing waitress, she wants to do it all the time. Of course it's nice to be idolized but it's not as much fun when you're not in control.

'Where?' I asked. 'The whole room's covered in glitter.'

But that wasn't really a response she tolerated. 'Sit down,' she said.

I sat down. At least I could sit down. With my legs bent in an Indian sitting position, I let my belly fold out. I do look pregnant. Holy cow, this little shitcake was right.

'What are we playing then?'

'Pizza Party,' she instructed. Kids love fake pizza parlors. I can't blame her though as I couldn't get enough of them when I was young, either, but then again who could have known if it was the game or Ernesto that kept me coming back. 'I'm going to take your order and when I ask you what you want, you're going to tell me what you want on your pizza. Okay?'

'Okay.'

I loved this game.

Now, instead of my voice asking for the order, it was Mary's. 'Are you ready?' she called out, making sure I was still paying attention.

God, I really do look pregnant, I thought. 'Of course,' I said, wondering why she'd question me. She had left the room and closed the door with her pen and paper in hand, only to turn around and re-enter. A clean slate, I supposed. I can respect that. She put on her half smile and approached me with determined steps.

'Hello. Welcome to my pizza restaurant.'

'Okay,' I said. 'Well . . . I'll have a pepperoni pizza with olives, cheese and tomatoes.'

'We're sold out of pizzas,' she said.

'What?'

'We just sold our last pizza. We're out.'

'But this is a pizza restaurant. An imaginary pizza restaurant.' She started to cry like a kid. 'Stop crying!'

'I'm only five!' she said. 'I'm allowed to cry!'

'Okay, okay. Jesus, Mary. What else do you have then? I'll take anything you suggest.'

'Well, you're too late now. The kitchen's closed.'

*

Mary held my hand as we walked at a pace too quick for her little legs to keep up with, forcing her body to lean forward with such diagonal force she looked like she would face-plant at any moment if she wasn't holding my hand. She kept telling me to stop laughing but I couldn't. I shouldn't laugh at children but sometimes I just can't help it.

Finally we arrived at the Tiny Horse, my favorite restaurant on Beverly Boulevard in Larchmont Village. Women in tight-fitting yoga outfits scurried past us, clutching on to their yoga mats and designer bags in an effort to not be late for Vinnie's class, the yoga God.

I peered into the cafe for a glimpse of Simon, the man with whom I've had a magical exchange for years. I was sticking my neck out so much it started to ache.

'You look like an ostrich!' Mary shouted. As I turned around, I lightly flicked her shoulder but then, just as she was about to scream, I put my fingers to my lips and shushed her. This made her understandably furious but sometimes you just have to do something drastic to make your point. When I turned back around, Simon was walking towards me.

'Hi, Lola,' he said, a notch too dimly, clearly a case of trying to cover up his excitement. I reminded myself that I was a catch. A ribbon-prize, a grouper, not your average trout or snapper. 'Take a seat and I'll come over in a minute.'

'Who's Lola?' Mary said. She's such a ball-buster.

I laughed out loud, negating her comment to throw Simon off. Sometimes you have to pretend you're someone else just for a little while to get a man's attention. Like a hook, I used interesting names.

There were two reasons why I frequented the aptly named Tiny Horse Cafe: 1. It was tiny, which meant the tables were fitted quite snugly against each other. Conversations were never more than half an arm's length away. There were no horses, but Simon was a stallion so the name made perfect sense. If you saw him, you'd agree. He had short curly blond hair and looked South African. I had this instinct that he was from Johannesburg even though he said he was from Indiana.

'I think Simon used to be a doctor,' I told Mary.

'Why do you think that?'

'We used to be lovers in a past life,' I said. 'I was doing some sort of Peace Corp work under the sweltering orange glow of the African sun, living in tents and feeling better about my life because I didn't have AIDS like everyone else around me.'

'What's AIDS?' she asked.

'Mary, focus! It's not an important part of the story. Can I go on?'

She nodded.

'So one day a South African doctor, ahem, Simon, dropped into camp to provide medical relief to the villagers. My memory of this past life is a little foggy so bear with me . . . He saw me feeding milk to some starving children and I knew that was the moment he fell for me. Their little stomachs were so empty. They were so helpless and gorgeous and their skin was so soft and mousse-like. At once I wanted to volunteer to save all the hungry children around the world. I could become the president of UNICEF (imagine all the doctors I'd meet there!). I had this primal urge to feed and nourish not just their bodies, but their self-esteem, and not just with milk but with love. I remember thinking it just wasn't possible, because I was scared I didn't have enough love to give – they needed so much and there were so many of them – but then one of the little kids looked at me with her huge, bulging eyes and said, "Of course it's possible; you can't run out of love."'

'Wow!' Mary said, impressed.

'Amazing, right?' I wondered at that moment if that's what parents of multiple children think: that after the first baby there couldn't possibly be more love in them to go around and that at some point the second and third and fourth child would get less love, but that is totally a myth. There is always more love! Amen.

'The story gets even better,' I said. 'One night Simon couldn't sleep and saw my lamp still flickering in my tent so he wandered over and snuck in. He told me he could hear rhinos and was scared to sleep alone. Then he asked if he could sleep with me.'

'Okay,' she said. 'Was he a prince? Because you can sleep with princes.'

'Who told you that?'

'Lucy from school.'

'No,' I said. 'He wasn't a prince. He was a talented doctor. Anyway, when he came in his clothes were dripping wet from sweat so he started to undress. I coaxed him to come closer, "Sit by me." I was pretty hot and bothered too but it was so freeing just feeling like we were two people who let our bodies do what they wanted to do naturally and to accept it. He lay by my side and we turned to look at each other. All without muttering a single word, we exchanged vows and hopes and dreams and had the types of conversations you know only a priest has had.'

'I don't understand,' Mary said.

I was on a roll and didn't want to stop so I just kept going. 'And then we made passionate love for hours. It was so animalistic, so pure and true; we even made the lions jealous. Sometimes I felt embarrassed, I was sweating so profusely, but he said, "Women don't sweat, they glow." He was that romantic. I kept feeling little pinches on my skin throughout the night and remember thinking he was giving me love nips but when I awoke, I was covered in mosquito bites. Every time I itched them I thought of him instead of worrying about malaria.'

I paused, touching my legs, remembering those bumps. 'Do you want to know the craziest thing?' I asked Mary.

'Okay,' she said.

'I'm only admitting this to you because we are family, and most people don't understand matters of the heart, but I wouldn't have minded if I got malaria because it would have been a great excuse for him to take care of me.'

'What's malaria?' she said. She was so exhausting! I waved off her question.

'The next day Simon had to go back to the hospital he worked at in Zimbabwe and I never saw him again. It was okay, though, because our love was about the moment and never needed to be more than that.'

'Yeah, right!' Mary said.

'The problem, Mary, is that Simon doesn't remember what happened anymore. I do, because I have a great memory, but he's completely forgotten it.'

'Wait,' she said. 'I thought you just said your memory was foggy?'

'It's fine. There's a slight chance that he's just pretending we don't know each other from Africa because otherwise it would be too difficult to move on, but I really believe he's just buried it deep inside. Once you have those kinds of experiences, everything else pales in comparison. Forgetting about it is easier because otherwise you're trapped, as I am, knowing that it might be near impossible to find that again.'

'But you just said love never runs out,' Mary said. Shit, this kid was wise.

'That's true,' I said. 'What a relief!'

It was perfect I had Mary with me. Simon was used to seeing me here alone. I like to spend many afternoons going to restaurants by myself, a table for one calling out. I sit there, pretending to read a book, usually one that may encourage conversation, like a grammar handbook or something light and airy, like *The Bell Jar*. But I didn't have Sylvia Plath to help me; I only had Mary. So on this particularly textured day, one where speckles of the sun shone through the cafe's fogged windows, I realized Mary might be a bit more helpful in my fight to jog Simon's memory than I had originally thought.

'What can I get you?' Simon said, appearing out of nowhere.

'Simon says!' Mary exclaimed. 'I love this game!' She definitely was my niece.

'I'm so itchy!' I said, hoping it would trigger something. 'Insects love me. I must be too sweet!' I giggled but Simon just sighed. He must have been sad about something else going on in his life because there's no way in hell that wasn't a cute pick-up line.

'So, ladies, what would you like to eat?'

'I'll take the cock monsieur,' I said, staring into his eyes as deeply and powerfully as I could.

'One croque monsieur,' he corrected. 'And for you?'

Mary was gazing forward, which made me worry she was going to say something she wasn't supposed to.

'Chicken nuggets!' she said.

Chicken nuggets made me think of McDonald's, which made me think of fast food and obesity, which made me think of how many people die every minute. Simon was standing right in front of me and we were alive and thriving in that moment and I believed in rewarding expression, so I knew I needed to just get it out. You never hear anyone on his deathbed saying, 'I wish I never made a move!' Unless it was a bad move, which this wasn't, and even bad moves are good moves in retrospect. Basically, I couldn't go wrong by moving.

'Sy-Sy,' I said.

'Excuse me?' he said.

'You don't remember me calling you that?'

'I don't know what you're talking about,' he said.

'What's malaria?' Mary asked him.

'Mary, not important.'

'But you said he's a doctor,' she said.

'I'm what?' he said.

'Look!' Mary exclaimed, pointing to my belly again. 'It's your baby!'

Simon was flabbergasted; bringing Mary was probably not a good idea.

'For the second time, Mary, it's a food baby!' I said. I turned back to Simon. 'A fortuneteller told me once I was very, very fertile and my hips are wide enough to have a lot of babies. I'm just not pregnant. What if I told you I was ready, though? What would you say?'

No words dropped out of his gaping mouth, only a hand was lifted. He wiped the saliva that had started to dribble out of his mouth.

'Here,' I said, handing him a napkin. 'I've never asked you, Simon. What do you do? Are you interested in saving people?'

'I'm a voiceover actor,' he said.

Oh my lord, affirmations really do work.

'Are voiceover actors doctors?' Mary asked me.

'I'm gonna go put your order in,' Simon said.

As he walked away I looked over at Mary who was smiling. Not the I'm-going-to-kill-you smile but the kind of smile someone smiles when they first figure out how life works.

'A doctor of the heart is more like it,' I said.

For the rest of the meal, he'd catch me staring at him, but he'd look away quickly so as to play shy or something. He was going to be a hard nut to crack. Maybe he had moved on and had a family of his own because he knew he had to do whatever he could to forget our past. Maybe I needed to know he was a voiceover actor so I'd have faith in affirmations again. Before we left the restaurant, I took a notepad out of my bag and tore out a single sheet and wrote the following:

Dearest Sy-Sy,

If you ever want to come over and read Lolita to me, that would be okay. If not, I understand. You might even be married and have a wife you need to read to. Thanks for the delicious cock monsieur.

Love always, Lola

P.S. I will always remember our night in the African desert together. Don't be afraid to let the memories resurface. If that wasn't you, please let me know.

Leaving the note for Simon instilled in me this calmness, this serenity I'd never experienced before. I was so proud of myself for being alive and moving. I also learned three very valuable lessons from this experience:

1) You can't make someone remember something he has repressed out of fear.
2) Affirmation note-making really does work.
3) You don't actually need a voiceover actor when you already have Jeremy Irons.

When I went home, I wrote a list of all the things I wanted to come true. The list was long and imaginative, and my heart was open and ready for a surgeon to piece it together. Or if a doctor wasn't available, maybe Vinnie the yoga God could do it. Surely he'd be able to stretch and open anything else in me that needed realignment.

One should always remain quite flexible.

The Boss Man

Many intoxicating yoga sessions with Vinnie later, I find myself wired, excited, optimistic and extremely loose. And on this beautiful day, I happen to have some time to kill before I pick up Mary so I follow Al Pacino into a Russian bathhouse.

His virility tinges the air before me so palpably I am left with no choice but to trace his footsteps. The opportunity is so enticing, so entrancing and spiritual, so seemingly fated, it would be a sin not to be, well, opportunistic. His scent is driving me wild like a bitch in heat so I stick to his heels, fixated, nostrils flaring. I know he wants me to follow him because a man like that doesn't emit pheromones unless he wants a hound dog sniffing his trail. Looking at his head as his shiny, well-coiffed hair glistens in the sunlight, I can't help but mimic his pacing and the rhythm by which his hands slap the pockets of air around him.

Al's movements begin to change slightly. Suddenly he stops and turns around.

'Are you following me?' he asks.

'Following you?' I say, as if shocked, appalled at the thought.

I feel like we are acting in a movie together, only this time the title is *Scent of a Man* and I've forgotten my lines. 'Of course not! I have been planning to go to the sauna anyway.' This is a lie – a white lie – but my mom has always said white lies are perfectly acceptable if it's for a good reason. Getting Al Pacino to fall in love with me is the best reason I can think of.

'Okay,' he says, turning around. Then he stops again.

'How do you know I was going to the sauna?' he asks.

I just start laughing to buy time because I don't want to tell him that I'd seen him go into the bathhouse before and had thus assumed, being only a block away, he was on his way there now. That would have made me look like a creep.

I send him a shrug.

We approach the door of the bathhouse. It is an extra-ordinarily ugly building, hinged on the corner of a busy inter-section in a part of the city you would never see on a postcard. The door is heavy and I struggle to keep it open. Two big Russians at the front nod to Al as they let him through. I try to sneak in behind him like I am his bodyguard, but they stop me.

'Ten dollars,' Moscow says. He has a few exciting tattoos on his neck that make me feel like I am in *Eastern Promises*. I hand him a crinkled ten like it's drug money, letting the sweat from our hands fuse together in a swift but solid grip. I feel like we're tight now, the guard and I, but when I look up to lock eyes he's already turned around, asking Al if he wants to get Platza.

I know exactly what he is talking about so I don't feel left out. Platza is when you get pummeled by boiling oak leaves in a sauna by big, fat, sweaty Russians – just my sort of therapy. I had to see Al get beaten up, as this would be the next step of our relationship. I think about what it would be like to tell people how my love with Al Pacino began, and now I hope I'll be able to burst out, 'It began with oak leaves and heat!' You can't go wrong when it starts in the steam room. I don't have much experience with relationships but in the movies love begins when someone shows some skin. My mother told me once that when my dad saw her naked he told her he loved her. It didn't last long, their marriage, but the thing to note here is that it started with the birthday suit, which means I have a chance. I pray my relationship with Al will end in a divorce-less marriage and summers in France at the Cannes Film Festival drinking Kir Royals. This must be an omen, or else why would Al be here with me right now, if we weren't meant to be together?

I slip my clothes off and put on a little red bikini. It's tricky because I know the key is to reveal flesh but I've had this rash recently from eating too much gluten and it's spread across my stomach. At least I'm feeling loose! The rash just looks like hives though, so I'm hoping Al won't think I have a disease. I once made out with a guy who had a wildly visible case of psoriasis. I tried to pretend it wasn't there but it was definitely there. It was all I could look at, like when you aren't supposed to look at someone's pimple because you know it's rude but all you can see is that giant red, blistering mountain. The point is my rash looks nothing like his psoriasis.

I hang my bag up on one of the shower hooks outside the main sauna room and walk in; the old-man body odor immediately hits me hard. The visibility is cloudy, which is a good sign for my temporary rash, and it covers my cellulite. I look pretty good in this fog. I should probably arrange to have all my first dates in this sauna. I lay my towel down and lower myself onto it with a sigh loud enough to sound like someone's hand is creeping up my leg, the beginning of foreplay. A few heads turn and I watch them as I pretend to mind my own business. I feel like I've been here forever but I guess it's only been four minutes. I'm sweating quite heavily, which I'm hoping also makes them think this is a sexual moment. I'm trying to get Al to look at me but he's keeping to himself. Goddammit, Al, I think. Look at me!

I inch a bit further towards him. When I recline like this my body looks slimmer. I'm liking this angle and I think, if he only were to look this way, he would like it too. I think about how the yoga is working already. I start to moan a bit to get his attention but it's still not working, so I start saying things he might know like, 'You fuck with me, you fucking with The Best.' A few bald fat guys turn to me, wondering if I'm talking to them, but I just ignore them. 'Okay!' I say. 'You wanna play rough? Okay! Come say hello to my little friend.' I feel like I'm messing up the delivery but Al finally looks over. I've got his attention – at last – but I think my words are muffled with the thickness of the air so he isn't really sure what's going on.

'Excuse me?' he says.

'Huh?' I fake innocence. 'I didn't say anything.'

Shit, I'm blowing this. I freeze.

'I really want to get some ovah here!' I say as tough and Bronx-like as I can, even though we're on the other side of the country.

'Igor, who the hell is this girl?' Al asks. The ground below me is getting very thin. My body is becoming so heavy it's going to give way any moment now and I'm going to fall through these cracks into some other universe. Hopefully, a universe wherein Al Pacino likes me.

One of the large men with hairy chests, his especially greying, starts to signal to one of the other men to pay me some attention. They're coming around.

'You want something?' he says.

'I want that!' I say, pointing to Al but unfortunately the large Russian thinks I'm pointing to the Platza bucket on the table in the middle of the sauna, not realizing I meant the sexy, Oscar-winning actor on the other side.

'Manny, Platza!' he yells.

A man I assume is Manny sits me down on a slab in front of everyone, including Al, face down. Within seconds he starts to beat me with prickly, scalding oak leaves that have been soaked in hot water to expedite the healing process (i.e. circulation). I start to feel like I'm about to be tarred and feathered in front of a medieval crowd for some ridiculous crime, like adultery.

I scream. It hurts. Russians are crazy. The men start to laugh; it makes me unsettled. I don't understand what's going on but I think Al would do something if anything were going wrong so I just try to relax and experience it. I want to be tough. I want to feel the pain so I get the heartache of our relationship out of the way. I look over at Al but he's gone. I pounce up off the table and run around in the fog and thick heat looking for him, yelling, 'Al! Al!'

Manny tells me he's not done yet but I don't care because there's no point in finishing if the man I was showing my penchant for masochism to is out of sight. I put my towel around me and go outside to splash some cold water on myself. My body is still burning from the heat so I go to the shower area to rinse off. I pull back one of the curtains and see Al standing there, naked, covered in bubbles. He is glorious. For a few moments we just look at each other, allowing the fire inside us and the water around us to cohabitate. I am waiting for him to invite me in but he's momentarily speechless.

I think he's going to say, 'What the fuck?' in a really Italian way, but he doesn't.

'Can you please shut the curtain and let me finish showering?' Al eventually says, as if this situation isn't weird. He asks so nicely I want to follow his orders and close it but I get this sense that he's saying No even though he's meaning Yes. I'm a woman, we all send mixed signals, so I get it. I move in closer and push him up against the wall and let the warm water fall over us. It's a really small shower with little room for two people so we keep having to push each other back and forth around the water because it gets really cold when it's the other person's turn. They get all the water and you're just left there, shivering, watching them stay warm. I push back in.

'Let the water wash away our sins,' I say. He looks shocked but I think it's because he's never seen anyone so beautiful.

'What the fuck is wrong with you?' he says.

'Doesn't it feel so good?' Before I give him a chance to reply I start swinging my hair around and circling my hips like I'm spinning a hula hoop, the more I do it the more energized I get. I feel really alive and excited about my life and my future with Al and I can feel myself getting stronger, my moves more wild and interpretive dance-like.

'Whoa!' he says. 'Calm down. You're scaring me!'

The more he pulls back the more I want him, so I jump onto him and straddle his smallish frame, my thighs clenching the sides of his waist with all my strength.

'Are you on PCP?' he asks. I'm not sure to whom he's talking so I just ignore it. Maybe he has Tourette's syndrome and never told anyone. I grab both of his shoulders to brace myself and start thrashing my body about so he knows how great in bed I'd be. At this point I'm riding him pretty hard. It's scary but fun . . . like all relationships.

'Yes, Al!' I scream. 'Give it to me hard! Woo! Giddy up!' I start laughing and whip my body around again to give my hair as much momentum as I can so it's almost exactly like a Pantene Pro-V commercial, secretly thinking 'What am I doing?' but before I can stop, check myself, I accidentally hit him in the jaw with my elbow mid-swing. I hear a loud crack and his body gives way below me and we both fall to the ground. I lift up and see his nose looks like it's on the other side of his face. Blood is streaming down with ferocity but it keeps getting washed away by the shower so I hope he doesn't notice how bad it is.

His eyes are closed for a second and I am scared I might have killed Al Pacino. I imagine what the headlines would read: AL PACINO DIES WHILE HAVING SEX WITH A MODEL IN A RUDDIAN BATHHOUSE. I guess it could be worse!

'What the fuck?' Al says, waking up. He looks around haphazardly and sees the color red wash through the puddle of water he's sitting in and quickly, intuitively, touches his nose. 'It's broken!' he screams. 'You broke my fucking nose!' He's going from really sexy to mad and scary in a matter of seconds – I'd say about thirty seconds – and now I'm worried. Before I can even think of a comeback, we're surrounded by a group of men who start screaming for me to get out of the way. I start lifting my hands up, saying things that just come to me, like,

'I'm so glad you're here! I just found him like this! He must have slipped on the tiles, they're so slippery!'

'She broke my nose!' Al keeps yelling. 'She broke my goddamned nose!'

I see one man coming towards me so I duck through his legs and start running. I grab my bag and run as fast as I can. It feels like I'm being chased by sharks, only we're on land. They're on my heels and they're yelling at me to get out, which is annoying because obviously I'm leaving. I see the exit sign and, thank God, the big Russian man from earlier is distracted again by people coming in. I weave around him and don't look back until I'm on the street. When I turn around, I see him talking to the guys who were chasing me and they start pointing in my direction.

'I wasn't trying to hurt Al!' I exclaim. 'I just got too excited!'

'Who's Al?' he yells. Everyone's confused.

When Al comes out, nudging himself through the bouncers, holding his nose, eyeing me, people start calling him Miguel for some reason. I take out my phone and google a picture of Al Pacino. I realize I might have made a mistake.

'You try to come back here and we call police!' the big one says. He tries to look intimidating but I'm not scared; he's so hairy he just looks like a big teddy bear!

'You mean THE police!' I retort confidently.

On the way home, I feel like I am missing something. I feel naked, and then I look down and realize I'm still in my little red bikini. My sister calls just when I need a pick me up.

'Where are you?' Brenda asks. I can tell she is mad because I can feel her lips curl through the phone.

'I'm downtown.'

'Mary's ballet teacher called and said she's waiting for someone to get Mary and can't find you. Are you almost there?'

Shit. I look at my watch and realize I should have been there thirty minutes ago. I'm a terrible auntie sometimes, but thank God I remembered my bag; that would have been so embarrassing. I slide into my flip-flops, put my clothes on over my wet bikini – which is a really uncomfortable and sticky project in itself – shake the wet out of my hair and head towards her ballet school.

When I finally arrive, Mary is sitting in the corner waiting patiently. Her little legs brush the floor below her in rhythm, slapping the air just like Al did this morning. I remember the way I followed him, how good it felt to weave around the second-hand pockets of his air. I remember how we tangoed in the shower together, how right it had felt. And I remember how shy he was with me; how I made him blush.

'I have some big news,' I say as I take her hand and help her off the bench.

'Why are you so wet?' she asks, eyes wide and captured. 'Did you go swimming?'

'I made love with Al Pacino today in the shower of a Russian bathhouse.' It felt so good to tell someone. To say it out loud, to proclaim it to the universe! Sure, his name might have been Miguel but she didn't need to know it was just his doppelganger.

'Who's Al Pacino?' she asks.

'Are you serious? Don't be pathetic!' I say, laughing for a moment, forgetting I'm talking to a child. 'Oh right, you're only five.' I take another minute to think about her question. 'He's a very talented man. He's the boss.'

'Whose boss?'

'I'm not sure,' I say. 'Mine?' I guess. 'Ours? Everyone's?'

'Are you gonna get married?' Mary asks me.

'I have a feeling it was just one of those magical moments in life that aren't meant to be anything other than just a moment. A perfect moment.'

'But what about your other boyfriends?' she says.

'I haven't met them yet.'

'Oh,' she huffs. 'But I thought Milk was going to be your boyfriend?'

'Milk?' I exclaim. 'What are you, high?'

She frowns and scowls and says, 'But he's the best.'

'He's just a friend. That's it. And anyway, he's a doll but, you know, he's young. He's a boy. I need a man. Al, now he was a man. We had passion.'

'I thought you're not supposed to be in love with your boss.'

'What I had with Al has really boosted my confidence and now I'm ready to get out there again! I'm not in love with him anymore, although the heart can take time to heal. I'm free to meet the right one now. Who knows, if I meet Al again by chance, then it means he's probably my soul mate but for now, I'm unattached. I'm available.'

I sense bemusement from Mary as she looks at me with pursed lips. 'The lesson here, Mary,' I continue, 'is that it's important not to be bogged down with doomed relationships and commitments and ties to the wrong person because then you're unavailable to meet the right one.'

'But how do you meet the right one?'

'You just date everyone you can and eventually it works out. I mean, you have to be resourceful and imaginative; you have to think outside the box. For example, I never would have thought I would have had an affair with an aging movie star but love can surprise you.' I grab her shoulders and look her straight in the eye. 'You have to get out there and try because people who don't try are losers.'

'So you're living a dream?' she asks. That's right, I think. She's a smart little shit, that Mary. Then a few seconds later she tacks on a heartbreaker: 'Mom says dreams aren't real.'

'That's because your mom doesn't allow herself to dream,' I explain. 'She only has nightmares. And people who have nightmares don't want to believe they're real because what you imagine can actually come true.'

I pick her up and give her a hug so tight I can feel her legs loosen in the air. I spin her around in circles, pretending Al is with us and we're all together, enjoying happiness as a family. 'Do you know what you call people who live their dreams?'

'What?' she asks.

'Winners.'

'Oh, okay,' Mary says. 'Do winners make up their own rules, then?'

'Yes.'

'Okay,' she decides. 'Then I want to be a winner, too.'

'You want to know something?' I ask.

'Yeah,' she says, eyes wide. Burning.

'On a scale of one to ten, you're twenty-seven thousand,' I tell her. 'Got it?'

She smiles. She gets it.

I can't wait to get home to tell my mom about my adventure. I think this one would really knock her socks off, give us something to relate about, show her I am not just following in her footsteps but stepping it up a notch. Leading. I am hovering from my Al Pacino high like she did after each affair when we walk into the house.

'You're never going to guess, Mom!' I exclaim. 'I've been doing what you said, making the magic happen. Taking charge. Making romance.'

She is, unfortunately, reading Dorothy Parker again on the couch, tissues and wine in hand, sniffling. This isn't a good sign. I know it means she'll be cynical.

'And how did it turn out for you?' she says, eventually, not looking up from her book. I want her to jump up, grab me, hug me, be proud of me, but she doesn't.

'It didn't work out, per se,' I explain, 'if you were to judge it in the standard sense of a successful relationship, but it made a great story. Just like all your stories.'

'Ha!' She smirks.

'I just think I wasn't trying hard enough. I probably approached it in the wrong way but I wanted you to know I went after it. I wanted Hollywood romance and got it, fleeting as it was. It was just like you said, you know, when you dated Frank Sinatra? It was a whirlwind!'

I feel bad for not telling her that Al was in fact Miguel, but the truth would only derail my point.

'Well, he's an idiot if he didn't see what a catch you are. I'm telling you, men are just downright baffling. Can't see a good thing when it's in front of them. No imagination.'

'No imagination?' Mary asks, butting in.

'That's the problem,' I explain to her. Turning back to Mom, I add, 'But the good sign is that he went along with it for a while. I'm going to find someone who can see just who I am, and I promise you will too.'

But the wine switches her, pulling out from under her the rug of hope, making it harder for her to see what my adventures mean for her future.

'You sound like your father,' she says, blowing smoke out of her nose, 'making promises you can't keep. All this time, I resisted settling. Now I get it. The fantasy of love gnaws its serrated teeth until you have nothing left in you to imagine any outcome other than what's in front of you. How plebeian!'

'Oh, Mom,' I say. 'Don't say that. You can't give up now, after all this time of trying. It's still possible.'

'The only thing that's possible is that it's never going to be as good as you hoped it would be. You better get used to it, girls,' she says, licking her index finger and flipping a page, countering everything she's ever seemed to represent. Everything she used to teach us. 'There's what you hope for, what you pray for, and eventually what you get.' She was doing what she did when she was sad: paraphrasing lines from Parker, as if she meant them, understood them.

Mary and I stand there, watching the smoke form patterns in the living room, wondering when we'd meet our Rainbow Dans who wouldn't stop delivering pizza, when we'd be able to ride that rollercoaster wind. I've had some setbacks, but I'm not going to give up. I have to find my love fast, because with each one of these failed relationships, my mother loses steam, becoming colorless. He's right around the corner, my dreamboat, I'm sure of it, I just haven't met him yet; a man who will understand me in ways men haven't understood my mother or my sister. I remind myself it only takes one, just *one* man!

'Will you go buy me a pack of cigarettes at Sun's before you sit down?' my mother begs me. 'I've been drinking so I can't drive!' It's not a good excuse because she is always drinking and therefore is never fit to drive.

Sun's is a small convenience store at the bottom of our road in Topanga, selling an eye-opening if not alarming array of goods ranging from almond oil to organic cat food to processed jerky. I walk down the aisles of the store, wondering if, since I don't want to be here, it might be exactly that moment when something big happens that changes my life. Realizing no one else is in there except for the owner, a sweetly worn man named Sunny, I head to the checkout to buy my mom's smokes.

I had been feeling so good with Mary just moments ago but my mother's bitterness has burned me a bit, and now I can't shake it off. She can stop a party as well as she can start it. There's this seed she's planted in me that's growing, that's needling my insides, urging me to water it but I won't. If I do, it might grow too big. It might grow so big it will push all of me out of my own body until it overtakes me all together. Basically, and I say this without being dramatic, I'll die.

I'm still aiming for the top; for the man I hope for, because even if Dorothy's lines masticate at my insides, vowel by vowel, twisting me, the truth is that she must have known there was something to hope for, to pray for, in order to know she didn't get it. She knew it existed or else she wouldn't know there was a deficit. Thinking about it, I dodged a bullet with the Al Pacino lookalike. Miguel was definitely not what I had hoped for.

Just as Sunny hands me my change, the pennies slotting into the cracks between my fingers, Delina and Julia walk in, my pseudo aunties, their backs straight, unabashedly bright. They are dressed, as always, in women's clothes. I call them pseudo aunties because of the lack of blood relation, but my mother is an only child and they are her best friends, so it works. I use the she pronoun with them because that's what they are now: they're women. Delina's an ex-pat British transgender woman and Julia's from Spain, also a transgender woman, and both are in their early seventies. They aren't together, they're just friends. Best friends, they say.

Delina wears a trench coat in lilac (she loves pastels), with wedges to give her height (a must for a woman, she insists), with wild, frizzy, electric-purple hair. She doesn't wear make-up except for lipstick because she says she doesn't want to do anything to distract from her lips, but really it's because she's lost all her eyelashes. Delina looks like a grandmother and walks around freely, proudly, unapologetically. It's taken her years to get here, and she feels great.

'For Heaven's sake, a goddess is among us, Julia!' Delina screams out, raising her hands over her head as she spots me. Shuffling towards me in shoes that don't quite fit. Shifting. Bopping. Deliriously happy, a meerkat on speed, and one of my favorite people.

'I'm so happy to see you!' I explode.

They are the two people I seek out when I need a pep talk because they've already lived many lives and therefore have great advice, like my very own Gandalfs. The only issue is that they can read me too well, they can pick up on everything, and being that I'm an atrocious liar around people I know, I might as well be translucent when I'm around them. They also happen to be clairvoyants and astrologers.

'*Hola, mamacita!*' cries Julia, popping out from behind Delina's subdued garb, leaning in to inspect me. She grabs my face and kisses my cheeks as Delina holds on to my hands. Warming them up as if it were winter. As if it were winter in Vermont.

'Ay, Delina,' Julia says, spotting something in me she doesn't like. 'Tabbycita's got something going on I don't like so much.' Delina joins her up close; nods her head. Calculating.

'You are looking so much like your mother the older you get,' Delina says. 'You look like a movie star!' I don't look bad, but I still know this is an exaggeration. 'Are you going to tell us what's going on or am I going to have to borrow Sunny's chair to sit down while you make me wait?' She is so pushy.

'I thought I was close to love today,' I spill, their eagerness to talk opening me up. 'I keep messing up, though. I don't mean to hurt anyone, but I think I'm coming at them from angles they don't expect. I'm going about it the wrong way somehow but I'm just wracking my brain and can't figure out what I'm doing wrong. Maybe it's because I get a little too excited?'

'If getting too excited is a sin then I'm going straight to Hell!' Delina says. She and Julia look at each other and start making sad faces, experimenting with the depths their frowns can reach.

'Oh my God,' Julia says. 'It's so ugly! I hate being sad!'

'Me too!' Delina adds, feigning melancholy. 'Look, you could settle with a numbnut like that.' She stops to point to a really good-looking guy getting out of a Hummer SUV in the parking lot, snapping her fingers for emphasis. 'But would you want that? No!'

I'm thinking, Yes? Maybe? But I know what she means.

'You know what? I think it's because you don't want it yet,' Julia surmises, her eyes flying around her sockets as she returns to Inspector Gadget mode. 'Ah, that's it. Delina, she's not ready.' She's been saying I'm not ready for years.

'One day someone is gonna get that bonkers brain of yours,' Delina says. 'Don't change! Until then, just live! Enjoy!'

'Let's live!' Julia exclaims. Sunny isn't even paying attention.

'You know,' I say, feeling better. Feeling like I didn't make a mistake. 'When I think about it, I knew he wasn't the one from the get go. I just wanted him to be so right that I made my idea of him fit the reality I chose . . .'

'Well that's it!' Julia yells passionately. 'It's all a choice! Love, happiness; they are all choices and you're making the choice to be happy.'

'Here's the truth,' Delina says as she leans back against a wall of tampons because her legs are getting tired. Every now and then her knees give out. You'll be talking to her and you'll be thinking, *Where'd Delina go?* And then you look down. 'It took us most of our lives to realize that the only way to be happy was to be true to ourselves. Of course, we knew it wouldn't be easy. We knew we'd find it a struggle to deal with the bastards who'd make fun of us, the stares, the homophobia, even our families who might not understand, but really, who cares? We're happy.'

'We're just three proud women,' Julia says, beaming. Grabbing us both by the shoulder in solidarity. 'Three happy women.'

Delina and Julia have parallel stories despite not becoming friends until they were about fifty years old. Delina was married for thirty-three years, as a straight man, to a woman named Trixie and together they had six children: Peter (forty-nine), Georgie (forty-six), Polly (forty-two), Henry (thirty-nine), Ruthie (thirty-six) and Harriet, the youngest (thirty-three). All of them have come around to accepting their dad as their other mom. As it's been revealed to me, Delina was originally Donald and was a banker in London straight out of university. He went to a good school though he was never aristocratic, hailing from a well-educated middle-class family. He met Trixie at a dance in 1963 when he was twenty-two years old, and they got married a year later and popped out Peter. Delina says she never even thought about being gay or not, not only because it wasn't an option at that time, but because it was more an issue of sexual identity than orientation. Before she realised she was playing the wrong role, she thought that was just what love and marriage was supposed to feel like: empty. Unsexual. Towards the end of their marriage, in the last few years I think, Delina started going through Trixie's closet. A pair of stockings under a suit here, a bra under a shirt there . . . until eventually he started wearing her earrings to work. That was the dead giveaway. Trixie couldn't ignore it at that point, and, after what I hear was about six months of hysterical crying, they began their ending. Trixie soon after remarried and Donald dumped his banking life to study numerology, collect healing crystals, move to California and change his name to Delina.

When Delina laughs, she laughs with her whole body, curves over, sometimes frighteningly. At times I've known her to heave. Each laugh comes out like a bullet, making you jump. You're silent, shocked, as you digest the shrieking that inevitably follows. It takes getting used to, but it's infectious. You can't help but love her and want her to be your aunt. Her last name is Hart. Delina Hart. She hasn't been in a relationship since she had her gender reassignment surgery ten years ago.

And then we have Julia. Julia Garcia from Madrid. Julia used to be Julio (makes sense, not too imaginative a name change), and was an insurance salesman married to a Spanish woman named Rosa. They had three children together: Juan (thirty-eight), Talia (thirty-four) and Javier (thirty-two). I recall Julia's transition being similar to Delina's in that it all started quite casually, quite slowly, until it became so obvious it was unavoidable. It wasn't just an elephant in the room. He was a bedazzled, high-heeled and false-eyelash-wearing elephant. Julio moved to London after he felt he couldn't be Julia in Madrid, and one night out in Soho, he befriended Delina and ended up following her to California. The 'land of the free-sexuals!' they love to say while driving down Pacific Coast Highway from Topanga back to West Hollywood; their thin, brittle hair under chiffon scarves, blowing in the wind like Thelma and Louise gone awry. I'm not quite sure what happened to Rosa, but I'm sure she's fine. I'm sure she cried, too, but she's fine. Women are always okay. We cry but we get over it. It's the men we have to worry about.

'So what you're saying is,' I ask, just to be sure I understand them, 'is that even if people think I am crazy, even if I am going about this all the wrong way, it doesn't matter as long as I'm being authentic to myself?' They are nodding throughout my recap so I know they agree; they know they got through to me.

'For years, we lived the way everyone else told us to,' Delina says. 'We did what was expected. We didn't shout too loudly—'

'No we didn't!' Julia interrupts.

'—we lived inside the lines, we were black and white, we fit in, but we were forgettable. We were miserable because we weren't being ourselves at the risk of causing a stir. Never change, darling. You've always been you and you have to keep being that divine creature you've always been.' She slips off the tampon shelf abruptly, it no longer comfortably able to support her. A few boxes fall and Sunny rolls his eyes.

'Cleanup, aisle one,' he says to someone in the back.

'I mean,' Julia says, wrapping it up as I can tell she's getting tired too. 'It will pay off in the end. Just look at us!'

And I do. I look at them for a while because they're so magnetic it's impossible not to. They leave me with no choice but to see how I must keep being myself as it's unmistakably, unequivocally, the only road open. Besides, all the other turn-offs along the way have been closed. No one warns you there might be roadblocks at every exit and that you might have to drive to the next town before you can turn around.

Delina grabs me by the arm just before I go. She's much stronger than she looks and often forgets the power in her wrists. 'Just remember,' she says, gripping tightly, 'one man's crazy is another man's dream.' Delina and Julia are my gas-station pit stops along this dimly lit path, keeping me straight and narrow; giving me somewhere to pull over and refuel before I break down further along the road. I'm pumped now, energized and ready to get back behind the wheel and drive, drive, drive.

The Rastafarian

Lately, I just can't get the image of dicks out of my head. Every bus ride I take, every elevator I get into, every supermarket line I wait in, I size up dicks. Old dicks, young dicks, big dicks, small dicks. It all started when I got a text from an unknown number with a picture of a big, black penis. I was walking down the street when the beep lured me in and the picture caught me by surprise. It took my breath away; made me dizzy. So loopy, I literally almost walked into a pole in the middle of the sidewalk. Now I know what it feels like to be stopped in my tracks, not just by signposts but by dick pics, too.

There was no face, no text – only a beautiful penis peeking out from colorfully patterned bed linens with a few fingers around it so it didn't just look like a floating dick. It filled up the entire screen. You look at it and *Pow!* A penis. Right there, just staring back at you. Every time I'd glance at it, I would cover my mouth and giggle, my smile surfacing between the cracks in my fingers like that dick did among its disheveled pile of sheets. It was like having a huge secret that only you can keep. You feel big just holding it in you.

I've never even searched for dick pics online. Not that I didn't want to, I just never thought about it. At first of course I imagined it was a prank from one of those porn telemarketers. So tentatively, naturally, calmly, I replied, 'Hi.' If you had asked me earlier what I would have replied to this kind of text, I would have thought I'd use an exclamation point. 'Hi!' felt a lot more appropriate. It matched the level of arousal that cycled, virtually, between us. But, because I didn't know him and because I didn't want him to think I was too keen, too soon, I avoided the exclamation. For the next hour, I couldn't stop looking at his two-dimensional cock – so strangely alien, so exciting – and then searching the faces of passersby to see who I could share it with. I wanted to scream with joy and run up to strangers and shake them because I believed in them and in their ability to be alive in the way I felt alive.

But no one made eye contact with me, despite my peering, so I kept on moving forward. I frantically plugged the photo into Google images to search and see if any other penises matched so I could determine whether or not it was indeed a porn telemarketer or just some man clowning. Some lonely guy in India texting numbers he got from a call-center station he worked at, thinking his own penis wouldn't incite such a visceral reaction. At least I knew he was smart, either way. No images matched my pic so I knew it was real, and it definitely wasn't photoshopped because it had this cute little bend to the left, which I found quite endearing. It was full of character. Straight penises are so dull! 'Veering left,' I'd say to him when we'd be united in the flesh, as I'd pretend to drive his stick. I imagined what he looked like, how his neck and head and chest and hands all fit into each other like a perfectly designed puzzle.

About an hour later, I got a text back saying, 'What up hot gyal' but the question mark at the end must have been cut off. I wondered if he wasn't very grammatically minded, or if he was lazy or if indeed it was just a texting malfunction. I hoped for the latter.

'Do I know you?' I asked.

'Don't remember me?'

I'm pretty sure I'd remember a charmingly asymmetrical dick, so I said, 'No.'

Two minutes later, I got another reply: 'Met u outside the Mexican place on Franklin in Hollywood a few years ago. Your so beautiful.'

I still couldn't quite recall the moment he was referring to because all I could think about was how he incorrectly used 'your' when it should have been 'you're.' Poor grammar kills me but he thought I was beautiful so he had my interest, and maybe he was cleverly giving me an in, showing me how I was needed in his life: sexpot and grammar teacher to the rescue.

'Are you sure you're not in India, feeling lonely?' I asked, just to be sure I was ruling it out. You have to be sure these days; there are so many creeps out there.

'DWRCL,' he replied.

'Ha,' I wrote back, having no idea what he meant. 'What's that mean?'

'Dead wid raas claat laff.'

I'm not sure if that was meant to clarify anything because I still had no idea what he was talking about. As I phonetically tried to work it out, bending my lips around the vowels, looking like I was warming up for vocal lessons, I realized what his accent was.

'Oh!' I exclaimed. 'Are you Jamaican?'

'Yah.'

Fabulous. I love Jamaicans.

'What r u doin?' he asked, texting me again before I had a chance to reply. That's guy code for: I'm interested.

'Why'd it take you so long to contact me?' I had to know. I had to figure this out. I felt like Sherlock Holmes in an erotic novel called *On the Hunt for the Face of the Man with the Fantastic Cock.*

'Cuz I was scared,' he said. I love a man who can own his emotions. I also want a man who is strong and capable and doesn't show his feelings to just anyone because he's so tough and rugged. That combination exists and this guy, he could be the one who embodies such a rare and delicate balance of sensitivity and manliness. I put the phone down for a minute as I let it sink in. My good karma is coming back.

Then another pic came through. This time it was more of a close-up, with some balls in the shot. The only problem now, though, was that his dick was half-hard.

'Did I do something wrong?' I replied.

'Naaah. Why?'

'You lost your hard-on,' I said, hoping he'd tell me how to make this right again. 'I've never had phone sex before, so you'll have to coach me a bit.'

'Ur turn now,' he wrote.

The exhilaration of the request disoriented me so. Every cell in my body was having the best party of their lives. They were so happy; they were even dancing the salsa, my cells. Everything was on fire, including my groin, despite not knowing what my turn meant.

'What do you mean?' I replied. 'Like a picture of me?'

'Yup. Da whole ass n de puss puss,' he wrote.

'It feels weird to send a picture of myself to someone I don't know,' I said. For some reason, I was a little embarrassed – an emotion I'm not used to. It's just that dick and ass shots were totally out of my comfort zone.

Silence. Dead zone. I waited. Was it because I hadn't complimented him?

'You have a great set of balls, and an awesome dick,' I wrote, trying to backtrack and steady the vibe again.

';)' he replied.

Again, silence. Then, 'You still owe me a pic . . .'

'I just want to know a bit more about you first,' I continued, trying to engage. Women need to talk, he should know this; surely he's a man with a lot of experience. Plus, I'm not just going to give it away. I'm letting him smell the bacon in my pocket. I'm not ready to show it just yet, but the point is that he knows it's there.

Silence.

'Where are you?' I asked.

'Home.'

'In Jamaica?' I asked.

'Yep.'

'Are you a Rastafarian?'

'Yep.'

He wasn't very talkative but I wasn't going to let that get in the way. Not everyone can be gregarious. That would be exhausting.

'Dreadlocks are an aphrodisiac for me,' I said, filling the gaps because we've already established it would be unwise for me to think he'd do so himself.

'Oh yeah?'

'Have you heard of a song called "Night Nurse" by Gregory Isaacs?' I asked.

'Dat be a classic. Mmmm I wish you wid be my night nurse.'

THIS IS SO EXCITING. I thought this was text foreplay, although I wasn't entirely sure. It was getting warmer, though.

'Are you a drummer?'

'Yes.'

It's amazing, he was saying 'Yes' to everything; it's as if I had prayed to the right Gods of romance this time. I couldn't have imagined answers more perfectly primed for my affection. My mom loves people who say, Yes! I think it's because she says yes to people. She's beautifully open, and that's why she's so lovable.

When my mom was twenty, she moved to Jamaica because she loved the colors and the people and the food. She used to tell me how the smell made her quiver and the sand smoothed her callouses, and how she fell for a local named Antony who played keys in a reggae band. 'I loved him,' she'd reminisce. 'He couldn't keep his dick in his pants but he taught me how to be a woman.' Real women have experiences across the board, I learned. Real women are women with stories. Women who can go to a party and tell a dirty joke well and know the exact right moment to leave just as the night is peaking. I wanted to date everyone and everything. I wanted to be the person I'd want to invite to a dinner party. What a story the Jamaican would be. Maybe I'd move to live with him in Kingston and just be one of those women with a million lives.

A cat woman, without the surgery, just the near-death adventures. This was how I'd relate to my mother.

'I bit you got a big bun in dah ass rit now?' he said.

I had absolutely no idea what he was saying but I tried again to pronounce it to myself to see if any of the words brightened up and took shape in my vocabulary, but the exercise proved unsuccessful. I took a breather, letting my head escape from the cramp-inducing downward position it was in to be able to see the screen. Being that the sun was shining quite brightly, I caught a glimpse of my ass's reflection in the window of a nearby clothing store. Ironically, the store was called Big Image. I turned around to see what kind of junk was hiding in my trunk and turns out, there was a lot! I started grabbing chunks of meat, imagining my hands were the Rastafarian's big, beautifully sculpted hands. I lost myself in the reflection for a moment, somewhere between LA and Jamaica. Somewhere between him and me, hope and reality, until I was rudely startled out of my trance by the shopkeeper knocking at the window.

'Are you for real?' I asked the Rastafarian as I skidded along the sidewalk, expressing my apologies to her in a dip and a wave.

'BOAL,' he replied, again using an acronym I couldn't follow.

'You're going to have to enlighten me with some of this slang!' I said, exclamation point purposely added.

'Buss out a laff,' he told me. Jamaicans are so happy and optimistic, living life the way it's meant to be lived. Plus, I love when someone thinks I'm hilarious. This relationship is going really well, although I must admit I'm not good at long distance.

'What's your name?'

'Jimar,' he said.

'Jimakin' me crazy,' I wrote, laughing to myself, but the joke is so old and boring, I got radio silence. No reply. Not even the three dots that show he's thinking, typing. Nothing.

I rationalized that if I never heard from him again, I would only be losing a fake boyfriend and that it wouldn't be so bad. Of course, I was hopeful, but I had to keep my roots intact because, well, we didn't really know each other. I'm looking for the big stuff, the stuff that moves you. Phone sexting could be a stepping stone; one I was willing to take in case I found paradise on the other side of this running creek. I got in my car and headed towards Mary's school as it was already ten to four in the afternoon. As I sat waiting for her in my car, I looked at all the other little kids coming out. I felt a level of solidarity with the little half-black, half-white kids running to their interracial parents. Beautiful mixed-race bundles of joy. I wanted to say, 'Yeah, I get it. It's good,' but I didn't want to create a divide between the humdrum white parents who just didn't get it and me. I wouldn't want to set the wrong example for Mary because I've always told her never to flaunt or gloat but just to know you're better inside.

Finally, Mary's little legs and belly came charging out towards me. Her backpack was so big it bounced from side to side, almost throwing her entire body weight off. This time she was with the new friend. He was downright adorable, sporting a short dark pseudo Mohawk. He looked like a rocker's kid, or more likely, the victim of a home haircut – the mother shaving the sides but forgetting the top. Either way, he had little man swagger.

'So is this the infamous Randall I've been hearing all about?' I asked.

'Can Randall come over to play?' Mary asked me. All I could think about was Rastafarian dick and Mary wanted me to plan a play date.

'I'm not sure. I have to ask his mom. Randall, honey, where is your mom?'

'She's in prison,' he said.

'Hahaha,' I laughed. Kids! The things they say! 'Well, you little wisecracker,' I started. 'I still need a number to call and ask permission to take you with us.'

He recited a number while looking at the sky, as if the clouds would help to remind him. As if the clouds and sun and stars and moon had answers.

I dialed the numbers to a ring . . . ring . . . ring . . .

'Hello?' said a man. His voice firm and deep, lethargic and wobbly.

'Hi,' I started, at first unsure. 'I'm Mary's aunt, Tabitha. I'm here at school to pick her up and she wants to have Randall come back with us to play for a bit. Are you on your way to get him?'

His only reply was a grumble as he sipped something. Ice cubes rattling. Clinking.

Catching on, I jutted in. 'Would it be okay for me to take him back for a bit? I'll drop him home in a few hours?'

'Yeah,' he said, bluntly, coldly, drunk.

Randall and Mary jumped in the back. I happened to have an extra car seat in the trunk and managed to strap them down despite their giggling and slippery bodies sliding and slithering around the seats. Trying to secure a seatbelt around a child is like trying to grab one jumping, psychotic frog out of a box without letting any of the others out. When you're done, you're sweaty and tired and you just want to sleep but you look at your watch and it's only been a few minutes. It's the moment when you can finally relate to boxers.

When I closed my driver's door, my phone beeped. I grabbed it so quickly with my salty palms it almost slipped right out of my hands. The jumping frog indeed. Good news: it was another dick picture, this time taken from far away so I get some face in the shot. He was beautiful. I couldn't see much but I saw dreadlocks united by big eyes to match his charismatic cock and that, that was just enough. I started giggling and felt this need to share his beauty, my luck, our love, with someone so I turned back towards Mary and Randall and said, 'You guys, I've had the best day.'

They both looked at me but their stares differed with peculiar measure: Randall's being inquisitive and open while Mary's was discerning and unflappable. I started to laugh because I was so giddy, reserved, knowing that I had in my hand something so naughty it would make the porn star Jenna Jameson blush. 'I met someone,' I said, smile bursting.

'Here we go again,' Mary said, eyes rolling towards that sky kids seemingly have a connection with. I believed she learned that phrase from my sister.

'Cool,' Randall piped in, pragmatically. I wanted to show them the pictures, because who wouldn't be desperate to show someone, to share her secret, but I knew I could have been arrested for showing Randall and Mary a picture of a giant cock, so I refrained.

'How did you meet him?' Mary asked.

'It's a sweet story, actually,' I began. 'We met years ago but he just reconnected with me because he couldn't get me off his mind!'

'Cute!' Mary said while Randall nodded his head, quietly in acceptance. He looked a bit tough, little Randall. He had these eyes rimmed with the longest eyelashes and the presence of a soul who's lived many times in bodies that became much bigger than his. I bet in a past life we knew each other.

'Randall's six,' Mary said, as if she knew I wished he were a grown-up.

'Oh, wow,' I exclaimed with believable enthusiasm. 'Six is big!'

We walked in the door and they whizzed around me, decking it to the playroom like it was about to expire in a few minutes. I checked to make sure they were okay, and, most importantly, preoccupied, so I could go into the bathroom and take an ass shot to send to Jimar.

I looked at myself in the mirror and grabbed the cheeks of flesh I discovered on myself earlier with outstretched hands. I had forgotten what color underwear I put on so I pulled down my pants and saw I had on my granny panties: Hanes white cotton high-waisted briefs because I was out of all my other clean ones. Of course, on the one day I needed to take an ass shot, I had on the most unattractive underwear. There's always the possibility that he is into some kinky stuff, like grandma porn, so instead of raiding my mom's drawers I choose to just be real. Be me. I pulled my pants down halfway to my knees, right at that position where if you were attacked and had to run, you couldn't. With the mirror behind me, I turned to see how my butt would look in the shot and tried to angle myself rightly. I don't like the kind of selfies where you can see yourself holding your phone in the mirror; I prefer the ones when you just take a picture of yourself with the camera reversed. So, I reversed the camera.

Ass shots are harder to do than they look. Ass shots are not for the weak but rather the trained and secure. The good news was that my butt, being slightly meaty and wrinkly around the thigh zone, would look better if the picture captured just a part of it; an excuse to get right up in it, personal. I'm better up close because then I'm abstract, like a beautiful painting you have to figure out using texture clues and speculation and postulation because no one really can be sure of the answer. You win when you're abstract because it's the most arbitrary of art styles. You could walk right past me at an estate sale but once you knew what you had, you'd be the richest person in the world. My ass is basically Jackson Pollack's artwork, personified.

Apparently, Jamaican men appreciate a juicy, round butt on a woman, which is another reason why I held a newfound confidence about sending Jimar a photo of my Botticelli ass. I drew my leg up on the sink because I figured, Let's make this interesting. I moved around, feeling quite flexible and proud, wishing a handsome, Paul Newman-type man across the street with a cigarette would be watching me. Wishing he'd see me in the same light I saw my big-breasted neighbor:

naked and flaunting, flirting furiously, most infuriatingly because she does it with total disregard for anyone else's feelings. I wished that man with the cigarette would call out, 'Great show,' from across the road as he inhaled richly. I wished he'd tell me he'd been watching me all night from his window and the thought of it would make me so confident I'd uncontrollably cream in my pants. That didn't happen.

My moving became increasingly unpredictable, more wild and free, each twist and leg lift more dramatic and whimsical than the last, like a modern dancer alone in a room searching for new moves of expression. Beads of sweat collected at my heels, behind my neck and in the cracking lifelines in my palms from tapping into all my physical reserves at once. I was so close but still didn't have the right angle, so I arched my back as I pivoted my left foot, bending my vertebrae so much that my head dropped into an upright bridge position. My head faced the window behind me in one quick turn and, from upside down, I could see Milk staring at me from his window. Not Paul Newman, but Milk, who was about as sexy as a potato.

I saw him immediately turn away, pretending to act casual as if I hadn't just caught him but you can't kid a kidder. I watched him brush his hair with his hand, turning slightly to the side as if he were looking for raccoons or squirrels in my front yard. I reached to close the curtains while in this contorted pose and, because the movement was determined and quick, I locked my spine into a fantastic position I couldn't get out of. I heard it crack and snap. My arms and legs reached out like a frozen ballerina until my foot eventually slipped on the tile, which was lubricated by my sweat, and as I fell backwards, grabbing at perfume bottles and makeup and anything I could grab onto, I hit my head on the shower door handle.

I was out cold.

I was gone for a few minutes, although I can't be sure. When I looked up, Mary and Randall hovered above me, staring, expressionless, as Milk bent over all of us. I could see this scene from above, as if I were the angel in the room as witness. Two curious kids and Milk over a sprawled-out Tabby whose pants were halfway down her legs while her underwear was pulled so far up her waist it was like God gave her a wedgie. And among the spilled bottles and brushes that once adorned the countertop rested a distorted photo of my ass, front and center on my phone.

'Are you okay?' Milk asked me. 'Looked like a bad fall.'

'I'm fine, thanks,' I said, trying to lift my head up but unable to do so. I let it rest back on the ground for another second while I re-oriented myself.

'What's that?' Mary asked, pointing to the photo.

'Huh?' I said. A headache started to creep into the room, just to annoy me.

'That's your butt!' she yelled. 'Gross! I'm telling Mom!'

'If you do, you know what can happen?'

'What?' She looked stern but frightened.

'You'll never be able to take a photo of your own butt,' I proclaimed, lost in my own argument. Randall was avoiding eye contact, staring at his toes.

'Why would I want to do that?'

'Because, Mary,' I said. 'Adults take photos of themselves. Some of them are called "selfies" and women do these weird duck-face poses because they think it makes their cheeks and lips look better. They're wrong. Don't do that. That looks desperate.'

'Like Grandma?' Mary questioned.

'Grandma's not desperate!' I fumed. 'We're a lot alike, and she's amazing.'

'You're a lot different from your mom,' Milk interjected as he used the back of his palm to check my temperature.

'You can't say that,' I interjected, insulted. 'You can never talk about someone else's family, even if the person is complaining about them, because they're not your family.'

'I meant it in a good way,' he said, grabbing my hand to help me up.

'She's just trying to be happy and hasn't figured it out yet. I don't get it because she's so much fun.'

'Why are you taking ass photos anyway?' Milk asked.

'You're really asking me this in front of the kids?' I said, exasperated. He threw an expression back to remind me of the fact that if I weren't taking photos of my ass while watching over children in the first place, it wouldn't even be a conversation.

'Why do adults take pictures of their butts, though?' Mary and Randall asked in unison.

'Because that's how people have relationships now,' I said.

'Why?'

'I don't know why,' I said, not explaining why at all. 'Because it's less scary than doing it in real life?' Now I'm asking her all of a sudden. Children have a way of asking you so many questions you end up getting to a point where your answers are also questions. Everyone ends up profoundly more baffled.

Milk seemed to disagree – the curl in his lip and glassiness of his eyes belying his cluelessness. He always has this annoying way of looking at me like he's confused but about to laugh. Mid-point between a smile and an open-mouthed gape. 'You don't date, Milk.'

'Yes, he does,' Mary said. 'I see girls go into his house all the time.'

'Oh come on, Mary, you don't need to make him feel better,' I said. 'Don't lie, it's unbecoming. No offense, Milk.'

'None taken,' he said again, smiling.

'It's just, you have to know what we want, how to talk to us, what feeds us.' I looked over at Mary for her help. I needed backup. 'Right, Mary? We're women. Brave, complicated, exciting women, right?'

'What are you talking about?' Mary said.

Ignoring her, I returned to Milk, and said, 'Chin up, Milkman. You're a catch, don't worry.' Again, though, I was met with that dreaded half smile. The bewildered stare of a giant puppy lost in some woods in the middle of absolutely nowhere. Bless him.

'Stop looking at me like that,' I said when the stare wouldn't break. 'You look at me sometimes like you think I'm crazy.'

Randall chimed in like a man and asked me if I was okay. His youth takes you by surprise. I reassured him it was only a little fall, nothing big. When I reached for my phone, I realized I must have accidentally sent the photo to Jimar on my fall. He now had not only a blurry photo of my ass, but because it was in movement, a stretched one.

Feeling insecure for a brief, unusual moment, I did what the master politicians do when there's too much heat under them: I switched topics. 'So were you spying on me?' I started at Milk. 'You saw me fall and ran over?'

'I was just checking you were okay.'

'You really are a big creep,' I said. 'You know that? Big old creepy stalker.'

Brows fluted. Mouths winced. 'But you . . .' Mary began before a beep on my phone silenced her.

It was from Jimar. In slow motion, I opened his message. It read: 'What am I looking at?'

I was embarrassed that my nudie pic wasn't strong enough for him to even know what it was. 'Why can't I just take a nice ass shot like every other women trying to flirt with a stranger via text message?' I said out loud. 'I want to have sext already.' Milk, Mary and Randall started to laugh.

'Never mind!' I wrote back, air-fluffing it off as if the picture were never taken, never sent. As if it were a joke. I waved and laughed to myself as if Jimar were right in front of me and I was in on the laugh, too.

'Did you just fart?' Mary asked, Milk and Randall still giggling under their breath.

'Why would you say that?' I asked.

'You're pushing fart around the air,' she accused me. How kind she was.

'Okay, Milk,' I said. 'Thanks for coming over. I think we're all good here now.'

'Hey, can we speak for a minute?' he asked me.

'Well . . . I'm busy,' I said. Mary gave me a frown. 'Okay, quickly.'

'I have Friday night off and wanted to see a movie at that new theatre with the reclining seats and cocktails,' he said.

'Okay,' I said, confused. 'Do you need me to take care of something for you?'

'No, I wanted to see if you wanted to go with me.'

I stared at him blankly.

'A date?' Mary asked. 'Does that mean you send Milk pictures of your butt too?'

'It's not a date, Mary!' I said.

'They're playing *Some Like It Hot* and I know you love that movie,' he explained.

'Oh,' I said, confused, unsure why he'd want to go to the movies together. We never went to the movies together. 'Well, thank you, Milk, but I'm in a long-distance relationship.' It was sweet of him to ask, but I had to keep myself focused on going on dates with men who I'd actually be able to be with one day. A date with Milk would distract me, and I was already running out of time.

And once more, I guess, for the road, he shot me the look again, the glassy-eyed deer, but this time his smile came through more visibly.

'Okay, bye, little man,' he said, turning to Randall and giving him a high five. 'Mary,' he said. 'You know where to find me if,' (nodding towards me), 'she starts acting up, right?'

Mary giggled like a little schoolgirl, like he was Prince Charming or something ridiculous. I guess that's the beauty in being naïve. Just then, when I was feeling cold and old and lonely, Jimar picked me up and threw me into the next stratosphere. 'Wait,' Jimar wrote. 'Is that wut I think it is?'

Bingo. I had no idea the illusion of ass was going to be far more provocative than a clear ass itself. Without even knowing it, I was drawing him in, luring him close to the bacon in my pocket. Close enough to be able to smell it even though he couldn't see it. Tapping into the allure of the mirage.

This is how you seduce people. This is how you become happy. My mom's mom was very religious, very, very Christian. She lived a calculated, slow life in fear of what would happen if she indulged, all of which made my mother more extreme in her reaction to prove she could instead be rewarded for her decadence. Now that my grandma's memory wavered, she forgot to give me the bad advice she gave my mother. She used to tell her she'd never be happy until she became realistic about love, about life; that my mother's dissatisfaction was the product of her inability to settle, as if dreaming big was a setback. I guess I'm trying to prove what she couldn't prove to Grandma. I'm designing my own kind of happy.

I was thinking this could go on for days, weeks, years. I was thinking there's a strong potential for longevity here but at some point, something's got to move forward. My head was banging from the fall when Mary and Randall told me they were hungry. I hurried them downstairs to continue playing while I fixed them something to eat. Bent over the saucepan, I boiled some water to make macaroni and cheese because in times like these, I turn to the food Ernesto used to talk to me about when we'd play waitress. When I see it, it elicits a response in me. I can hear him saying it in his soothing and Mexican way and somehow, I feel invincible. Less alone. Less fragmented. Less embarrassed about things gone wrong in the past, like an unflattering ass photo sent into the ether. I looked out the kitchen window and imagined being my mother, having looked out at me in the garden with Ernesto from that same vantage point many years ago, and I wondered what I would have thought if I were her, back then.

I was thinking that from now on, I was going to be more thoughtful. Being more thoughtful than I already was might seem impossible but there are always ways to improve. I gave Mary her favorite plastic cartoon spork when the mac 'n' cheese was ready. 'But I hate Ariel!' she yelled as she threw it across the table.

'Seriously?' I said. 'Last week you only ate with this spork!'

My phone, resting face up on the table, beeped and a picture of Jimar's penis flashed to the screen. I chuckled from the shock and grabbed it away as soon as I could, though looking at Randall's contorted facial expression, I didn't pick it up quickly enough. But who cares! 'Nothing to be afraid of, Randall!' I shouted, so pleased my wobbly, distorted ass didn't end my relationship with the sultry Rastafarian.

'Ariel believed in love, Mary,' I said. 'You should be lucky to use her figurine as a spoon!'

Mary did that weird scrunched-up face again where she purses her lips into a line that's oddly straight. One of her eyes bent down from the pull. 'Why don't you and Milk get married?'

I couldn't help but let out a hearty laugh, so deep it would have fit my body better to have a barrel gut. My shock and surprise quickly morphed into annoyance. Kids don't understand anything. 'Well,' I began. 'You know how Grandma Twilda has had so many romantic adventures? It's because she knows what she wants and she goes for it. That's where I get it from. Milk is nice, but he really just wouldn't understand me. I'm attracted to men who know what they want.'

'But he just said he wanted to take you out,' Randall said.

'Is Mom like Grandma, too?' Mary asked.

'Your mom may as well have been adopted,' I told her. 'She's possibly a different species. I'm not even sure if she's human.'

'Why?'

'Because she's not interested in love.' Just as I said it, Brenda opened the front door and collapsed inside, still in her nurse's scrubs. I ran over to her, phone out, picture forward. 'A beautiful Rastafarian in Jamaica sent me a picture of his dick today!' I exclaimed.

She wafted it away in a panicked reflex, worried Mary and

Randall could see it. 'What's wrong with you?' She looked over at Randall, who stood with his legs a little further apart than the width of his hips. She took another look at my photo and winced. 'Ugh. Gross. Who does that?'

'I think it's great,' I bristled back.

'Hey, Mary, are you going to introduce me to your friend?' Brenda asked as she walked towards them.

'This is Randall,' Mary said. 'Aunt Tabby asked his dad and he said it was fine to come over.'

Brenda looked over at me to confirm its truth and I did with a quick nod.

'He's not my dad,' Randall snuck in, but the comment slid under the mat as soon as it came out.

'Who is sending you vulgar pictures anyway?' Brenda asked me as I watched Randall's eyes drop to the floor again where they seemed to find their home.

'This guy in Jamaica named Jimar,' I said proudly. Shoulders back.

'Ah, I see,' she said. 'So my sister gets penis pictures from a stranger who's probably working in a random customer-service call center in Mumbai pretending to have that big a cock in front of not only my daughter but her new friend and you think this is how adults behave?' She said it all in one go without taking a breath.

'I thought that too!' I exclaimed, eager to find a thought between us in common. 'But a lot of Indian men have big dongs, you know. I mean, they must be pretty good. They invented the *Kama Sutra.*'

'Ugh,' she sighed. 'You're disgusting and pathetic. If you're not careful, you're going to wind up like Mom.'

My smile flatlined and I was just left there, in the hallway, feeling a half of myself.

'Please tell me you didn't send him a picture back?' she added in afterthought.

'Well . . .' I began but it was too late. She could read it on my face.

'We have to go,' Brenda said as she grabbed Mary. 'Mary, come on. We have to go home now.'

'What about Randall?' I asked.

'You can take him home, right?' She delivered me a look that gave me no other option but to take him home. 'I would,' Brenda explained. 'It's just I'm exhausted from a fourteen-hour shift.'

'Of course I can take him,' I said. I winked at Randall to let him know it was okay, that fun was still to be had.

On the ride home, I asked Randall how his heart was.

'What do you mean?' he said.

'I want to know if your heart's okay. Is it big? Is it alive? Is it sad?'

'I guess,' he started. 'I guess it's okay.'

I let the lack of details go because I sensed his hesitation.

I've realized a lot of men, despite their age, cannot connect with their hearts. I wanted to get Randall thinking of it now, rather than later before it was too late. Before high-school heartbreaks and adulthood mistakes closed it up and locked it down for good.

'Where are the dads and husbands in your home?' Randall asked me, as if it were a normal question.

'Milk came,' I said. 'But I guess he doesn't count. I'm not sure where the rest of them went. They left a long time ago.'

He sat there quietly.

'What's your family like?' I asked, unafraid of whether or not it was an appropriate question.

He silently looked out the window as we traversed over cracks in pavements, past stoplights and yellow signs and missing-cat posters stuck to trees. I stuck my hand out behind me to reach him and it landed on his head. I brushed his hair as well as I could given I was driving with the other hand which meant that my affectionate strokes sometimes ended up in his eyes. When I walked him up to his house, a dreary brown one-story, he still didn't answer me and, in turn, I didn't push it. I just waited for him to say something to point me in a direction like those signposts I ran into earlier.

Randall pushed the unlocked door open and I peered in to look around. The television light was glaring from the other room. Instead of the sounds of a family inside, I only heard a few beer bottles tap against each other. I was surprised to see his house was as dark as mine can get, given that he had both a mom and a dad, biological or not.

'Bye, kid,' I said as he went to walk upstairs. Before he got too far, though, he turned around to me.

'I don't like Jimar,' he said.

'Okay,' I replied. He climbed up the stairs quietly, as if not to wake up the house. I wondered where the cheer was. Where the family dinners were. I wondered why there was no one to greet him but a gloomy blue light.

I got another text from Jimar just before I started the engine. I thought it was going to be something romantic this time. I imagined he'd describe my hair flowing beachside at sunset and how my lips would stay perpetually cherry-colored because they'd reflect the love he had for me in his heart. Instead, he told me he was jerking off, thinking of me with another man. I wanted to flick it off, the sadness that came over me, but I couldn't. I didn't want to be shared. I wanted him to want me. I wanted him to want to beat the shit out of any other man who'd try to touch me. The guy who is going to plan a flash mob for his proposal isn't the same guy who wants to watch the woman with whom he's in love be intimate with another man.

When I pulled into my driveway, I saw somebody swaying around the house. It was obvious after watching a few dance moves that it was my mother. Tonight she wore a tweed coat she bought from an exclusive dealer in London some years ago. Her black hair was a few steps outside a tightly groomed bob, with just enough flare and personality to let a stranger know she had a story. A glass of red wine, half consumed, was balancing dangerously between her fingers. She was dancing to Sam Cooke's 'Sad Mood' on vinyl, her knees giving out to the beats in rhythm, her hips swaying to the right and left, wine glass moving around her invisible dance partner.

'Mom,' I said. She never looked over but kept dancing. 'I want to ask you something, about your time in Jamaica.' I was starting to question whether or not these adventures had made her better, more adventurous, more wildly attractive, as I had hoped they were making me.

After a few delayed beats, she glanced at me through her coal-colored hair. Her lips wine-stained, as usual, and eye-makeup smeared.

'Come dance with me, baby,' she said, holding out her hand.

I started to move my hips with her, to meet her wherever she was, tossing my hair around to ruff it up a bit.

'But I . . .' I started.

'You really are your father's daughter, aren't you?' she sighed, ignoring me. 'Two brick legs. I guess it makes sense, why he never wanted to dance. I just wanted him to grab me though, you know, out of nowhere and start dancing. I didn't even care that he was terrible at it. I wanted him to want to dance.'

She gets sentimental when she drinks; which means she's pretty much always emotional now. I went to turn on the lights but she yelled out to stop me. 'Leave them off, I've lit candles,' she said, waving for me to come join her again. To fill the gap. 'It's a full moon. We have to dance when it's a full moon.'

When her eyes were closed, I looked out the window. The moon was, indeed, full. It was swollen and shiny, storing secrets against a stark, ebony sky. A big, black sparkling spatial landscape freckled with stars of varying brightness. Some big, some beaming, but most were dull set against the moon. The small ones just as bright, but too far away to tell. Those faint stars were like us, I thought, dim from afar but bright up close. All kinds of stars were out there; and it was magical. Most often, the way I picture things in my head trumps what I actually see (therein lies my disappointment), but this time, I didn't need to change a thing.

I took a moment to think about what I'd learned from my time with Jimar. Some men, like him, wanted to share love with other partners. I wasn't upset, though, because that's just how he loved (how Rastafarian of him!). I was grateful for the experience because it made me realize I didn't like that kind of sharing. But that moon, knowing others around the world were experiencing that view with me at that exact moment, well that was a different kind of love. A love, in fact, I couldn't wait to share.

The Breast Man

My neighbor's breasts are impossible. I used to think mine
were pretty fantastic until my breasts caught sight of her confidently, magically, painfully buoyant breasts in the window.
She dresses and undresses without pulling the curtains, on
purpose, to gloat. I feel mine drop and sag, dejectedly, every
time; I even hear them whimper. I knew I needed to give
them back their swagger, especially after everything that just
happened with Jimar, so when I woke up I looked out to the
street and saw her leaving the house for work. I couldn't just
sit back any longer and let my boobs get bullied like that so I
ran outside, chest up, nips high, while she was walking to her
car and I asked her if those bad boys were real.

'Tubby Tabby, the puffer penguin!' Margot said, ignoring my
question.

It was hard to run whilst sticking my breasts out like this,
in self-defense, but I persevered.

'Come on!' I begged. 'Tell me!'

'You really are a Cadbury Fruit and Nut bar, you know that?'
I hated it when she flaunted her Britishness. Even her

insults were cool. We get it, you're English! You have an adorable accent, men love it. You have great tits. We get it!

'I think you owe my chest an apology,' I said.

'Why?'

'Because your breasts are insulting them! They're insulting women everywhere and natural breasts just can't look at themselves in the mirror anymore without wanting to commit suicide.'

She looked down to consult her beautiful rack, appeared pleased with what she saw, lifted her head up again smugly and said, 'If you really must know, ask my boyfriend.' Her eyebrow slithered around her temples.

This could have all been solved quite simply, quite quickly, but no, she wanted me to talk to her boyfriend and hear it from the man who knows breasts best: The Breast Man. Milk came out of his house as the two of us were tits up and forward.

'Hi, Milk!' Margot gurgled, annoyingly and flirtatiously waving to him for some reason, tossing and flipping her long hair over her shoulder as she got in her flashy red car and drove off, leaving me and my underdeveloped nips to recoil into their padded bra and cry. Milk waved at me, his eyes wide and hopeful, smiling as he held a bag of garbage.

'Oh, so now you're laughing at my breasts, too?' I yelled out, still reeling from my altercation moments before.

'I'm not laughing,' he said, laughing, as he dumped the

trash. His hair was messy and he was wearing sweatpants and heavy black-rimmed glasses.

'It's almost noon and you're still in your pajamas! You're a grown thirty-one-year-old man!' I swear if I didn't say it, no one else would. I've known him too long; it's almost my job.

'It's my day off.' He always thinks he has a valid comeback but I was not buying it.

'I'm going to the gym!' I shouted defensively, letting him know I take care of myself, that I put my health first. When I'm feeling momentarily insecure, an emotion usually lost on me, telling people I'm going to work out makes me feel like a woman in control.

'Yeah, yeah,' he said, 'you've been saying that for years.' He never believes me. One day I'm going to go to the gym everyday. Starting tomorrow.

Pumped and vexed, I turned to the house and noticed some mail sticking out of Margot's mailbox and I imagined the type of mail she gets. It was probably all about her breasts. I bet her breasts have no idea they were getting fan mail because she most likely forgets to tell them because she thinks it's all about her, anyway. Maybe I've been getting fan mail, too, just like her breasts, but I had no idea because it was getting intercepted.

I did receive a love letter once. It was from a wiggly boy named Barry in fourth grade. I spent the entire summer memorizing what he wrote, twisting the letters backwards so they could even be read from the inside out, you know, so my heart could read them. I knew not just every line but every word and rhythm, the way the vowels tipped and dragged on my tongue when I spoke them. The way they tasted together and apart.

We spent that summer making our Barbies have sex with each other, not really understanding what was going on but feeling like it somehow made us closer because that's what Brenda told me adults do when they love each other. Now Barry's gay and I've lost the letter and the dolls but it's okay, it wasn't the best letter anyway: *'Hello, Tabby. Your hair is nice. You look like my hamster. His name is Steve. He poops a lot. Love, Barry.'* I found out later Steve was so fat he died shortly after. That was the only love letter I've ever received (of course, not counting the ones I don't know about).

Margot's boyfriend works at Whole Foods, where all the good-looking men work. His name is Richard and he is in the prepared-foods section, dicing, slicing, mixing, serving. A part of his left ear is missing. Just the tip. I heard it was cut off in a street fight with a butcher's knife, ironically. Needless to say, he is extremely sexy.

All I've ever dreamed about was being kissed in a super-market. It's quite possibly the most romantic place to kiss because it's romance where it doesn't usually exist; it's being loved during the mundane errands we have to do. I sometimes just walk around the aisles and imagine shopping with my husband, and as I'm blabbering on about ingredients for a meal he'd grab me and kiss me, right there in front of the world. We would be *that* couple.

I steadied myself at the entrance before going through, letting the automatic doors sense my readiness. They opened and I walked through casually, as if to just pick up some eggs on my way to work. I've had jobs before so I knew how to play this up, the whole 'excuse me, I'm on my way to work because I'm a real adult' vibe. I didn't have to act too much because I nanny, and nannying requires protein, too, just like any other job.

My first stop was the fresh fruit and vegetables section, directly across from the prepared foods. I slid from mound to mound, pretending to assess the ripeness of avocados and the amount of green on the lemons while I looked around stealthily for Richard.

From my periphery, I saw him. I could admit I'd like to climb him like a koala but I don't believe in adultery, tempting as it is, so I didn't. I did, however, need him to notice me so I stood up tall to make myself look as slim as possible, turning my hips to the side as if someone were about to take a photo. I learned this trick from my mother. She always crosses her legs in pictures and has her arms on her hips with a side twist to make her figure look svelte. She lives by the motto that if you think you're the best, everyone else will, too. Oh, and to never point out your faults; no one likes an insecure woman.

'If you've got a big butt,' she'd say, 'never, ever, ask a man if it looks big. Just wear a tight belt and he'll never notice because all he'll be able to see is how small your waist is.'

Growing up, my mother had a palpable hatred of insecurity. One time she slapped me when I said no boys would ever like me because of my gapped tooth. 'You're different!' she yelled. 'And thank God for that or else you'd be a real bore! Someone's going to love the shit out of that little gap.' I pondered this as I let my tongue slip through the space in my teeth with the tentativeness of an eel gathering its confidence to surface from a cave. I thought of my mother, of her current suffering self-esteem – she was just dumped by another lover, whom she referred to as Timbo; oh, how she oscillates with ease! I thought of how she needs me to be strong as she inexorably slips back into one of her depressions. I didn't mind looking after her when she was in between men, though, because it gave me an excuse to help her and be needed.

I gave up posing for a moment because it was really hard work (I have no idea how street performers do it), so I started juggling avocados for a minute or two. I dropped one inevitably each attempt, but that was only because I was out of practice. I thought it might startle Richard, the noise the avocados made as they fell, but he was not looking my way. If Richard would have only seen me juggling atrociously, he might have offered to help me get better. He might then even have asked to start meeting me after his shifts to practice and that's how we'd fall for each other (of course, my neighbor would be out of the picture by then). That's another lesson from my mother: Men love a project, something to fix. Sometimes, and I know this from experience, you need to give a man a way to feel needed. You have to create space for someone to come into your life and you do that through need. That's why I cleared room in my closet for a man's clothes. I didn't know what man would need to put his clothes in there but the point was that the room had been created for him for whenever he decided to show up. The moment was nearing and it could even have been that moment, which was quite thrilling. Just like how my mother gives me a reason to be needed, I was giving Richard one. I wanted to write Post-it notes with the words 'It could be now!' on them and stick them all over the city to inspire and remind humans that the best is around the corner. Hope is addictive.

'Wow,' someone said, catching me off guard because no one ever talks to me first, 'you're quite coordinated.' I turned and found a man and he was smiling at me. I wasn't sure if he was playing a game or being real but I would rather assume the best so I relaxed and let myself feel flattered. My cheeks were swelling and I was getting red and it felt good to be alive again.

'I'm juggling,' I said in a fake English accent, trying to invoke the Margot in me, but it came out a little like Dick Van Dyke from *Mary Poppins*. 'But I am doing so terribly, aren't I?' I added, giving him an in. Between him thinking I was British and having a flaw he could fix, I was definitely irresistible. He wasn't Richard, but sometimes we are brought down certain paths and we don't know why until we look at them in retrospect. I thought I was coming to Whole Foods for Richard, but maybe I wasn't. Maybe it was for this guy with the pithy observations. Not knowing was what kept me going.

He didn't tell me I was good at juggling or that I had a cute accent but that was okay because at least he was not an empty flatterer. I'd much rather be patient and let him compliment me when he wanted to, when he was ready.

'Where's that accent from?' he asked.

'London,' I said quickly, effortlessly. 'I'm from Chiswick.' I actually had no idea where Chiswick was but I knew a girl once who said she was from there, and I had to think on my feet.

'No shit. I actually lived in Chiswick for two years. What street?'

I desperately picked up a handful of raspberries and forced them onto each of my fingers so that I could re-enact that moment in *Curly Sue* when the little girl picks off each raspberry and manages to shove them all into her mouth in one go. Almost as soon as they were on my fingers they were in my mouth because I was panicking and needed a few seconds to strategize. I looked like I was storing nuts in my cheeks at this point, all squirrel faced, full of raspberries. I peeked over to see Richard but he must have been in the back room, washing and sorting.

'Oh,' I said, quite pained, trying to keep up my English accent while my mouth was still full. 'You know, just off the main road. The one with the shops. Lovely area!' I had never even been to England before but I was praying there was a main road in Chiswick. He looked at me with a hint of confusion but I stuck my tits out and arched my back because the sweetness of his face made him look like a man who might be distracted by the suppleness and shape of natural breasts.

'What's your name?' he asked.

'Tabitha,' I said. 'And yours?' I couldn't believe this accent was working.

'James. Nice to meet you.' His arm was extended to shake mine so I wiped off the berry juice on my jeans and latched on.

I was looking at this man in front of me and I almost forgot that I was there to stand up for my breasts because I could see James and I together. I could see us cutting wood outside a cabin. Well, I could see him chopping wood outside while I had a fire going inside, cooking some roast dinner, drinking a glass of Prosecco. Good Prosecco, too. I imagined calling out to him from the cabin doors, rusty and in need of WD40 like the Tin Man. And then I realized he was like my lion in need of a heart. 'You can have my heart,' I imagined saying, gladly.

Exuberantly. Proudly. Wildly, until I realized I was saying it out loud.

'Wow . . .' he said, chuckling. 'You move fast, don't you.' I thought at first that he was still charmed but then it hit me: Something must be wrong. He was just too cute and nice, and he was talking to me . . . there had to be a catch. Something must be off. I was so used to men not being interested that when they were, well, I assumed the worst.

'Are you sober?' I asked.

'What?'

'How big is your willy?' I went on, searching for the kicker because he was sounding way too perfect. Inhuman almost. There must have been a catch. 'I just mean roughly.'

'Excuse me?' He was starting to back away from me in small, measured steps, as if I were now the lion and he was walking backwards to keep me calm but really, you knew, he wanted to run.

'Or maybe it's a weird fetish? You like midget porn, don't you? Wait! You have a terrible mother?' I paused for a moment, collecting myself, then said, 'I'm sorry. I'm not used to dating.'

He still looked perplexed but I didn't blame him because it felt like we were in a parallel dimension, one that was cloudy and humid, one wherein you couldn't feel your body but somehow you knew it was tingling. Maybe that was what love felt like.

James was basically around the corner at this point, halfway down the next aisle, when I heard another guy say, 'Excuse me.' When I turned around, it was Richard. He was right up next to me and I couldn't stop looking at his ear.

'Excuse me,' he repeated. He was carrying what appeared to be an enormous tray of chicken salad. It looked heavy and I forgot to move out of the way because I was so distracted by his half-ear. He was sweating and nervous, probably because I looked so good up close.

'Hey, can you please step over a bit. I just need to put this tray down,' he said. I looked over and there was a gap where the chicken salad was supposed to go. While James and I were talking, we must have floated upstream towards the self-serve salad area where you can make your own lunch.

'I'm just here to buy some eggs!' I shouted because I didn't want him to suspect anything.

'Cool,' he said. 'But can you move over a bit so I can slide this in?'

'I thought you'd never ask!' I said, stepping to the side, laughing a little, all of a sudden quite timid. Quite self-conscious that I was coming in too hot, too strong, messing it up before it had begun. Sometimes I hear myself talk and wonder where the words come from. I get embarrassed but figure they're already out, so go with it.

'I know your girlfriend,' I said.

'Margot?' he asked. I watched as his eyebrows engaged in their own version of Downward Dog.

'Well, yes, unless you have another one.' Philanderers! 'Basically,' I paused. 'The point is, Margot's, you know. They're so . . . perfect and—'

I was puffing my chest out again, like the penguin Margot said I was, trying to reinvigorate the confidence of my breasts around The Breast Man but he was ignoring me, trying to place the tray into the slot but it wouldn't fit right because some food was lodged in the hole. I had to get him to talk to me, to tell me what I needed to hear so my boobs didn't slip into their own depression.

'Can you hold this for a sec?' he asked, because he couldn't dislodge and hold at the same time. Clearly he wasn't a multitasker and I wondered how that affected his moves in the bedroom.

'Sure,' I said, holding out my hands, taking the tray. It actually was really heavy so I balanced it on the corner while his fingers fished out remnants of a past dish in the crevices between metal trays.

'So who are you?' he asked, looking at me sideways. Checking me out. Oh, Richard!

'I'm Margot's neighbor,' I said, unsure of how to continue. 'I see why you like her. Her breasts are perfect.'

'Uh, that's a weird thing to say but . . .' he stopped. 'But yeah, they're pretty great.'

'Are they hard when you touch them?' I asked. 'I mean, sure, they look great but are they just as nice as the soft puppies on a natural girl?' I lifted my hands out widely to gesture my boobs but, as soon as I did, the tray abruptly fell off the counter before I could compute what was happening.

'Fuck!' he screamed as salad with nuts flew everywhere, sliding across Whole Foods, landing on shoes. Chunks of chicken sprayed across the floor, mayonnaise everywhere. Cream. Guts. Gross. The vibe was tense, jumpy. Whole Foods employees swarmed the area like flies on shit, and to my dismay, I was being pushed out of the private cleanup party that shortly after ensued.

'It's okay,' I said to no one. 'I've been pushed out by the best of them!' Richard was shouting, hands flailing, as the others screamed at him, berating. Shoppers looked on, rubbernecking, annoyed because they wanted that salad. I noticed my hands sinking in my pant pockets, searching. I found an avocado from earlier that I must have accidentally, distractedly, put in my pocket when James was after me. I guess I really *was* nervous.

I looked at the avocado and I wanted to join the pit in its cocoon of warmth and soft green but I was not sure how I was going to get there. I wanted to have a strong core, to be constantly, unconditionally cradled by velvet. I wanted to know what it was like to expire and be past my best-before date only to taste even better because I was so ripe. I squeezed the avocado as hard as I could until the fat started to seep through my fastened fingers. I was thinking I was never going to stop squeezing, even when I hit the pit, hit rock bottom; I was going to keep squeezing as hard as I could, getting every last bit, because once it stopped I'd have to live in the world again. I'd have to face Richard, chicken breasts, Margot and her perky breasts. And of course, I'd have to deal with my own, less pronounced, less aggressive, less offensive breasts, sweet as they were.

I kept my fists tight as people continued to fuss around me, as if I was not even there. I felt myself perspire and my hands tremble. I had this feeling that if I didn't release my clasp soon, I'd die from sheer exhaustion. I thought then that I was dying but when I looked down, all the green was on the floor, alongside the broken pit, and there was nothing left in my hand to squeeze. Somehow, though, I was still alive.

Richard looked up and asked me if I was going to pay for that avocado and it crystallized at once the whole situation. Instantly I became very aware of my value, how mature I really was (I thought maybe being in a natural foods store, without a processed item in sight, also made me feel better). And so I grabbed my boobs and yelled out, 'See these melons? They're real and they're beautiful! They're just as good as jaunty breasts because they have their own unique disposition and personality. They might not be hard, but they rock!' When I looked down, I saw I'd stained my shirt with the remains of avocado green on my fingers. Two painted hands on my boobs; too bad they were my own.

James must have been close enough to witness me drop the accent because I could faintly hear him telling someone, 'Hey, wait, she said she was British,' but it was okay because I just didn't care. It was so exhilarating to be proud of my breasts again that, all of a sudden, I could feel them lifting. Expanding. Growing not just bigger than they've ever been but bigger than all the biggest breasts in the world. Bigger than Pamela Anderson's. More bouncy than Jennifer Love Hewitt's. And most importantly, more fabulous than Margot's miraculous breasts, real or fake, because they were mine. I didn't find love but I did learn to love myself even a little bit more. If only my mother could see me now, she'd be so proud.

The Dancer

The charity event my sister invited me to was looming and I had less than an hour to get ready. My mom was screaming out obscenities because she couldn't find anything to wear as my sister drowned out her moaning with a hair dryer. I put on some bright red lipstick because I know red lips lure in eyes and it's a perfect way to draw attention when you're not on a date and know that no one is going to kiss you. I put on my wedges but they're too high for me to walk comfortably in and I had to hold on to the sides of the walls and anyone around me to keep me from falling, but hey, the extra height always helps.

'Hey, Randall,' I said, steadying myself as I bent down to give him a hug.

'Spin me!' he said, to which Mary of course added, 'Me too! Spin me too!'

I slipped off my shoes because, if I didn't, I'd break all my bones, and picked up Randall.

'You first,' I said. 'Ready?' I grabbed him and had his elbows secure themselves on top of my forearms, and started to spin.

The faster I went the more free I felt as he squealed and winced at the increasing speed at which we flew around together in circles. I stopped as soon as I felt light-headed and we wobbled from side to side to steady ourselves. I took a few minutes before doing it to Mary as you couldn't spin one kid without the other.

Milk walked in through the front door and within minutes the two kids were on him like bees on a syrup-laden pancake and I watched them crawl all over him, pawing in plea for more spins. I noticed he was holding a backgammon set.

'Hey,' he said to me as he hugged them. 'You look great.'

'Thanks, Milk,' I said, quite bashfully for some reason. I started patting my dress down to give my hands something to do.

'Is that backgammon?' I asked, shocked he'd have such a game.

'Yeah, it's my dad's old set. He's had it for ever. I thought maybe I'd teach it to Mary and Randall.'

'But you don't know how to play!' I laughed.

'I play all the time,' he said.

'Are you any good?'

'I'm not gonna lie, I'm not the worst.' He winked at me but all I could do was laugh at his confidence.

'Can I ask you something?' There's a question bursting at my seams. 'Am I intense?'

He snorted at first. 'Absolutely.'

'I mean it!'

'I'm serious, you're totally intense and insane.'

'This isn't comforting, Milk.'

'But, you know, you're also the most fascinating person in the world, right? Everyone else is super-boring next to you.'

'You don't need to lie to make me feel better,' I said. 'I can handle it. Do I scare men off because I'm so, you know, in their face?'

'Breathe,' he said, interrupting me. I was out of breath, and the more aware of it I became the harder it was to catch it. 'You think way too much about all of this.'

'Come on! I'm dying here!'

'Okay,' he started, 'well, yeah. Most guys want simple girls and you're like a big, giant rolling rock of complexity, bull-dozing everything in its path and you're probably just too much work for most men. It's a compliment, believe me.'

'Hmmmm . . .' I said, because how else would I follow that. I couldn't tell if my heart hurt or if it was happy or if I was just pre-menstrual. 'Thanks for looking after Mary and Randall,' I added. Before our smiles faded, my mom and Brenda came downstairs.

'We shouldn't be home late,' Brenda told Milk. 'Eat whatever you want in the kitchen. I've left you some food but if you don't like it just make whatever you feel like. Thank you so, so much.'

In the car, Brenda drove, Mom took the passenger seat and I sat in the back. I loved the back because you could look out the car window and imagine you're going anywhere with anyone and just ignore the conversation up front without needing any other excuse except that you can't hear them. It reminded me a little of when I'd drive away from Ernesto, waving my special wave.

'So,' my mom began in her sinuous way. 'I snooped. I know, I know, I shouldn't have, but I did.'

'What are you talking about?' Brenda said.

'I wanted to know about Randall's background, what with Mary and him hanging out all the time now, I just wanted to know more about his situation.'

'Mom,' Brenda replied. 'They're in kindergarten. It's not like they're dating and sneaking out of the house to get high. He's a cute little kid.'

'Ah, yes, but parents influence their kids a tremendous amount.'

'You can say that again,' Brenda chimed in.

'I just wanted to know, okay?' my mom said histrionically. 'I'm curious, sue me.'

'So what did you find out?' I asked. The wind whipped my hair around my face, arousing and punishing me at the same time.

'Well I called Jenny, Victoria's mother, who lives next to

them and she told me Randall's a foster kid. But it's a little different because he used to be at this group home for kids who keep failing placements in the system. Poor little guy. He's a wild one.'

'I'd be a wild one, too,' I piped in, 'if I were thrown into homes with weird-ass strangers all the time.' As I said it, I realized that Randall probably wasn't joking the other day about where his mother was.

'You were born wild, Tabby, and you had biological parents,' Brenda said before turning back to Mom. 'But it's good he's finally found a home, right? I mean, after all that shuffling and state government bullshit and stuff, it's great he has somewhere stable now.'

'Yes, darling, but that's not entirely the point. They didn't bring him home because they wanted a kid,' Mom said. 'I'll tell you that much right now.' She paused and lit a cigarette, tapping the ash out the window on her exhale. 'Their place is a pigsty. Disgusting. It's sad, really, when I think about how there are so many people abusing the foster system just because it's an extra way to make some money. God knows what they're doing with it.'

'That's jumping a bit, Mom,' Brenda suggested. 'They might be good people. Messy, but good hearted. You can't assume that all foster parents are in it for the money.'

'The dad always sounds drunk when I call the house to see if it's okay if I take Randall out after school,' I added.

'Nothing wrong with a few drinks,' Mom said.

'We're not talking about you,' Brenda retorted.

'Well we have to get him out of there,' I said. 'But it's such a stupidly twisted system. I've already looked into it.'

'You've looked into foster care?' Brenda asked, shocked.

'I just don't feel good dropping him off,' I said. 'When I took him home the other night, the house was so eerie, so spooky, lonely and dark. I didn't want to leave him there, but of course, I had to. Otherwise I'd be kidnapping him.'

'At least he looks well fed,' my mom added, characteristically switching her side of the argument halfway through. 'This could all be a grand miscalculation of character.'

'I just hope that even if they're doing it for the money, they love him,' I said. 'So, if there's one thing we actually *can* do, it's shower that little sweet soul with some love. By the way, have you seen his eyelashes? They're longer than RuPaul's. So jealous.'

As I looked out the window, I could see in my flickering reflection that my cheeks looked less defined. I really should be running every day. Milk was right; I never go to the gym. I knew I only needed one, just one man to work out . . . but in seeing this face in the window, some girl I don't really recognize, I wondered if she'll find him. I wondered if the chances were on her side. I also wondered if she should dye her hair lilac, just to change things up. I couldn't tell if I got all soppy and self-reflective and sad because we were talking about Randall, or because one of my favorite love songs was playing on the radio and it made me feel like I was in a movie. Just a girl staring out a window after her lover died at war. I wasn't entirely sure why I was down, especially after having such a wonderfully exhilarating and confidence-boosting experience at Whole Foods. I was starting to think too much, tired from all the effort. Maybe I was beginning to flip-flop like my mother. I was running out of time.

We arrived at the party: a decadent mansion in the Hollywood Hills overlooking the sprawling sea of lights that is night-time Los Angeles. It was a breast cancer fundraiser, so pink was everywhere. On the rare occasions I go to parties, I always have that sickly feeling, plagued with the fear that someone will come and eject me, claiming I was never invited in the first place. Admittedly, this has never happened, but the worry is always there.

I heard myself talking under my breath about how I shouldn't have eaten that whole can of broad beans before I came out because they were making me not just bloat, but steadily expand to the point that my stomach was stretched taut; I might have just blown up in one big fart. I had become obsessive recently about white beans with rosemary, dressed in oil and tossed with copious amount of salt. I couldn't get enough but I was bearing the consequences and feared that at any moment I would regret following those beans with too many prunes. If Mary were here she'd definitely start jumping in celebration of my looking pregnant and be on the road to naming my twins.

Trays of Prosecco were being passed around by gorgeous people in penguin suits and I thought, when locking eyes with one penguin in particular as I thanked him for the bubbly glass, that maybe tonight was just what I needed. His smile infused in me a feeling of possibility; that was usually all I needed. My sister was on her second already and I would bet my fifth can of beans in the pantry that my mom was on her third.

It drove me crazy when I saw people not taking sips of their drink after they clinked glasses; it's less a pet peeve and more of an actual concern that their wish won't come true. I mean, that's why we cheers.

'So, why are we here again?' I asked.

My mom waved the bubbly around as she took a thespian breath, as if the party were her audience and she was ready for her performance.

'Do we ever know why we are anywhere?' She sent me one of her winks, and even though I didn't get the answer I asked for, it was somehow okay. She was right; who cared? The point was that we were all there, having Prosecco like we were on a mini-holiday. The three of us, alcoholic ducks in a row, all scanning the room from the sidelines. Before long, my mom was dancing with a man twenty years her junior and her laugh sustained the energy of the crowd as it has never failed to do.

'Come on, girls!' she yelled from across the room. 'Grab someone and get dancing!'

'I'm so hungry,' Brenda said as she started to wander away in search of sustenance. Once she starts, she keeps going. 'I need food.'

I kept trying to make eyes with someone attractive, well, let's be honest, with *anyone* at that party but no one was paying any attention so I started to look for Brenda near the buffet table. I couldn't find her but I did find the shrimp skewers and bowls of risotto and started to scoop up as much as I could while juggling my champagne glass under my armpit. I wasn't even hungry. I looked up and behind the bar was a huge mirror. I couldn't quite believe my sight. Looking ahead at the life behind me, I saw myself stuffing and stacking plates of food with booze under my arm, alone, while the room partied on behind me. I was so bloated from the beans, and the prunes were going to make me wish I'd invested in Depends. I couldn't for the life of me understand why I was still stuffing. I was so full but I was feeling sad about my plummeting love life so I just kept stuffing. I tried to understand why I wasn't able to hold on to the success of The Breast Man this time, but I think even for an optimist, little wins lose their staying power when there are enough big fails.

Then I saw it: three girls I went to Malibu High School with were walking towards the buffet table, towards me, and it set me into panic mode but I couldn't put anything down because I was holding too much. No free hands. I was frozen and so to empty a plate, I shoved down a few of the pastries by bending over and grabbing them with my mouth. I was chewing and chewing furiously with my head down to avoid their recognition and it was working until Felicia Adams literally bumped into me, sending her cocktail all over my outfit.

'Oh my God,' she yelped, 'I'm so sorr— wait, Tabitha . . . Gray? From Malibu?'

'Tanker Tabby,' Juniper Wilson added, eyeing me up and down. She thought she was so clever because they both started with the letter T. And then there was Alexa Brimstone, the width of my anklebone, in a stunning skin-tight dress, the kind I thought were designed only for mannequins (until now). I was still chewing; I couldn't stop. There was too much in my mouth. I almost couldn't swallow and that in itself made my eyes flutter. I was dying again. Surely, I was dying.

All three of them were staring at me, mouths agape, as I attempted to swallow the rest of my food. I assumed high school was the same for everyone, until I realized it wasn't. I never had enemies or bullies. I had lots of friends! That time when Felicia and Rebecca told me that I should sing the National Anthem in front of the entire Malibu High School at assembly because my voice was so amazing was just a mistake; they didn't mean to embarrass me! Come to think of it, maybe they weren't so nice. Goddammit, I've always been too optimistic.

'How have you all been?' I eventually said, my gulp louder than I'd hoped.

'You look exactly the same!' Alexa burst out.

'I've been great,' Felicia answered, throwing out her hand. 'Just got engaged!'

'Congrats!' I said with forced enthusiasm. It was a standard diamond ring. Everything you're told to want by De Beers except originality. I managed to set the rest of my plates down and grabbed another passing Prosecco.

The server looked at me and handed me a napkin with a wink. He could tell I was being faced with my past and it was not a good look.

'I'm married,' Juniper said, patting her belly. 'I've got a little one on the way. Already getting those stretch marks that will never go away.' She smiled ever so smugly.

'I had two kids already and I'm the thinnest I've ever been!' Alexa chimed in, making you want to punch her. 'It's like being a mom *helped* me to lose weight. Crazy, right? Donnie always says I'm the sexiest I've ever been.'

Donnie and Alexa met each other in college, at the University of Southern California. It was the typical fraternity/sorority setup, with bulging muscles, thigh gaps, anorexia and beer pong to thank for their everlasting love. They were everything I wanted to avoid in college, although now, being a face-stuffing, Prosecco-downing single and soon-to-be-unemployed nanny in front of them, I considered possibly having made the wrong choice. I knew about Donnie and their kids from her pictures on Facebook during one of my late-night prowls.

'What about you, TT?' Juniper asked me. 'All I can remember in high school was you getting detention for indecent conduct or something.' She let out a few high-pitched laughs as she reminisced on my unfortunate time in school.

'Oh yeah!' Felicia said, the light in her brain illuminating her bulb-like bobble head, intermittently giggling. 'You were so weird!' she exclaimed, patronizingly hitting the top of my shoulder. 'Like making up stories and following people around with that big smile on your face like a creep!'

'You know I can hear you, right?'

'Sorry,' they said in unison behind glasses and poorly upheld personas.

'Hey,' Felicia chuckled, ridiculing. 'What was that thing you'd always say? "I have a big crush on life?" Was that it?'

'Yeah,' I said, feeling like I was seventeen again. 'It's a good thing to have, you know.'

I guess these girls weren't so nice to me in school. I must have blocked it out. The blind spot, the Achilles heel of optimism. I wasn't the outcast, but when I tried to remember it I couldn't recall much other than not understanding why they were calling me weird. I just remembered being happy. I remembered smiling.

I wanted to say something better, to come back with some witty phrase to shut them up and defend my name, my memory. I wanted to be Dorothy Parker at the Algonquin Round Table, but I was frozen, paralyzed, hypnotized by their deprecating humor. I wanted to expel confidence but that kind of humor was lost on me and, unusually, I had nothing to say. I knew when they left I'd think of the best line but in that moment, I had nothing. I kept forgetting to breathe and then all of a sudden I would have to take in a huge breath to accommodate the fact that I had not been breathing; each time it would freak me out. The more I breathed, the more panicked I would get.

They scooted off before I realized I'd been left so I turned around to my right and saw a guy wearing a sweet suit.

'I like your bow tie,' I told him. He looked at me and smiled, holding his tray of Prosecco flutes.

'God, I hate these people,' he said, smiling at me.

'Oh, they're not so bad.'

Every party I go to, albeit rare, I inevitably end up hanging out with the crew working it, as they are undeniably more interesting than anyone else at the party. I looked out over the heads in the room, through to the back and out the window where the night met the moon and everything else had a place to disappear.

'I went to school with some of those girls over there,' I explained, pointing as indiscreetly as possible as he followed my finger to the three of them. 'They used to sit in the back of the classroom and throw things at my head. Usually Tic Tacs or something. Anything small so the teacher couldn't see.'

'Girls are mean,' he said.

'And then I'd turn around and ask them to stop, and the teacher would throw me out of the classroom for interrupting,' I told him. 'This happened most days. There's a huge part of American History I missed out on because of them.'

'Well, shit,' he said. 'Now that's what I call a real setback.' He laughed slowly and deeply, and its weight lulled me for a moment as I tried to regain my confidence in the middle of that uneven crowd. The man with the tray was named Gerald, but, 'People call me Gerry,' he told me. He was probably, if I were to guess, in his middle twenties. Really cute, looked like he was from Japan but I learned he was from El Salvador.

'Gerald's a funny name,' I said.

'It's kind of old, right?' he admitted.

'Ha, yeah.'

Guests walked by and I watched them pick up from his tray without even making eye contact with him. It really upset me so I started to bully them with my eyes but they were not looking at me either.

This one girl came up and said, 'Can I give this to you?' in the whiniest voice you could imagine while she set her glass down on his clean platter before giving him a chance to respond. He smiled as she turned her back on us, moving her hair off and around her shoulder.

'I'm sorry,' I said to Gerry.

'What for?'

'Her,' I said, referring to all people who didn't look party staff in the eye. 'I'm a nanny. I'm used to being bossed around and walked all over. I also used to wait tables for a while and I've never wanted to right-hand someone so badly as I did when I got a condescending thank you from people like that. It's almost worse than no thank you at all, because you know they think they're being nice but it's patronizing as hell.'

We watched the crowd as I learned about growing up in El Salvador. I told him about my former, now outgrown, proclivity for Mexicans and he laughed, at first startled, but then he relaxed when he realized it was a compliment. He told me his uncle was an outlaw and his mother shipped him to the States before she could come, to protect him first. Start a new life with better odds. I spotted my mother, guzzling down wine in the middle of the dance floor, dancing all by herself. Swaying back and forth to the jazzy beat of the swing band, whose name, apparently, was Afternoon in Paris.

'She looks like the only one having fun,' he said, looking at my mother. Seeing me, she hovered across the room towards us, dancing with each step to the rhythm of the acoustic guitars.

'Oh, I remember those girls. They were awful to you in school!' she said, dipping around, swaying. 'I remember when Milk found you in the bathroom wrapped in toilet paper. You couldn't move.'

'Why didn't he do anything?' I asked.

'You don't remember? He did. Took the poor guy ages to untangle you and I think he threatened to do the same to the girls if they did it again. I'm pretty sure they stopped bothering you after that.'

'When I think about it, high school was the worst,' I said. 'I used to think hindsight was 20/20 but it all seems pretty blurry to me. Maybe I blocked it all out.'

'Well, darling, at least you didn't have my mom for a mother. High school is a respite when home is the real nightmare.' She scooted off before I had the chance to tell her that Grandma was just trying. She didn't know better. It was her way of doing her best.

'That's my mom,' I told Gerald. 'She's always like that.'

'If I were here as a guest,' he began. 'I'd be the first one dancing with her. All these chumps are too stiff. She can move.'

'It's interesting because I look at her and I don't get why she doesn't have more attention.'

'These kind of men want the safe choice. They're boring, they want the trophy wives. They want to play the part and have someone to play the part with them. Doesn't matter how fun or cool your mom is because she'll always be a risk.' He stops to take a breath, survey the room while I wonder if he's talking about me just as much as he is my mother. 'Some fuckers think they play better than the rest of them, and because of that, they do. It's like soccer. Have you been watching the World Cup?'

'God no,' I said, confused.

'Okay, just go with me on this. Some of the weaker players play the best because they're the most confident. They perform above the standard.'

'But are they the ones who actually are scoring the goals?'

'Sometimes,' Gerry said. 'But overall, they play better and smarter than the guys at their skill level, but who aren't as arrogant.'

'Huh,' I said. 'I get your point, but is that a real fact?'

'I'm not sure,' he admitted. 'Actually, I have no idea if it's true. A buddy told me that once and it made sense.' I pondered this for a moment, kicking it around like the players do with their balls on the field, trying to deconstruct it. The idea that the confident ones finish first didn't make sense to me though, because I've always been the one with confidence, I've always been the aggressor, and it was not working out so well. Perhaps it was because I was just not playing the game right, or I wasn't arrogant enough. I was already pretty optimistic but maybe my doubts were being detected, like a bull sniffing fear from an enemy.

I grabbed a muffin from the table and offered it to him.

'Hungry?' I asked, holding it up.

'I can't eat while I'm working.'

'Tell them I made you eat it,' I said as I took the tray from him and held it while he looked around the room to make sure his supervisor wasn't around. He shoved it into his mouth in two bites like a shark eating a seal, gulping it down before it was really chewed properly. Or chewed at all.

'Impressive!' I said, eyes wide.

'Ha,' he laughed, wiping the crumbs from his face and tightening up his jacket. 'Thank you. I was starving.'

We just stood there side by side. Every time someone came up and took a glass without thanking him I said, 'You're welcome,' on his behalf.

I saw my mom start to lose it. She was very off balance at this point in the evening, and I felt I must go save her.

'Okay,' I said. 'Now my duty calls.'

'Hey,' he said, stopping me. 'Thanks for talking to me for a minute.'

'Are you kidding?' I exclaimed. 'You're the best conversationalist here.'

I pushed past all the glitter and jackets towards my mother, parting botoxed faces and Rolexes like the sea.

The closer I got, the more in focus my mother became. She was proudly grabbing her crotch with her free hand, the other one waving the wine glass in the air to the music. She was the only one who didn't know she was dancing alone.

She noticed me walking towards her through the crowd and saluted me, her wine horns around her mouth more pronounced and comforting than ever. As the glass was held high over her head, her other hand quickly reached for her heart. Clutching. I thought she was just so in love with the moment she was wanting to warm her chest, but then, as if in slow motion, her face contorted, wincing, wrinkles scurrying around her face. Her high smile dropped to a pained expression and all at once she fell to the ground, her hand still on her heart, wine glass breaking in every direction.

'Help!' I screamed out, running towards her. My body hot, tingling, panicked. 'Mom!'

Everyone in the middle of the room stopped and looked at my mother, frozen as they figured out what was happening. Gerry started yelling out for someone to call 911 and a few others rushed over to her side as I knelt down beside her.

'Mom!' I shouted, grabbing her head and placing it between

my hands. Her stare was empty, disconnected. 'Mom, what's wrong? What's wrong?'

'She's having a heart attack!' someone screamed, inciting the room into chaos.

'Brenda! Where's Brenda? My sister's a nurse. Brenda!' I pleaded as my hands shook, trying to figure out what had happened, what to do. I couldn't think straight because my mind was racing hysterically. Brenda yelled out from the other side of the room; her volume moving from faint to full blast as she reached us.

I moved to the side as Brenda checked her vitals. I looked back between my mother and the crowd, and realized no one had called the ambulance so I dialled 911.

'What's your emergency?' the operator asked.

'My mother, she was dancing and then, then she grabbed her heart, and collapsed—'

'Is she breathing, ma'am?' My mom's eyes came back to us, darting around the room as she realized what was going on. She was breathing heavily, panting in short bursts.

'Yes, yes she is.' I watched as Brenda did what nurses do, checking her pulse, her chest, her breathing, her temperature with the back of her hand. She looked over to me and let out a giant sigh of relief.

'She's okay,' Brenda said. 'We still need to get her checked out but it's not an emergency. She's okay.'

'Oh thank God,' the party host said off to our left as

he looked over at us, not helping. The crowd, once stiff and breath-halted, returned to a stir as they scattered off to their glasses and party snacks.

'Are you there?' the operator asked. 'What is your location?'

'I think,' I started, unsure of what to say, unsure if we needed to go to the hospital, but I trusted that if Brenda said she was fine, she was. 'I think she's okay now. I'm sorry.'

I hung up and looked back to my sister, who was still holding Mom's hand. 'So what happened?'

'I think she was having a panic attack.'

'Mom, are you okay?' I asked. 'You were holding on to your heart . . .'

'I, I . . .' she began, 'I don't know. I was dancing and then out of nowhere had this sharp pain in my chest.'

'You were having a panic attack,' Brenda explained. 'Thankfully, it wasn't a heart attack.'

My mom tried to get up but Brenda told her to stay where she was until she collected herself, in case she banged her head too hard on the fall. 'Just to be sure, stay lying down for another minute or so, okay, Mom? You'll be okay. We're here with you.'

I looked at her spread out on the ground, helpless as I hadn't seen her before, like a child. I wondered what could have spurred it on.

'You were having such a good time,' I said.

'I was having a heart attack!' Mom yelled out, wanting to make the most of it, annoyed it was only a panic attack, searching for a reason her heart would give out over her nerves. 'My nerves betray me,' was all she came up with.

'You know she gets panic attacks, Tabby,' Brenda said. 'She needs to stop smoking and drinking so much, too. All that just makes it worse.'

'I'd rather die than stop drinking!' my mom said with renewed vigor.

'Pump the brakes, Mom,' Brenda said, fragile still and caring in a way only disaster can bring about.

'We need to figure this out,' I said. 'I know she gets freaked out sometimes but it doesn't make sense for it to happen here. She was having a ball.'

Brenda looked at me with her heavy eyes, now flattened. 'I think we need to go home. Mom needs to rest.'

On the way back, Brenda insisted Mom begin to find a way to de-stress naturally. Try yoga and meditation, maybe, before rushing into anti-anxiety medication again. 'Klonopin really fucked you up, remember?' We all know what she was like on Klonopin. We didn't need that again. It disconnected her from a reality she already tried to distance herself from. If she started using again now, I'd never get through to her.

Mom's phone started to ring and it was Delina. I grabbed it from her before it went to voicemail.

'Hi, Delina, it's me,' I said.

'Oh, darling, hello! It was such a treat to see you the other day! Just checking on how the big party is going?'

'Not so well. Mom had a panic attack,' I said. 'I thought she was dying, Delina. I thought we lost her. I thought she was having a heart attack.'

'Dear, dear, don't worry,' she said, trying to comfort me from afar. 'Oh, what a worry this all is. She really is so extreme, our Twilda, isn't she? All or nothing. Her body can't handle the highs too high or lows too low. I've told her this!'

I was so shaken up, the only thing I knew how to do was let it all out.

'Oh cut out the dramatics, Tabby,' Mom said from the front seat. 'I'm fine!'

Hearing her say she was fine only made me worry about her more. Delina let me sniffle for a minute longer.

'Can your mother hear me if I say something?'

'No,' I whimpered.

'You know I love you, and love you exactly as you are, right?' she began. 'And I couldn't love your mother any more than I do, but I am concerned about her unraveling. Julia and I both are. We know how you idolize her so, and,' she stopped to sigh. 'Well, we worry, darling, that she's slipping away. She's getting worse, it seems.'

'Yeah, I know,' I agreed.

'We're going to come over soon, okay?'

'Please. We need you.'

My mother was undoubtedly losing it and that naturally set me spinning because everything was slipping from me, too. I had two choices: Become my mother or rebel against her. But I loved how she was just as she was. I wanted her to be right because I also knew I was so much like her, which meant that if I was going to be okay, then I damned well hoped my mom had it right.

All this time, I thought I was doing it for her, to prove to her that love exists. Finding my own love was just a pawn in a larger game. I didn't think about its repercussions on my life, how I would become her if my luck didn't change, and if she couldn't handle reality, then how would I ever cope, and not just on my own but in a world without her? I wanted to want to be her, just as I'd want my children to want one day to be like me. I needed her to be right. If she had it wrong after all, then I was fucked.

I was left, therefore, with the only option of trying harder, although to be honest, I was already trying so hard I wasn't really sure what trying harder would look like. I'd still be me, like Delina and Julia said, but with no holds barred. Surely I was holding something back. I had to get in the ring and be the fighter because everyone else was in the bar drinking.

The Ju-jitsu Master

The good news is that there are still men out there who like to wrestle, and there is nothing like a grappler to reinvigorate one's optimism and confidence. I was watching mixed martial arts on cable the other day (because I had to learn how this whole fighting thing worked) and, well, let me just say, I exploded with excitement. I saw these big, bicep-bulging, ferociously primal men grabbing at each other and just thought, why have I not signed up for ju-jitsu before?

'Oh, yes, I do love blood sports,' my mom said as she passed by, cigarette bouncing on her lips like big tits on a Punjabi bus ride. 'Beautiful bodies, all that contact!' She was looking for something, a lost bangle or earring. She always thinks she's lost something, turning pillows over and searching under tables.

'It's just so manly!' I gushed. 'Not bar fighting, that would make me sick. Just the idea of someone being able to stand up for me if I needed him to. It's quintessential romance.'

'Most men cut and run, baby,' she said as smoke danced its famous dance around the shape of her face. 'You need to find someone who will fight for you or else you'll be the only one swinging.' She stopped at the mirror, grabbed her boobs and turned to the side while lifting them up and down. Up and down, shoulders back. Upright. Smoke and mirrors. 'Someone who can take the challenge. Someone who isn't afraid to put his hands up!' She paused and held her reflection, keeping it in her lungs before letting out her breath. At least she was looking in mirrors again. That was a good sign.

'I'm just not sure men who will fight for you exist anymore. So it's just up to us now, it's just you and me, baby,' she yelled, thumping her chest like she did when heated. 'You and I, we're the ones who will have to fight. You can't rely on anyone else to, that's the quickest way you end up alone.'

She was so dramatic; it was fun to listen to. Sometimes she talked with this slightly Southern twang, although it could have just been the wine slurring her speech. It was relaxing, though, the way she spoke, despite her histrionics. Half of the time, I didn't have to listen to what she was saying because I got what I needed from her cadence.

'Aha!' she squealed, finding her lost bangle in her coat pocket. 'I found it!' She never actually loses anything. She just has this fear she always has and if something does actually get lost, it turns into a meltdown centered around the despair of all the other things she might have lost that she doesn't know about.

'But just because Dad never fought for us doesn't mean there aren't men out there who will, right?'

She smiled, not in fond memory of him but more because

doing things with emphasis made her feel powerful. She took a deep breath in as she fluffed pillows around the living room, moving from slow to fast at a woozy pace.

'I'm losing my faith in it,' she told me, pausing again for a moment. I was used to the speed at which her demeanor could switch without warning. How fast she could move from frantic to calm, relaxed to panicked. 'But life is a funny thing,' she continued. 'Nothing is black and white. It's all in the grey, like our last name.'

It was the first time in a while I'd heard my mom talk about being a Gray without wanting to throw a plate across the room. She hadn't changed her name after Dad left because she didn't want Brenda or me to have a different last name from her. It was her way of holding on.

'It's weird how Brenda doesn't like blurred lines,' I interjected, trying to find a way to connect us. 'She wants everything sharp and defined.'

'And where's the fun in that?' she said. 'The funky shit in the middle is where the good stuff is. That's where you become a real woman.'

'Yeah,' I said.

Mom had a new boyfriend this week. His name was Donald. Terrible name. I wondered what they used to call him as a child. Donald isn't a kid's name. That's probably why he was so boring now, because he's been old forever. 'He's not a fighter, quite the opposite actually, but like I said, they don't exist anymore. At least, well, at least he's very established,' she told me, but all it did was cement his senescence. She was settling. I could tell from how her face dilated that she was exaggerating to make him sound better. She kept dating men too rich, too useless, too sad. She would get up so close that her vision would obscure to the point she would no longer be able to see them in full frame. The cracks I could see were, to her, softened and blurred. I supposed it was because she wanted them to be. My mom used to be so wild, what with all those stories she's told me, but I think my dad took her adventurous spirit with his coat and socks when he left.

'But the guys you're dating now,' I started. 'They're not like the ones in your adventures.'

'That's because I was ignorant before. Stability can be really exciting. Donald is F.U.N.,' she lied. 'Okay, sometimes he's a bit stiff – in the wrong way – but he's an accurate lover.' I knew she was miserable because she always reserved terms of measurement for when she was settling. I could tell just by the way she fluffed those pillows. She was so anxious to fill in the gap of space Dad once took that she pulled at everything around her until it became all but a mound of tangled string. I can see it clearly because, of course, I have perspective from my vantage point. I needed to prove to her that men who will fight for you still exist before all the fighting she did alone exhausted her, and it just so conveniently happened that there was a ju-jitsu school right around the corner from our house.

THE OPTIMIST

I imagined there would be a roundup of muscly, tattoo-covered guys with names like Moracio (from Italy) and Alain (from France) because they were so cool and multi-cultural. I walked in under a decrepit sign that said, 'Ju-jitsu World' painted on a wood panel. I loved the rough and gruff of this place; someone really thought about how to make it authentic, and I appreciated that attention to detail. Great signs, literally.

A sweet, chiseled Asian dude sat behind a desk as he yelled out to the other guys. He had a very strong East Coast accent.

'New Jersey?' I asked as I approached him.

'Boston,' he corrected. 'You here for the 3:30?'

I had on tight, *Grease*-like spandex pants. You know, the ones Sandy wore in the final dance scene? Those. Tight. Pants. I could barely get them over my thighs so the mere prospect of having to pee at some random moment during class made me anxious. That anxiousness actually made me feel like I had to pee. Good thing the pants were black. On top, I had on a white tank with no bra. My nipples were saluting with such patriotic zest they could have been confused for concealed weapons. I was already having fun and class hadn't even begun yet.

'Sign the waiver here,' East Coast told me. 'You done this before?'

'Not exactly,' I said, giggling a little. 'Unless you count bedroom wrestling!'

He looked at me blankly and then said, 'Take your shoes off, lockers in back, class starts in three minutes.'

At least he was direct. I headed over to where the rest of the gang congregated and pretended to warm up. A little forward hang towards the toes, a little arm and elbow stretch. My pants were too tight but at least they showed off my womanly figure. To my right stood an older, silver-haired fox. His hair was greying and a few chest hairs sprouted from his formidable torso, his body defying the age his hair's loss of pigment suggested. I looked down and discovered his wedding ring: a fox doesn't stay single for long.

To my left was a tall, skinny young black kid with an Afro. He looked over and gave me a 'what's up' nod then turned away before I could return one. The rest of the room was populated by: a rotund Persian man, the Asian East Coaster from the front who joined the class, and a butch but annoyingly attractive girl around my age with blonde hair. Okay, she wasn't so butch. In fact, she was half my size, but she looked tough. The blonde pulled her hair back as she rose and fell on her tiptoes, apparently her misguided method of warming up. She had a tattoo on the inside of her wrist of two interlocking infinity symbols. What does that even mean? It was hard to know if you liked her or you hated her. She had a scary bitch vibe, but I also wanted to be her friend. And last but not least, our teacher. The man fiddling with the stereo in the corner of the room, whom I had overlooked because his back was towards me, turned around in slow motion and faced us. He was a most beautiful specimen of man. When the music came on, it was like watching Jesus with the music crescendo-ing as he took center stage, the room going black save for the bright light around him.

'I'm Moses,' he said as I melted. You've got to be kidding me, I thought. Moses! Moses! I moaned under my breath, imagining, mind wrestling. I couldn't tell where he was from. I thought he could be Israeli, with his dark curly hair. 'I think I want to focus on take-downs today,' he announced. 'First we're going to go through form, then we'll move it into the ring. Okay?' It was the kind of question that required no answer.

The room clapped in unison. Grunting was detected, as was the patting of men's shoulders in some show of camaraderie as my heart widened looking at the man who would become the love of my life. Tabitha and Moses. I kept repeating it to myself and, I have to admit, it sounded pretty smooth. Then, just as I was starting to feel comfortable, the door opened and slammed shut and in walked Milk.

'Milk?' I said. 'What are you doing here?'

When he saw me, he paused for a moment and did a double take as if it were strange to see me in there. 'What do you mean?' he countered as he took off his shoes at the edge of the mat. He threw his keys onto the desk and looked around the room. Everyone was facing him, hands at their hips. 'Hey guys,' he said.

'Hey, Milken,' the room replied as he walked towards the front mirrors.

'The man himself,' Moses said as they embraced with a secret handshake and bow. I couldn't believe this. How did all these guys, especially Moses, know Milk?

'So you want to learn how to fight?' he eventually asked me. 'Or are you here to meet some fighters?' He might be dense, but he's pretty savvy sometimes.

'I'm already a fighter,' I said, leaning in. His eyebrows moved up his forehead as his chin and lips moved down into what seemed like an impressed expression. 'But love is a tango, Milk. My mom thinks that you can just have one fighter in a relationship, but I think both people need . . .'

'Let's get started then,' Milk interrupted, springing into jumping jacks, blowing bursts of air out of his chest. He kept his gaze forward but I could see the grin inching across his face.

Moses immediately followed and by the beat after, everyone in the class had joined in before I could even finish my thought. After about ten jumps I was wasted. The more I jumped, the more jelly-like my limbs became. The bend in my knees dipped increasingly deep, so much so I felt at any moment I might end up sitting on the floor in one quick drop. Finally, we stopped. When I looked in the mirror in front of me, I was beet red.

'Okay, grab a partner,' Moses said.

I looked around and wished there were uneven numbers so Moses could practice with me, the new kid, but I was out of luck with a perfect six. There was a moment of slight chaos as people spun in circles, awkwardly looking for a partner. I was thinking about how to tell Milk, 'No thanks,' but then I saw Blondie grab his arm and smile her ask. Phew, I thought, wiping my forehead. I turned around and everyone was paired up except for the Persian man and me. He was really hairy.

'I'm Farid,' he said.

'Tabitha,' I replied. 'Nice to meet you. What do we do now?'

Before I knew it, Farid's chest hair was accosting me like a starved homeless man attacks a bucket of chicken wings and I was on the floor, pinned with my arms out. Immobile. Helpless. Confused.

'Farid!' Moses called out. His tone indicated that this was something of a recurring incident.

'Sorry, boss,' Farid said as his head cowered apologetically. 'I thought you said go.'

Moses took center stage again and explained a move I couldn't follow, probably because I had just been unexpectedly body slammed. What I could gather was that Farid and I were practicing what was called a 'take-down.' Oh, the men I couldn't wait to take down. I faced him with my legs wider than hip distance, fearful of the moments to come, face-to-face with this Iranian bull. I looked over Farid's shoulder for a moment and saw Milk half-smiling at me, half-curious. He winked just as Moses said, 'Go,' as if to distract me from my opponent. Milk wanted me to get floored by this giant but he was oh, so, wrong. There was absolutely no way I was going down. I couldn't for the life of me understand why Blondie would choose to partner with him but I guess he was so meek, so feeble, so brittle, that it was probably a choice to stroke her ego. I looked back at Farid and – probably because we both thought it was our turn at the same exact moment – we darted towards each other's legs in unison, but instead of grabbing his heel as we were instructed to do, I was once again pounded by a block of bristly black chest hair, body odor and sweat. I bounced off him like a ricocheting shuttlecock. Pop. Land. Skip. Slide, I went, across the floor.

'It was still my turn!' Farid yelled at me. I nodded to let him know I was okay, and he hadn't hurt me, in case he was wondering.

I looked over at Milk, furiously. 'You winked to distract me!' I accused him.

Of course, I would have loved it if it were Moses's soft fuzz, sweet smell, and glorious sweat. An imagined world in which he and I wrapped around each other like monkeys in heat warmed me, taking me away from the harsh realities of my opposing partner in this less romantic world. I wanted Moses to show me the moves, to grab one of my legs and take me to the floor. Pin me while twisting arms behind my neck and giving me no place to go but to submit to his domination. I looked over to Moses again and said, 'Hey! Can you—' but before I even finished Farid had a hold of my ankle and I was whipped to the ground with brute force. Why people don't use deodorant I will never know.

Farid was over me now, breathing heavily. I thought he might even collapse on top of me and that would be my death.

'Nice work, Farid,' Moses said as I got up again from the floor. It was like no one noticed I was being tossed around like a rag doll. Milk was ignoring me now, pretending to be taking his take-downs seriously. He clearly had no idea what he was doing because he was being so gentle and tentative with Blondie. I overheard him saying things like, 'Are you okay?' to her every now and then, and, 'Tap out if it hurts.' Of course she didn't because she was trying to show how tough she was.

'Okay, everyone,' Moses instructed. 'Let's switch.'

I was hoping he meant switch partners, but I soon realized he just meant it was my turn to take Farid down. I caught a glimpse of myself in the mirror: my hair was disassembled from its original ponytail, so much so that most of it was sticking out, flying up and around my head, a remnant of a former bun. I looked like Bill Murray in *Kingpin*. My complexion was splotchy. I was itchy all over. This was no way to start a Wednesday, let alone a relationship.

'Do you have chicken pox?' Farid asked me. The guy with the Afro behind me laughed.

'Give her a break,' Milk intercepted. 'She's never done it before.'

'I'm fine!' I said as I pulled my top down and rearranged

myself into my fighting stance. I saw Moses nod to the class to indicate a 'Go' and I was off, dipping, pulling at Farid's heels but his feet were so slippery from sweat I couldn't grab on. Each time, I face-planted. Each time, I ate shit.

'I need some help,' I said with bursts of breath, whatever I had left in me. From my periphery I witnessed Milk teaching Blondie how to maneuver around him with more efficiency. 'You have to use my body weight against me,' he told her. 'Otherwise, it's not a fair fight because biologically I have more strength. You have to be strategic about it. It's physics.' I couldn't believe it; he was flirting with her. I always thought of Milk as being small but next to Blondie he was towering.

Farid must have caught me listening and said, 'Milken is a master at Wing Chun.'

'At what?'

'A martial arts practice called Wing Chun. Bruce Lee did it. Milken teaches it here on Tuesday nights. He even has a free class on Sundays for women's self-defense.'

Is everyone stoned? Milk doesn't know a thing about martial arts! He's never been in a fight before! I think I would have known about this if it were true. I mean, I'm very observant.

'How do you know him?' Farid asked me, barely flinching as I mauled his heels.

'We grew up across the street from each other,' I huffed as my palms slapped together with each failed grab at his glistening, hairy feet.

'Terrible about his dad,' Farid said. 'My grandpa had Alzheimer's too, but Milk's dad is so young. Such a shame.'

Weird conversation to be having while trying to practice take-downs but at the same time, it seemed to flow effortlessly. Wait, what?

'Alzheimer's?' I said, inflecting up. 'Jeff?' I laughed. 'I think I'd know if he had Alzheimer's!' My laugh came out more like a cough from a lodged hairball.

Farid looked at me with eyes of an abandoned child. If I were a dog, I would be put to sleep. I looked over at Milk again, standing there in a headlock, letting Blondie have a go at him.

'Does she have a crush on him or something?' I asked Farid.

'Who doesn't,' he said. 'He's the king around here.'

'He's just a student!' I said, not understanding. 'If he were so great, he'd be the teacher.' I was ignoring the fact that Farid just said he taught Wing Chun.

'He owns the place,' he said, shutting me up. 'I thought you said you knew him.'

Milk owns a fighting school? Yeah, right. Like I'm going to believe that. How had he duped everyone into thinking he knew about martial arts?

'Well,' I said. 'If that's true, why is he in the class and not leading it?'

'It's his style. He likes to be immersed so that the teachers learn to teach better, so he can evaluate them from a student's perspective.'

'A bit relaxed, I'd think.' As I said this, I laughed. Throwing my head back for emphasis like Rainbow Dan did when he talked about being a lion. 'He's so annoying!' He's just so nice, it's infuriating. He needs more bite, more jazz. Some chili, some spice. Always has.

I jumped as Milk body-slammed Moses on the other side of the room in demonstration. I panicked at the thought of losing the man I'd love before we even had a chance so I tucked past Farid and ran to Moses, leaping into the air and landing on him and Milk. We were all screaming.

'Break it up!' I yelled. 'Break this shit up!'

'What the . . . ?!' Moses screamed.

'Tabby!' Milk shouted. 'What are you doing?'

As I was spread out like a stubborn starfish on top of the two of them, Milk and Moses started laughing, which confused and angered me at once. 'Milk, get off of Moses! You're hurting him!' I was the only one moving on the pile, legs and arms flapping around as Milk disentangled himself calmly and gently. He picked me up and placed me to the side. Moses scrambled away as he dealt with his confusion.

'Tabby,' Milk began. 'We weren't really fighting, you know. We were practicing because, well . . . that's what you do in fight class.' I was still on the ground, now turned over, facing up. Milk had his hands on his hips as he peered down at me and my legs and arms continued to flail in a silent room, kicking and punching the air.

'Are you done?' he asked. I stopped and let him help me get up.

I looked around the room and now everyone was chuckling. I even detected a faint eye-roll from Blondie which made me want to run over and punch her right square in the face, but I knew that wouldn't be a smart move in front of Moses since our relationship was so new and first impressions were everything. I realized I needed to do something to get him close. I had to be strategic.

Moses addressed the class. 'Let's move on to the single-leg take-down,' he said. 'So this move is one of the most effective, swift and powerful take-downs for grapplers. Single-leg take-downs can't be forced and you have to learn how to efficiently move with the power of your opponent for it to work. But when it does, it's deadly.'

Yes! I'm good at these.

'I'm going to demonstrate this once for the newbies,' Moses went on. 'Who wants to volunteer?'

I raised my hand so quickly it almost shot out of my shoulder socket. Moses looked despondently at Milk, then back at me.

'Anyone else?' Moses asked as I shouted, 'Hey! Me! Hey! I'm ready! Hey!'

'Moses,' Milk said firmly as he nodded in my direction.

'But, she . . .' he started but didn't know how to continue. He must have been choked up with emotion. Bless his little cotton socks! Milk motioned for me to join Moses at the front as Milk scratched his head, perplexed. His hand moved over his ear, through his scruffy chin and eventually across his mouth. I had never noticed his beard before, its dark blond freckled with hints of lighter and darker tones. He was also much taller than the other men in the room. One hand gripped his elbow as the other one stayed planted over his lips as he watched me walk to Moses. I turned around and smiled a thank you to Milk for letting me get this. He must really know how much this means to me. A good friend, indeed.

Moses's stance became wider the closer I moved in towards him.

'Okay, stop there,' he said, hands flexed. His stance was so wide it looked like he was about to take a standing poop or re-enact moments out of a western.

As he grabbed my left leg and picked it up into the air, he paused my body with his elbow to keep me at range. He said it was because he was leveraging his weight but I think it was because he wanted to be able to look at my face properly. 'Ah,' I said. 'Like missionary position.' I smiled to let him know I was cool with it. There we were, just two love cats holding each other in front of a room of animals, showing them that even tough fighters can be comfortable with public displays of affection. Moses still had his elbow on my chest and used his hand to grab the front of my T-shirt and aggressively yank at me to demonstrate his strength and hold. So glad I didn't wear a bra; he might even get an early-bird special. 'See how much more in control of her I am when her balance is off?' he addressed the class, moving me from side to side, pivoting me on my standing leg. 'I can do anything to her from this position.'

'Ready, able and willing!' I said, smiling. Joyous. In heaven. It was like being in a pornographic video with the commentator right next to you. My balance was, as planned, off but he was holding on to me so tightly I knew I wouldn't fall. This is what it feels like, I guess. This is what it feels like to be at the mercy of someone else and to be trusting them implicitly to not let you go. This trust, this love, made me so horny I used my abdominal muscles to bend towards him to sniff his neck. I wanted to smell his primal fragrance. As he was pushing me away, I was holding on to his strong trapezoids to hoister myself towards him but I couldn't get a proper grip as he kept shrugging me off every time.

Moses at once released me and let me drop to the floor, turning to Milk in defense. 'Dude,' he said. 'She's sniffing me!'

'It's some bunny-boiler shit!' the guy with the Afro said. 'Glenn Close kind of cray cray.'

'Thank you!' I said enthusiastically, because I knew 'crazy' was just another way of saying, 'This girl has mojo.'

I got up and resumed my position. 'I'm learning to work with your strength,' I whispered to him as I drove my head into his front deltoid area, allowing the strength of our bodies to feed off of each other. Moses scowled at me briefly but he was only doing that to keep the class engaged and to uphold the 'aggressor' and 'opponent' personas he had so cleverly and artistically created, although clearly we were fighting for the same thing.

'This is weird,' Blondie piped in, twisting her hair away from her face. 'Is she on something?'

'She's fine,' Milk said. 'Moses, let's move on.'

Moses pinched the back of my neck and picked me up like a puppy. I loved it, but it hurt. I consider myself open but I'm not into S&M. I do have boundaries, after all.

'You have to learn to read your opponent,' he said to the class while holding me, legs dangling. The air to my lungs was being cut off by the way he was hanging me and I started to choke. Milk told him to let me go and at once he dropped me. When I looked up, Milk asked if I was okay, doing that annoying half smile thing he did again.

'You see,' Moses continued. 'In a moment of distraction, I got her. You have to always pay attention because you never know when and how your opponent is going to attack.'

'I—' I started.

'Shush!' Moses snapped back. 'So not only do you have to always think ahead, you have to be prepared for a million possibilities at all times and be ready to deliver when you need to take action.' I perked up. He was speaking my language. That's exactly what I was doing here: preparing myself so that I'm ready for when the lucky break comes. I'm putting in the time, the effort, the due diligence . . . because I know it's going to happen to me and I want to know how to grab it when it does.

The class nodded, all scowling and frowning in a shared sense of agreement with the words of wisdom dispensed by Moses while Milk stood at the back, arms crossed.

'That's so right, Moses,' I joined in. 'When you are proactive, someone else will meet you halfway.' I started winking so he knew to pick up the reference.

'I don't think that's what we're talking about,' Farid said.

'Who is this chick?' Blondie added.

I'm all for sisterly love but this girl was really being aggressive. I don't know where it came from but from a deep part of myself leapt a ferocious animal. It was instinctual, like a cornered rat. I jumped, I barked, I screamed, and clawed my way towards Blondie . . . But I fell to the floor one foot too short of her.

The floor padding smelled of clammy feet.

'What's going on, Tabby?' Milk asked. The room was silent. I could hear the sound of feet sticking to the mat as the class shuffled in their awkward places.

'I'm fighting for someone so that person knows he can fight for me, too,' I shouted.

'Who?' he asked.

'I don't know!' Tears welled in my eyes and I started to cry. I didn't know I even could cry; I would have even thought my tear ducts didn't work until this point. 'If I don't fight for him in the first place,' I sobbed, 'he's never going to know he can fight back and then I'll be left alone to fight for the rest of my life like my mom and she's so tired. She's just so tired.' I paused with a hiccup.

'I think we're really off topic,' the Asian guy said.

'Let's pause here for a moment,' Milk said as he walked towards me to help me up. 'Farid, why don't you practice with Isabelle for a minute. Moses, take them through the next form. Tabby, come with me.'

I followed Milk into the back room with shoulders that hadn't sunk that low in years. He opened the door to a small office where he instructed me to take a seat. He was so bossy. I'd never seen that side of him before. I thought he was going to yell at me. I prepared myself for it as I sank lower and more deeply into the uncomfortable, plastic chair.

'You really should invest in better chairs,' I sniffled.

'Let's talk,' he said as he crossed his arms.

'I know,' I said. 'Moses is not the one for me.'

'Brenda told me what happened to your mom at the gala. She seemed a little more quiet than usual when you all came back. It must have given you a scare. Is she feeling okay?'

'Yeah, you know her. She gets right up again. And if you're wondering, I don't get panic attacks.'

He took a moment to adjust in his seat.

'So, I saw your dad the other day,' he said. 'Down at a bar in the valley.'

'Oh yeah?' I said, feigning lack of interest as my skin caught on fire. My eyes started to twitch and I felt a flood of emotion pouring towards those recently active tear ducts.

'Is he still friends with your dad?' I asked. 'I didn't think they'd still be friends, with how close my dad and your mom were and everything.'

'Nothing happened between them and you know it. They were just friends.'

'He went over there all the time without us,' I countered, blood getting hotter.

'My dad was there, too,' Milk said. 'The three of them. He just needed to get out of the house sometimes. To breathe a bit . . . do you understand what I mean?' The skin under his eyes sank into half moons. Like frog eyes, deeply embedded, heavy and round.

'I'm sorry,' I stopped him. 'I shouldn't bring up your mom. It's still so new. Like it was yesterday.'

'She died over ten years ago,' he said.

'Was it really that long ago?' It was so strange how it felt like a few weeks ago. Sometimes I feel like I keep waking up from dreams every day, as if I've just fallen asleep for an hour but find out I've been in another world for a year. Silence sat in between us.

'So do you really own this place?' I asked.

'Have done for years now,' he told me as the faintest outline of a smile crept its way out of the shadows once again.

What the hell? Wait a second . . . Milk really owns a fight school?

'Do you have a crush on Blondie?' I asked.

'Isabelle?' Milk said. 'Of course not. She's a student.'

'You were just paying so much attention to her, I thought—'

'Listen,' he said, lowering his eyes for the first time. 'Let's get something straight, okay?'

'Okay,' I said, confused by how in charge he was. 'What?'

He looked up and straight at me. He was staring so intently I, for a moment, wasn't sure if we were playing the blinking game or not. I looked away then back again but his eyes hadn't wavered.

'You aren't like normal girls. You're different. Very, very different.' His speech was slow and steady, but he kept taking big breaths as if he were running out of air. 'And you aren't going to have a life like most women because you're not normal.'

'Oh, thanks a lot, Milk,' I interjected.

'Will you just please shut up and listen?'

I nodded obediently.

'You're special and special people sometimes have a harder time finding the one because most people are typical. They're boring and they're predictable. It's easier for them to find someone because they are like most people so finding someone to be with is easy. So basically, it's going to be trickier for you. But I promise you're going to have a much richer, more interesting life than most and when you do get together with that guy who gets you,' he paused, looking down, took a breath and fidgeted in his seat. 'He's going to be one lucky bastard.'

He turned his head up and stared at me like no one has ever looked at me before. The twinkling wide-eyed glance was now softened, diluted. A sadness I hadn't traced before had, for the first time in years, resurfaced. I wasn't used to seeing him sad, and not knowing why made me feel even more unsettled. I lifted myself up out of the sticky plastic chair, my sweaty fat sticking to the seat, making a suction noise as I tore myself away from it. I felt the lines the chair's crosses had indented into the backs of my legs, through my spandex. I rubbed them but knew that no matter how much I massaged my skin, no matter how much I tried to make the impressions disappear, there was nothing I could do but wait for them to go away.

Those indentations were like all my experiences, all the things that hurt, that continued to dig into me, leaving marks that would only go away with time. I speculated, if only for a moment: was it a sign? Was I trying to speed up things that must wait? But then I snapped out of it before realistic thinking got the better of me. At least I knew one day the chair marks, like those other marks, would let up. That's the only way you can think about it or else it can really bring you down.

Maybe Milk wasn't sad either, but just waiting for something like I was, and waiting for something you can't even see in the distance can at times become quite lugubrious, even for the optimists. And then I drifted off, wondering what it was that Milk was waiting for.

The Pretender

Feeling nostalgic, I was going through some of my old keep-sake boxes that I store under my bed, and I found a ticket stub from many years ago from the night when Chrissie Hynde cornered me backstage at The Troubadour. She said it was because she saw me trying to take some of her food, but I think it's because I was the only one in the room who looked interesting. She needed someone fun to talk to.

'What are you doing?' she asked me, staring intently. Not moving. She was so intense I thought I might pass out. Her eyes were rimmed by her trademark black eyeliner, smudged in areas that didn't make sense. It added to her mystique.

'What?' I asked. When I looked down, I realized I must have buried a handful of food into my bag: Coconut water, two Popchips, a gluten-free granola bar, nuts, and sweet potato chips. I was hoarding and I didn't know why.

'Whoa!' I exclaimed. 'How'd they get in there?' I laughed wildly and potentially insensitively as her gaze never faltered. She eyed me up and down, moved her hips to the right, embodying sass and confidence. She would love Delina and Julia.

'That's my fucking food,' she said. I had snuck in there because I knew the place. It was one of my first jobs after turning twenty-one, so I knew my way around this endearingly scummy music establishment in Hollywood. I knew that if I went up the stairs and pretended to go into the Ladies but actually dipped into the backstage area, no one would notice. It was the back entrance. The secret entrance. I'd seen all sorts of people, but Chrissie Hynde was the only one who spoke to me.

I panicked about how to explain my unexplainable hoarding but then thankfully remembered reading something about how she was vegan. I said, 'I was just so excited to see such a socially conscious array of vegan food that I grabbed a few to check the labels, you know, just to make sure they were cruelty-free.'

Her eyes opened up. Finally, she was intrigued.

'I am so against palm oil!' I added.

'Huh,' she said, adjusting her weight to the other hip. 'Me too.'

'All those poor orangutans. It's just awful. I can barely sleep at night!'

And at once, because of our shared love of animals, she forgave me for stealing her backstage food and we became friends. I went to give her a hug, because it felt right, but she just stood there with her hands hanging limply. When I let go, she said, 'Don't touch me.'

We sat down together and I thought, 'This is a perfect opportunity to get some advice about love.' I'm going to ask her because she's talented and cool and tough and probably has it all figured out. But I'm not so sure she did.

'Love sucks, man,' she said, lighting a rolled cigarette, but I didn't believe she meant it. How could she? Everyone wants to believe in love. Rock stars are no exception, but maybe she was just scarred and tainted, blasé and heartbroken one too many times, like Dorothy Parker. Beneath the wit and sarcasm, they were humans like me, wanting to connect with someone. She held out the cigarette towards me.

'Want a drag?' she asked.

I took the cigarette off her with easy, graceful movements and hit it like nobody's business. I was already cool, but bonding like this blasted me out of the universe. As the smoke flooded through my organs and circled around my brain, I was overwhelmed with affection for her. I kept trying to give her hugs but each time she told me to stop.

I was so hungry, and then I remembered I had thankfully stuffed my bag full of vegan treats. That's why I was hoarding! It was as if I secretly knew this would happen and I prepared myself for it. Luck favors the prepared, they say. People were milling about, buzzing around Chrissie, asking questions, but she kept ignoring them. Her eyes still on me, sharp. I was so glad we were friends.

'You're a pretender,' I said, passing her back the cigarette, 'like me.' She was scowling at this point in my story, not understanding, so I hurried to make myself clear.

'I mean, we're all pretenders, until we don't have to pretend anymore.' She started nodding and bobbing her head in agreement, black hair moving about the room like a beginners ballroom-dancing class. Her heart was leathery, but in that way you're drawn to, like the girl at school who sits behind you, her Doc Martens tapping against the back of your seat while she chews gum against the rules and smokes cigarettes in the parking lot. You think she hates you until you realize she's an outcast, like you. Only you play the victim while she revels in not being like the rest. You start to see how much more power you'd have if you just sat up straight and let rumors and gossip fly over your head than try to bend your neck to hear them. Once you do, you get the cool girl's nod and that's all you need to get through high school. Chrissie was like that girl in high school whom you wanted to be friends with. You think she rules the world and has it figured out because she doesn't give a shit but you know deep down, she does.

'So are we friends yet?' I asked her.

'Not yet,' she said. A hint of a smile unburied itself from the corners of her mouth.

I cracked open a bag of Popchips and started stuffing them in my face. I'd never been so starving. 'So really,' I pushed with a mouth full of food. 'Don't you have any advice for me about being in love?'

The cigarette was depleting, nearing her fingers, but the heat didn't seem to bother her.

'You're really hung up on this love thing, aren't you?' she said.

I wanted to tell her it wasn't my age. It wasn't about status or diamonds or weekend trips to Napa with a 'husband' or having a nice house with a dog and two kids. I didn't care about those things. I wanted the kind of romance that would twist me inside out. I wanted a funky cabin on a small plot of land, with chickens and pigs instead of dogs and cats, and I wanted to wake up on Sunday mornings to the smell of freshly brewed coffee and the voice of a husband who says, 'Sugar?' as he's pouring your cup because he thinks it's cute you change your diet daily. (Okay, I'll admit it: I'd like to live in a Folgers coffee commercial.) I saw it: the person I loved and me, under the covers as our children – adopted, mixed, bio-logical – ran into the room and jumped on our bed. Kids and mattress springing together. Joyous. I could see us all laughing. I could see it all so clearly that I could almost taste it, like the smell of croissants drifting down a Parisian street at 5 a.m. Just the smell of it would be enough to make you feel like you were having it. But eventually, your stomach would gurgle. You'd be so hungry you'd have to go into the patisserie and you'd have to buy one and eat it. I'd spent my life smelling romance and at this point I was clawing at the pastry chef's doors.

My eyes pleaded for her to go on. Please, they screamed. Give me something, Chrissie. A few moments passed, and eventually, she looked around the room, taking in the crowd.

'You see all these people?' she said. I nodded, following. 'We're all looking for the same thing. Everyone's a fucking mess.'

At first, it delighted me, this camaraderie, until I realized – taking stock of the faces around the room – that in many ways, I was just like them: lost. The only thing that I had continued to hold on to was the belief that life could be as magical as I wanted it to be. We're all born with that; they just let it go. They let it slip away. 'That's life,' they'd say, but it wasn't true. That Folgers coffee commercial? That really happened. Those butterflies? They don't go away after the honeymoon. I clung on to the hope that we're not all just going through the paces. Some of us are living.

The room became smaller when I thought I was a part of it, like my dad in our house growing up, and bigger when I thought I wasn't. When I looked back at Chrissie, she stopped me as I was about to say goodbye, see you later, nice to meet you.

'You want to know my real advice?' she said.

Yeah, yeah, I did. I nodded furiously, eager for a morsel of truth, of guidance. She blew a ball of smoke towards me.

'We're all just little chickens waiting for a fucking rooster to love us. Do you know how mad that makes me to say? I'm tough, you know, but shit, there are times I want to be vulnerable. But goddamn, I don't know how to be both without getting torn apart in some direction.'

'So if you, the queen of cool, of rock, of badass, can't figure it out, then what's in store for the rest of us?' I asked, scrabbling for the pieces of my heart that had started to fall onto the crusty, beer-spilled floor.

'All I know is that your heart's gonna get ripped open and that baby girl inside of you, she's going to get hurt no matter which way she plays the game, so you might as well enjoy the ride.'

I'm not entirely sure if Chrissie ever said this or if I imagined it because I loved her, but I'm pretty sure she did. I am completely certain, however, that something happened because I woke up the next morning on a pile of empty bottles of coconut water and covered in broken remains of Popchips. I remember thinking that maybe my heart had already been ripped open. That I'd already been hurt and broken, over and over again, so maybe the worst was over. But then, what if the ride was more fun than the ending? What if I was so used to the adrenaline that I wouldn't be able to handle how it felt when the cart stopped moving?

The Blind Man

After a recent intervention with my mom from Delina and Julia, following her doctor's suggestion of possible psychiatric evaluation, I knew I had to start getting creative because nothing was working. Phrases like *Well, that's life* were being thrown around the house in regard to dying alone. It was getting really bad. So, when I heard that blind men make great lovers, I decided to sign up to be a volunteer at the Braille Institute.

I was ushered into the main reading room where Sandy, a busty woman in her fifties, made an announcement that I was the new volunteer. All heads turned in different directions as if someone had spotted a mouse but no one knew where to look. Instinctively, I started checking over my right shoulder, then my left, looking around for that invisible mouse with the rest of them.

'What's your name again?' she asked as her brow slithered like a snake until it fully arched in repugnance. Sandy looked me up and down like I was the new girl at school who just transferred from a shitty neighborhood. I started to panic.

This bitch was on to me. She knew what I was after because she wanted a blind man, too.

'Lauren Bacall!' I blurted out. It was the first name that came to me. As I said it, I shook my head and grinned widely as if to say, We're all in this together! 'I know,' I continued, trying to crawl out of my hole. 'It's weird. Same name as the famous actress, but we're not related.' I put my hands up. 'It's just a coincidence!'

The room was saturated in a jaundiced glow and smelled exactly how my grandma's house used to smell: a musty concoction of stale perfume, Ritz Crackers, animal fur and old carpet. That made me curious, though, because the floors were laminate. I was feeling really good about myself because I had stopped off at the department store on my way over and sprayed on the best perfume I could find since I knew, with these guys especially, scent would make it or break it.

'So how does this work?' I asked, scouting the room for eligible men. She smiled and handed me her sticky grin along with a sign-up sheet. I picked up a volunteer brochure on a nearby desk and opened it to a delightful spread of snapshots featuring colorfully dressed couples, laughing and hugging and reading and pointing at things that were outside the frame of the picture. I really wanted to know what they were pointing at. Whoever made this brochure knew what they were doing.

'Why are you here?' Sandy asked me, dubiously.

'To . . .' I stammered, searching for a reason she'd accept.

Then I remembered the faces on the brochure and how happy they'd looked, '. . . to spread smiles?'

I wasn't exactly sure what I could help these blind people with as far as my skills were concerned, but I could see, and they couldn't, so I thought inherently I had something to offer. On top of the heightened-senses aspect – and what an asset indeed – was the idea that great sex happens when two people are connected in ways that go beyond the physical. Finally, a chance at meeting a man who would be able to see what's inside me first.

I got the idea from a seemingly dull conversation with Roselyn, a chipper lady who lives at the same old people's home as my grandma. Dull. Dull. Dull, peppered with updates about how her grandson never visits, anecdotes of her time as a backup dancer in the forties, and the ailments she now endures and how no one else notices. Dull, that is, until she told me that in her ninety-two years, her best lover was a blind Scottish man named Tom Patrick Ward.

'Oh how he could make me dance,' she said.

I brightened up. Intrigued.

'He was your dance partner?'

'How could he be my dance partner?' she asked, exasperated. Impatient. 'What a mess that would have been.' Images of a swiftly moving blind ballroom dancer whipped around me, legs and arms everywhere. I learned Tom Patrick Ward was a war veteran who apparently returned home without his eyes. They were blown off, she told me, whilst making explosion sounds with her wrinkled lips. Roselyn said the blindness made Tom's sense of touch so acute he could find her G-spot in one motion. She looked quite weird demonstrating this move to me as she covered both eyes with one hand while the other stretched out towards me, searching for what appeared to be the location of my nipple. Her pointed finger just jabbed the air in front of me without a freckle of precision. Her movements were hard to follow, but that may have been because she has Parkinson's.

'What are you doing?' I eventually asked.

'A one-jab knockout,' she said, punching the air, still a little irritated I wasn't following. 'Just like my Tommy used to do.'

I had hit a goldmine here and she was just waffling around the room like a drunken mime. When I told my grandma Roselyn's story, I thought she'd scoff at it and tell me she was losing it, that her Parkinson's had gone to her head, shaking things around too much or maybe it was the dementia setting in, confusing her. But she didn't. She just looked at me, cocked her head and patted me on the back.

'Roselyn's right, dear,' she consoled me as my concentration drifted to the bingo game going on behind her. 'The catches are the ones who aren't easily distracted.' One day I'd be old, too, with the highlight of my day being a bingo game. I was running out of time. I asked her how old she was when she met Grandpa.

'Twenty-one,' she said. Well, shit, I thought. That's young. 'It's okay, pet,' she continued, knowing I needed some tenderness, some reassurance that everything would be okay. 'As long as you keep looking for it, you'll find it.' The dementia helped her to remember things from when she was younger, but she couldn't recall much in the middle, like raising my mother and when everything went pear-shaped. She forgot about becoming a fanatical Christian when my mom was uncontrollably wild around fourteen. Now she rarely brings up Jesus. I was the only one who'd see her; my mom still blamed her for how she turned out and my sister was too busy. I wanted to tell Grandma about Moses but thought it might trigger memories of Jesus somewhere deep in her subconscious. If I did that, Mom might never visit her. It was exhausting trying to navigate around all the possible scenarios that might make my mother disappointed.

I took my grandma's advice, blindly. I know I'm not supposed to listen to her because of her dementia but my grandma and Roselyn are reliable confidantes in many ways. Not only have they been through the hoops of life themselves and have all the time in the world to just sit and listen, but they have sieves for brains so I'll never have to worry my secrets will get out. She told me love is always where you least expect it to be, so I've been expecting to find it hiding in some corner of a desolate alley or at a funeral. Her advice proved slightly dangerous when I mistook the attention of a crack addict for affection but this is how we learn.

Before I left, my grandma grabbed a hold of my jacket collar quite firmly – which both surprised and impressed me because I had no idea she was so strong – and told me she was going to hang on as long as she could, until she saw me married.

The stakes were high. And I'll admit it: I was nervous, hanging on to the hope of a forecast less dreary and blustery than predicted. But thanks to Roselyn I might be on the right track. Blind men were like artists. It's a girl's dream to be with an artist because they only see shapes and shadows, not flaws. You're a work of art, not a mess. The Institute was bustling with visually challenged men. I wanted to get a sense of what it would be like to make love to a blind man so I closed my eyes, right there in the room, and imagined myself spread out on a red satin bed while Stevie Wonder and Andrea Bocelli sang to me as Claude Monet painted my portrait, the vibrations of their notes and strokes hitting my heart over and over like an automatic weapon. If I died right there and then, the newspaper would have titled my obituary, 'A true victim of blind love.' I loved that title and thought it sounded like a romantic way to go but then the thought of all those sexually charged blind men became too intense so I opened my eyes again.

I looked around the room, hoping for a connection, but every eye was still facing a different direction, staring at something in the blackness. Sandy told me to feel free to wander around and make myself familiar with the premises while she processed my volunteer form. Everyone seemed to be quietly studying the shapes of letters in their Braille books. The floor was mine. I started to dance very subtly to test their reactions but not an eyebrow was raised, so I let it all pour out of me. I spun around with my arms lifted high above my head until I was spinning like a human dreidel.

The first person I approached was named Thompson. 'Is that a nickname?' I asked.

He shook his head, 'No.'

I searched for a better pick-up line. 'How do you know when it's night-time?' I asked.

'What?'

'The time. Can you tell when it's dark outside? Do you feel more tired? Is it a temperature thing?'

'Are you stupid?' Thompson replied.

I had more questions.

'Can you get vertigo?'

He just shook his head again, more annoyed than confused, as if he gets that a lot.

I didn't believe Thompson was his real first name and I couldn't work with liars, especially aggressive ones, so I moved on to the next one: Dwight.

Dwight had great hearing. He knew I was coming for him before I even pulled up the chair. He got up and bowed to me, his hand holding on to his invisible cowboy hat as his head dipped. Hearing well meant he had heightened senses, but I deduced that if his hearing were extraordinary, then his sense of touch would skate in around average. Dwight would make an excellent detective or best friend to talk to, but the best lover? I couldn't count on it. Despite Dwight's obvious interest, I had to remember why I was there. I needed to find my own Tom Patrick Ward. My decision-making had to be ruthless.

Musical chairs led me to my next bachelor, who introduced himself as George K. Not entirely sure why he didn't want to tell me the rest of his name but I understood his preference for anonymity. At first I thought George K was playing footsie with me under the table. Naturally, I smiled, flirting, tossing my hair back and forth over my shoulders with considerable ease for what seemed like an unusually long time before realizing that this would all be wasted on George K, the blind man. His cane moved around my foot under the table so fast I could barely keep up. It was like riding a bicycle downhill when your legs cycle faster than your brain can compute. Thinking about it too much ruined my rhythm and, before I knew it, my foot got caught in the spokes and I crashed. I had moved too quickly with George K. I realized it was strange he was using a cane since he was sitting down. He told me it was because he has vertigo.

'So you can get dizzy!' I said, excited, wanting to go run up to Thompson to tell him he was wrong.

'Vertigo has nothing to do with eyesight,' he said. 'I feel dizzy even when I'm sitting down.'

Poor guy. 'Sorry about the foot thing,' I said. George K reassured me that, 'These things happen,' and not to worry about it, but I had lost my cool and gotten carried away and now there was too much water under the bridge. I realized that maybe that's what I had been doing wrong when I was a kid and would crawl under the table to play footsie with my mom's visitors. My good intentions had ruined it.

I got up, turned around quickly and accidentally stood on the paws of a giant, slobbering German shepherd who had somehow snuck up behind me while I was fooling around with George K. The dog's consequent yelp ricocheted off the hardened walls so fast I ducked to avoid it hitting me on its swift return. I was a little embarrassed that my reaction was so severe, like when you see a bird's shadow and put your hands out in self-defense before realizing it is, in fact, just a shadow. But in this place of clouded vision, I was safe from ridicule. The dog's owner was tethered to him a few feet back. I had no idea how long they'd been there . . . Blind people are so quiet!

'Sit, Charles!' the owner said sharply. 'He likes you,' he said as the dog leaned his curious nose towards me, sniffing away like a truffle-hunting pig.

'Oh, hello, you!' I said, giggling – a reaction of the unavoidably ticklish. The shepherd's cold nose on my legs rekindled a slew of delightful images. I cycled through them quickly like an impatient kid views a flipbook, only this time, I was seeing snapshots of Andrea and Claude, painting and singing away. The dog stayed there sniffing for a while until his owner pulled him back. I had to continue this somehow; it was like the dog knew we needed to meet.

'You know what has the most discerning sense of smell?' I asked the man before me. 'Ants.' He looked at me, puzzled. 'I know you'd never think it but it's true,' I continued. 'You should watch this great documentary on it.' The man was silent. Oh right, I thought. Shit. Blind men!

'Want to sit down for a minute so we can chat?' I asked, but then Sandy came over and started hitting on him before I got too far. She was cock-blocking me!

'Richard! You're looking great today,' she said. Charles, sensing commotion, immediately lost interest in me and went to her, wagging his tail and proving to be just like all the other dogs and Dicks I'd met. She started to giggle. Richard and Sandy were both smiling and the dog's tongue was out of its mouth, happy. It was at that point that I knew I had lost my chance with the lover and the truffle hunter.

I stood up and headed towards the last blind man in the room: Sam. Sam is such a concrete, grounded name. You know what you are going to get when you get a Sam. There are no surprises with a Sam. Sams don't lie. They don't cheat. Your dad's name is probably Sam.

Sam was younger than the rest with a full set of coarse,

black hair and unruly eyebrows. Eyebrows so wild I felt compelled to pluck them, one hair at a time. I'd be the remora fish and he'd be the shark in our symbiotic relationship. He also wore sunglasses, which made looking at him less intimidating. He also had a beautifully big Texan smile. All the arrows were pointing to him as the one.

'Hi, Lauren,' he said as I sat down next to him. (Who's Lauren? Oh yes! He remembered my name!) 'Want to go over some Braille with me?'

I was so excited I basically levitated as I reached across the table to grab *The Burns Braille Transcription Dictionary*. When I leaned over, I grazed his elbow with every ounce of seduction in me. I apologized profusely when he jumped in shock at the touch, even though we both knew it was no accident. I took his finger between mine and began at the top of the page, tracing letters and uttering their sounds. I started to breathe deeply and told myself, Go slowly, Lauren. Go slowly. If it's going to be forever, we don't have to rush.

It was evident Sam liked this combination of finger tracing and heavy breathing because he just sat there limply, letting me lead. 'This is an R,' I said, rolling the R as long as I could before I ran out of breath. It felt like we were playing on a Ouija board and I was the ghost. I didn't know love could be this much fun. I moved his finger across raised letters and spelled out, D-O Y-O-U S-E-E M-E? Sometimes I'm so romantic I even shock myself.

He quickly retracted his finger.

'Too much, too soon?' I said, secretly hoping he'd interject and tell me he sees in me what's invisible to everyone else. Sam took off his sunglasses and let me look into his grey eyes before giving me back his finger. I wondered if this was the moment he would use his hands to search my face and identify my shape as the woman of his dreams.

I think Dwight overheard our conversation because he scoffed at us from the other side of the room. I felt sorry for Dwight and hoped he would one day find what we had found.

I knew my window was closing, especially with Dwight's rising jealousy, so I had to think of something quickly. I needed to get him to touch me so he knew how buttery my skin was.

'Play a game with me?' I asked Sam, whose gaze was still on me, steady. 'I'm going to put my arm out like this,' I said as I flipped my forearm over. 'Then, when my eyes are closed, you're going to walk your index and middle finger up from the inside of my wrist and I'll scream "Stop" when I think you've reached the crease in my elbow. Okay?' This is one of my favorite games.

He nodded and placed his two fingers at the start line. I closed my eyes to meet Sam in the dark. I wanted to live in that space with him forever. I could hear everything better all of a sudden, especially George K's cane still rummaging through the space on the floor under the table. Then it began. Sam's fingers commenced their creep. I could taste the salt in the misguided beads of sweat that ran down the sides of my temples. Good thing Sam was blind.

I thought he was nearing my elbow but I wasn't quite sure. It felt so close but love has felt close in the past and never been anywhere near it. It was hard to trust myself. My breathing pattern started to become irregular. I wanted more than anything to peek but I refused to. I couldn't. Not this far in. His fingers climbed further and further. My toes curled. The space behind my ears tingled and my spine arched in the wooden seat as if someone had poked me in the back with a needle. He was almost there. My left leg started to shake. I couldn't take it anymore.

'Stop!' I screamed. 'Yes! Stop! Yes! Yes! Stop!' Euphoria lapped through my veins. When I opened my eyes, I saw my very own Tom Patrick Ward before me, smiling contentedly as if he'd been watching me the whole time.

My heavy breathing started to settle but when I looked down at where his finger stopped, it was only halfway up my forearm, a good three inches from my elbow. I wasn't even in the ballpark.

Sam grabbed my elbow with his free hand and, gauging the gap between where his finger still lingered and my elbow, I thought he was going to say, 'If it felt like it, that's all that matters.'

Instead, he said, 'That was intense!' Finally, I was understood.

'How long have you been blind?' I asked him. He quieted me with his finger and held his Texan smile in place as he stood up. He was taller than I expected. He grabbed his cane, put his glasses back on, and shuffled out the door. He left me sitting there, drowning in my puddle of horror like a little boy who ejaculated too soon the first time he made out with a girl, but there was nothing left to say. As he waved goodnight to Sandy, I noticed The Braille Institute logo on the back of his shirt.

'See you tomorrow morning for our volunteer training seminar, Sammy!' she cried out. He was a *volunteer*? Not even blind at all?

I looked over to Dwight for answers but he just sat there laughing at me from afar, jubilant in his opaque bath of glory.

Turns out Roselyn didn't know much about love. I started to rifle through my Mary Poppins bag of personal baggage in an effort to find something, anything, that would justify why I kept doing this, but I had nothing except the lingering tingling sensation on my arm. I could still feel his fingers on my skin like a phantom limb. I was giving off some major sexual energy and I just had this feeling that something good was about to happen. Maybe my chakras were opening and I was becoming a real woman. It was in that moment I realized I wasn't heartbroken; I was heart-disappointed.

It was probably time for me to go home. My mom would be home soon and she hates it when I'm late because she feels like people who are late are lazy and lazy people never find happiness, even though she isn't particularly happy but always punctual. Tonight she was making lasagna, and that's what I was thinking about when Dwight grabbed my hand and said, 'I guess we're all just shooting in the dark.'

Funny, I never even saw him coming. It would be romantic if he were the one for me, fervent Dwight with the bad eyes. He was right; we are all just trying to get it right but none of us really know what we're doing. We're out there, putting ourselves on the line to make some sense of our worlds and why we're here. So I found out blind men didn't necessarily make good lovers, and that old people with dementia don't always know what's best, but at least I'm still trying. Hunter S. Thompson said we're all just figuring out 'whether to float with the tide or swim for a goal.' I'm swimming; I just don't have a life vest.

I ran outside as fast as I could. I was huffing and panting and about to pass out from shortness of breath when I noticed Milk driving by in his Ford Thunderbird. He caught my eye and slowed to a pause. He took in The Braille Institute sign above me and then looked back at me and smiled. I was alone, drowning in the middle of the sidewalk, unable to catch my breath, and this dude can't stop smiling.

He rolled down the window. 'Want a ride?'

I jumped in and banged the door shut, trying not to look at him. Brenda had to drive my car to work because hers was in the shop for maintenance, so I had taken the bus there and was quietly relieved I didn't have to take it back.

We rode in silence for a while, listening to Leadbelly. Nothing like a little blues to steer you through a comedown. Eventually I turned towards him at the same time he looked at me and all he said was, 'Hey.'

'How do you always seem to know where I am?' I said, annoyed that he always catches me at those fragile moments when I actually need some help. 'Are you following me?'

'Oh,' he joked. 'Was I not supposed to hack into your computer and look at your calendar?'

'Not funny,' I said.

'Let's call it fate. I thought you love that, anyway. Did your adventures with blind men not go as planned?' he said as his smile turned to laughter.

I was so mad I clenched my teeth. I was gritting them so hard my jaw eventually gave way. It's hard to be mad for too long.

'You're not helping my confidence, you know,' I said. 'I'm just trying to make shit happen. I'm trying to fall in love. All *The Secret* stuff, all these affirmations, and I still haven't found anyone. I don't get it.'

'You'll be fine,' he said, eyes focused on the road. Men simplify things so much. I needed to know I'd be fine, not just whimsically be told I would be, like what you tell a kid with a scrape. It's gonna be fine, you say, but do you really know? Are you absolutely sure?

'All I want is to play backgammon in the park with a fifties picnic set filled with treats, and for a guy I'm in love with to bring out a piece of paper and he'll draw a face and then I'll draw the neck and back and forth until we've drawn a couple – us! – while we enjoy the vodka-spiked elderflower pressé I would have packed – homemade, of course! – as he takes breaks to play his guitar. Is that too much to ask?'

'Haha,' Milk said. 'Well, yes.'

He didn't get it. 'But this kind of romance exists, Milk! It really does. It has to.' I kept looking over to see if he was going to say something but he didn't.

'I know it does,' he said, glancing over at me. 'Don't worry about it. It will happen when the time is right.'

'Thanks, Milky.'

'At the risk of sounding like a broken record, I've always said it would be hard for you.'

'Ugh. Yeah.'

'You have something very specific you want. You're not just looking for the hay. You're looking for the needle.'

We were quiet again for a while as we rode up the bends in the canyon.

'So then,' he said, 'tell me a story.'

He always did that. He always wanted to hear a good story.

The Passenger

When I think about flying, I never get scared – mostly because it means I am going to have to sit next to someone who's already dealt with the fact that his personal space will be invaded. He is prepared for it, which makes my encroaching upon his so-called 'boundaries' less invasive, less offensive. It will come as no surprise, therefore, when I accidentally push his elbow off our shared armrest and pretend to fall asleep on his shoulder so innocently, so naturally, that he'll feel like a dick waking me up.

I'm pushing the male pronoun here only because I had a premonition the other night that I was going to get on a plane and sit next to a man named Jimmy on a flight somewhere exotic and, because of turbulence, hand holding and a false sense of mortality, we would fall in love. The name Jimmy made me think about the pussy-twisting effect reggae music has on me, and its inevitable, albeit jumpy, connection to Jimmy Cliff. I've always loved rice and beans and the robust smell of dreadlocks so it all makes quite a lot of sense. The prospect of sitting next to a man is more exciting than sitting next to an attractive woman because I'm not into lipstick lesbians, although if she were butch enough I could get into it. When I was in my early twenties, I had a crush on a forty-year-old black lesbian named Sunshine, but that's another story.

When I told my mother in the kitchen, she looked at me with these round eyes that were once much bigger, much brighter. They had the same diameter, the same oaky color, but they were cloudy and distracted, as if she didn't use them to see anymore. She was moving around the room nervously. Feet never touching the ground, holding on to something I didn't understand. Reorganizing. Reshuffling. Reordering the placement of cups and saucers that had already been organized, shuffled and ordered earlier. She said she'd always dreamt of sitting next to a man on a plane who would become her soul mate, so if this omen were real, I could be – to some degree – fulfilling a multi-generational goal. An opportunity I had to take advantage of or else it could turn into the moment that, in retrospect, was the moment that changed my life but never did because I didn't take it. So this is me, seizing opportunities. Naturally, and I suppose as a consequence, I started googling the next available flight out of Los Angeles International Airport. I could barely wait to call Brenda and let her know I wouldn't be able to watch Mary for a few days because I had business out of town.

'But you don't work,' she said. 'That's why I pay you to take care of your niece.' She really just had no idea how much work I was putting into this, but I let it slide because she was tired and she is, after all, my sister.

'Yes I do!' I screamed. 'I coach teens with confidence issues. Plus, you're not really paying me right now for Mary anyway, remember?'

'You went to a meeting one time because you were bored and stood at the front to make a speech like you were in AA. I don't think that counts.'

I shrugged, unable to counter.

'Where are you going?' she continued.

I knew I was leaving, I just didn't know where I was going. 'I'm not entirely sure yet. I'm thinking of just showing up at the airport and seeing what the next flight is to really get fate into the picture.'

I heard her sigh through the phone. 'You're kidding, right?'

That's the problem with my sister.

'Of course I'm not kidding! There are so few real surprises in life, why should I get in the way of one of them? It's like waiting to name your baby until it's born. So much more interesting, real, spontaneous . . . right?'

'How can you say that? Mary was our great-grandmother's name!'

'I'm sorry. I know honoring ancestry is the kind of thing you have to plan.' I avoided the rest of the conversation before it escalated. 'I'll be back on Monday. Adios!'

'Wait, how can you afford to go on a trip anyway?' she said, just before hanging up. 'Given that I haven't been able to pay you lately with the whole ex-husband fiasco.'

'Savings,' I said. When our grandfather Morty died, he left each of us a modest sum, about $10,000, that was to be used only for 'a rainy day.' I've been waiting for that drizzly, wet day for two years and then realized I could die waiting for that day, the right time, so I might as well use the money to live while I'm alive.

I packed a small backpack's worth of clothes because I knew traveling light was a man's dream. I mean, it practically screams low maintenance. I put on my new bangles and did my hair just right with a little twist at the top to give myself elevation. I always wondered if I'd be more of a bitch if I were taller because height gives me so much confidence. I put on my sparkly skirt, despite it being a little inappropriate for a plane journey, because I needed pizazz. I looked really good; heck, I was sparkling!

When I arrived at the airport, I made a pact with myself as I approached the departures board that I was going to choose what city I'd go to by flipping a coin. Heads would mean that I'd go to the second one down the departures list, and tails would mean the fourth. Whatever city it would land on would determine where I would go. I knew it was crazy, but time was ticking. My mother had upped her Klonopin intake (against our wishes) from daily to twice daily, and that meant soon it would be three and four times daily. I had to make this work and had a feeling this time was it. I imagine it's like actresses who spend years auditioning without stopping, but they keep trying because they never know when they'll get their lucky break. What if I gave up right before landing my big role? I guess that was another thing I learned from the blind men: to just keep moving forward even if you can't see the light. And I was living in the dark now. Sure, I was learning and spots of light would sometimes get through the cracks, but I couldn't see anymore what was happening or where I was going. I had to trust the things that weren't yet in sight.

I tossed the coin and got tails. I was going to Frankfurt.

Rio de Janeiro was the second one, and Lisbon was third. I was a little upset that I chose fourth down for my coin toss rules because everyone knows Germans are terrible lovers (except if you are into fetish porn), but that was the game and I had to follow the rules and so Frankfurt it was. I walked up to the Virgin Airlines ticket counter with my carry-on, pass-port and the unadulterated air of someone about to find love, which you'd think would charm a nun, but the lady in the smart red suit with the matching handkerchief just tossed me a bitter look. I hoped it was only because I was looking so fantastic and going on an adventure and she was working, married to a man who wasn't her match and had blisters from having to wear those patent leather low heels all day. I felt bad for her. I looked down and took in her nametag: Tricia.

'What's your destination?' she asked.

'Frankfurt,' I said, sliding her my passport. 'I haven't purchased a ticket yet, but I'm hoping to get on the 14:25 flight.'

As she typed, her face showed no emotion. No flicker of the lids, no twitch at the edges of her mouth. Not even a wrinkle stretched or bent.

'I had an aunt named Tricia,' I said. 'My dad's sister. I always called her Tish.' Again, her face was sterile, detached. After a few moments, as Jimmy's mirage began to fade and hope was about to commit suicide, Tricia craned her neck around and said, 'Well, if it isn't your lucky day.'

I panicked when I entered the security line, thinking maybe the end of a joint I smoked five years ago was somehow, someway, tucked absentmindedly into my bag that I had forgotten about. I imagined life in jail; the people I'd meet. I had too many layers on. Too many scarves, too many jackets, too many technological appliances to place into separate containers. It was exhausting but I kept the finish line – the one with Bloody Marys at the end – in mind as I wrestled through the cattle in order to keep my belongings by me. As I went through the X-ray machines, hands extended, the alarm bells went off, making me jump. My panic settled, though, as I remembered not even having that bag the last time I smoked pot. Phew! Something about being questioned though, even if you're innocent, makes you nervous and act guilty.

'This way, ma'am,' the female security officer said. 'Are

these your bags?' She pointed towards my suitcase and purse. I nodded, Yes.

'Arms out!' she instructed. 'I'm going to search you now, is that okay?'

I didn't even realize what I was doing but I felt myself nodding so hysterically it were as if someone had just asked me if I'd like to jump into a lake of chocolate with a fleet of Olympic male swimmers. The security woman was patting me down – the back, the arms, the legs, under the bra, all the good spots – and I couldn't help but grin.

She looked at me, her demeanor still deadpan but moving, changing shape. She said: 'I've never seen anyone so excited to get frisked before.'

I was so happy I couldn't hide it. I didn't even want to hide it. Fuck it, I was alive and who wouldn't gobble up the physical attention given in a security search? We all want to be touched. That's why getting your hair washed at the hairdresser's is such a heavenly experience.

Two hours later I'm sitting in the lounge, ready to board with a to-go bag of niçoise salad from an awful airport restaurant called On The Fly. The smell of fish and hard-boiled eggs are already clinging to my clothes but there's no way I'm throwing this food away. It cost me twice as much as it would outside the airport; I know about being economical. I tie the knot tighter, hoping to trap the smell inside. I hear the announcement that my flight is about to board and that's where I am right now: in line, smelling like tuna and eggs.

I take the moment to size up my co-passengers. When you're in line at an airport, you realize there are two types of people: those who make you proud to be an American, and those who make you embarrassed to be one. I want the guy in front of me – the businessman – to just lighten up. Loosen his tie, unbutton his shirt, make me patriotic. I want to lean in and ask him if buttoning his top button made him feel contained, secure, safe, or if it held him back. I want to tell him that it does, in fact, hold him back, but I know it isn't my place. Adults know how to hold their tongue so I switch my attention to assess the woman behind me: a mother. She isn't just any mother, though. She is a hipster mother.

Hipster mothers have this wonderful way of making you feel terrible about where you're at in life without really ever saying anything. They're basically shouting, 'I'm cool and I'm fertile . . . fuck you.' The hipster mother in front of me has a pixie haircut and bright red lips and a stylish outfit she probably stole from some Instagram style blog by some anorexic Italian who takes selfies in clothes no one could ever afford or get into. I sound really awful; they're probably all quite nice. I think I just need to start running.

I look over to the first-class line because, well, who doesn't? You have to know what you want to affirm it. I see a beautiful man with a beard who looks like his name could be Jimmy but that may just be wishful thinking because he's gorgeous and in the first-class line. Don't get me wrong; it's not about money. It's about class. As I inch closer and closer to the air hostess, or flight attendant depending on how PC I'm feeling, I watch Jimmy board ahead of me with so much swagger it makes my cookie tingle. I say cookie because it sounds substantially more classy than pussy. Jimmy's got a leather jacket on and a bachelor vibe, plus no ring: perfect. He's got a nose ring (I'll deal), a few tattoos inching around the top of his V-neck T-shirt. His hair is messy and curly, like a musician's, ready and asking for hands of screaming girls or one screaming Tabby. His locks rest dark and silky. I imagine rolling around on a bed of guitar strings, pulling on his hair like he pulls at those strings, the tension screaming out of him with pleasure. Pleasure that bursts from his roots to the extremities of his limbs and makes his whole body tingle and shake. I'll use the opportunity to nurture him and embrace his lost soul and tell him, 'Baby, home is where you hang your hat.' He'll look at me and sign, 'I love you' because he can't breathe, let alone talk. But when he does catch his breath, he'll remind me that we won't burst. That the love will just keep growing and growing, like a big man's belly. People always say that things go sour, after you peak, but that's the best thing about always being at the bottom.

I hand my ticket to one of the stewardesses who I have to admit is pretty hot – Claudia Schiffer hot, so boiling in fact that I'm slightly worried she might get Jimmy's attention before I do, but I tell myself she probably has a smelly pussy. That makes me feel better.

'Welcome to Virgin,' she says, cookie wafting, although it may just be the tuna from my bag. 'You're in 23C. Enjoy your flight.' She gestures in the direction of the back of the plane and I want to just turn around and say, 'Who am I? Dick Gregory?' But I don't; I just keep walking. I look around first class and spot Jimmy in the last row of Premium Economy. It's okay; it's still classy. My eyes are fixed on him like a cop tracking a suspect until he looks up. He smiles and I can't believe it but he's looking at me with the best face I've ever seen and he's moving his hair around, pushing man fragrance towards me. 'Jimmy?' I say, still unbelieving but confident that the omen is actually coming true. He just keeps smiling and now he's lifting his hand up and starting to wave. I pick my hand up, too, and wave back. I knew we had something.

Sometimes you just know you're going to know someone for a while. Like when you are certain you'll be with someone the first time you see him playing the keys. He's there, sweating and tapping and banging and you could bet your life on the story you'll have because you know a man with hands like that means a lifetime of rhythmic pleasure. Then you break up because he says he might be a bit more gay than straight. Someone gives you a handmade present that says, 'I knew you once' to hang on your wall, to remind you of the times you shared with people who are now strangers. You think it's sweet at first but then it reminds you only of what you had so you throw it away. I've never dated a pianist but the point is that sometimes you just know, and with Jimmy, I can see our story's shape before it's even been drawn out, like a gift waiting to be opened.

He's looking at me still; he won't take his sparkling eyes off me.

He gets up.

'I thought you were going to bail on me,' he says.

I drop my light baggage and run up and bear hug him, screaming with joy. I wrap my left leg around his and lock my feet behind his calf like a wrestler in an upright death match because I'm so happy I could squeeze all the life out of both of us – my nickname in high school was Python. When I pull back though, his once joyful expression drops to a slip of itself. I realize he's not holding on to me, only I to him. I turn around because he's looking behind me now and I see the horrifying sight of another woman.

'He was talking to me,' she says, close to laughing. There's more condescension in her tone than the condensation I could lick off a warm beer bottle in Miami during the hottest summer of the past thirty years. I'm talking about global-warming heat. Hot. And it hits me hard, this heat, this hot, hot heat, as I process the miserable fact that I've jumped into the arms of a man thinking he was talking to me when he was celebrating the arrival of someone else. My heart freezes. I collapse inside, quietly. But it's okay; I'm still breathing.

I take a step back. 'I'm so sorry,' I say. 'I didn't realize you were talking to your older sister!' I mean, she has to be. He is Jimmy and Jimmy is meant to be my soul mate, so the only possible conclusion is that she is a sibling. She moves around me and I watch them, like a train wreck, move towards each other in slow motion and delicately weave into their own sort of odd embrace. Way too close for siblings, but who am I to judge? Maybe they were from the South and that's how brothers and sisters say hello.

I nod at Jimmy, to say, I know, babe. I know. He doesn't understand yet but he will once we have learned to speak each other's body language. Looking at his stance right now, I cannot wait to be fluent in Jimmy. It's tough to know what to do but I pull my shoulders back and exude lion-level confidence so his sister doesn't think she's the alpha female in our triangle.

My seat is further back from Jimmy than I had hoped so I go up to the lady sitting in the first row in Economy, right behind Premium, right behind Jimmy, and I tap her on the shoulder. She looks like she's flying solo.

'Excuse me,' I start. 'My son is flying upper class and I need to be closer to him because he's epileptic. If he starts having a fit I need to be as close as possible and the airline made a mistake with my ticket.' I point back towards my seat. 'They've put me so far away! Would you by any chance like to swap seats with me?'

My eyes search in hope for sympathy as I stand, waiting, for a response. She looks back towards where I pointed, then back to me. Then back again to my seat.

'Well,' she says. 'I guess, if you need to be close to your son, I could switch seats.'

'You are so kind. Thank you so much!' I say, joyously, gratefully. 'You're going to get a lot of good karma points for this. Believe me, I've racked up quite a few for good deeds done and I can say without hesitation that my life has changed for the better because of it.'

She collects her bags and shuffles towards my empty 23C as I take her place. She's warmed the seat up so much I wonder if she's just eaten a packet of fruit cake and farted all over it. I sink in cozily as my heart's temperature rises from my proximity to Jimmy.

My neighbor looks nice. 'Hi,' I say. 'I'm KK.' I once met a woman named KK and thought she sounded fun so I'm adopting it now, for short-term use, to try it out. See how it goes over. He's older, the man next to me, probably early eighties. He holds out his hand.

'Tony,' he says. 'I hate flying so don't be startled if I faint on you or have to hold on.' This guy sounds like me. Such a little old pervert! I love him.

'Sure thing, Tony. Grab away.'

About an hour into the flight, Tony's grabbing my wrist like it's his only lifeline – which, based on his age, is probably true – and then tells me he can't see very well.

'I have to take ten medications a day,' he says. I'm starting to wonder if switching with the Fruitcake was a wise idea. He takes out a plastic container with slots filled with colored pills to take at different times during the day. He starts fumbling around and dropping them on his lap without realizing it. I grab the box, somewhat impatiently, and say, 'What colors do you need now? I'll get them for you.'

'One blue and one pink,' he says. 'Thank you, KK.'

'My boyfriend is in upper class,' I tell him as I hand him a few pills along with a glass of water. 'Well, Premium Economy.'

'Is he sitting with your son?'

'No, no. I was just lying to get this seat.' I stop, worrying I've said too much, but then I realize he wouldn't have anyone to help him with his pills if he told on me. Plus, they'd all think he was senile. I honestly can't wait until I'm senile; no one will ever be able to blame me for anything. I get up and slide the curtain over a tad to check on Jimmy, who's now asleep. He's so coy! I inch over another foot and see his sister is asleep on his shoulder.

'Psst!' I say. 'Jimmy.' No answer, just a little snore. Well, that's something I'll have to talk to him about when we're sleeping together because I cannot sleep with a man who snores. Before Brenda and her husband split up, she used to have to sleep in Mary's room because he'd snore so loudly. Not my idea of an ideal marriage! Jimmy jumps and turns around, piercing my heart with his lagoon-colored eyes and says, 'My name's not Jimmy.'

Hold on. What? It has to be Jimmy. All you have to do is look around the rest of the plane – over the shoulders of the moms and the hairy backs of the old dads and the food-spilt laps of their kids, around the general vicinity of gross people – and you will know why Jimmy has to be Jimmy. There are no other options. I start to panic and take a bite of my tuna salad when it hits me: He's undercover.

I lean in again. 'Come on, baby,' I say. 'Let's get wild.'

Jimmy's eyes widen then his face contorts into a pained look, as if he were going to the toilet in his seat. I hope he doesn't have gas too! That can be really painful, believe me.

Poor Jimmy turns around and whispers something to his sister but I can't get in close enough to hear. A flight attendant pops her face around the corner and stares at me with violent intentions as I sit back, quietly growling.

'Please don't bother the upper-class flyers, ma'am,' she says, awfully loudly, making me so mad all I can do is look like an old woman with her dentures out eating an orange, top lip curled around my gums. Turn around, Jimmy. Turn around.

He never does turn around so I wait patiently. I take the napkin from under my vodka tonic and write him a note. It says, 'I want to fa-uh-uh-uk-uk you (I like the song), x' and

I fold it into a little paper airplane. I check to make sure the flight attendant isn't looking and send it sailing through the stagnant air towards him. It's flying, my ironic plane within a plane, gliding effortlessly towards his head, but then it hits the armrest in front of him and ricochets off to the left where it dips and slides under a seat to be found, surely, by a janitor.

Tony is nudging me to help him find his next round of pills. I fish out a few and try to shove them into his mouth but, because I'm distracted by thoughts of Jimmy, I accidentally push them into his nostrils. He blows them out in a sneeze. As I realize what I've done, I quickly wipe them off and redirect them into the right hole.

'Are you trying to get someone's attention?' he asks me. Tony has this way of not really looking at me but for some reason it feels like he sees more of me than anyone else. Why on earth is the old man with the bad eyes and pockets of medication getting me more than Jimmy?

'Yes,' I reply. 'My boyfriend is sleeping and keeps forgetting his name and it's driving me crazy because I just want to talk.'

Tony gives me a counseling look, somewhere between concern and intrigue.

I hear Jimmy's seatbelt unbuckle, cha-ching! He stands up and walks towards the bathroom in the front of the cabin, the one I can't get to. But then, as if divine intervention were at hand, the occupied light flashes on just before he reaches the door. Yes! God really does exist. He circles around and heads back as the only vacant toilet is the one right in front of me. He's avoiding eye contact with me, but only because he's shy. We've gathered that by now so it doesn't worry me.

He enters the tiny stall at which point I turn to Tony and say, 'Excuse me, sweet man. Got to go work my magic.' I check to see if Jimmy's sister is watching and, good thing, she's asleep. Snoring with her mouth open like an old lady.

Tony looks puzzled, again, but it doesn't matter because I'm my own quarterback and my team is losing and if I don't do something drastic I'm going to lose this game. I hate that I'm even referencing this whole love mission as a game, anyway. It's not a game. I can't play games anymore.

I pop up from my seat effervescently and just before the green vacancy light turns to red, occupied, I open the door before he has a chance to lock it and slide in like a cockroach through a vent.

Jimmy's back is towards me, standing over the toilet with his hands engaged on his dick to direct the flow of piss as I stealthily approach him from behind. I lock the door – why do men always forget to lock doors? Maybe he knew I'd follow him in – and pounce on him like how I imagine a black widow approaches her mate in one swift, accurate move, securing him down with her overbearing weight before he has a chance to process what's happening. And like its deep sting, I thrust my arms around him. He jumps, startled, as I say, 'It's way more cramped in here than I'd imagined!' My hands are now making circles around his clothes to warm him up. Big, sweeping circles to penetrate deep into his heart. He spins around but hasn't let go of his dick yet so his pee sprays all over me and the walls and the floor. I had no idea my Mile High Club experience would include a golden shower! I love surprises! He's swearing now, but swearing quietly because he knows being in here with me puts him at risk. It makes him an accomplice. 'What are you doing?' he whisper-screams. 'This is crazy, get out!' But I can't respond; all I can do is look at his penis.

I smile in the sexiest way I can while also sucking my cheeks in to look more chiseled. He reaches for the door handle but I block it with my ass – thank God it's big – and I shush him with one hand while the other pins him in the corner. His eyes are rolling around, searching, so I lessen my grip so he can breathe. He starts panting.

'There we go,' I say, motioning towards his short breath. 'First step to the Mile High Club.' Oh God, I know I'm going too far now. But what can I do at this point? I have to see where it takes me. Maybe I'm meant to be acting this all out. A part of me knows it's wrong but at the same time the whole situation is so exciting and raw and real and the fact that I feel so alive means I'm doing something right.

He grabs me by the shoulders and tries to move me to the side so he can get out but there's nowhere for my body to go so it just lodges both of us into a more complicated pretzel-like formation. I try to lean in more closely, to feel his warmth, but every time I do he pulls his head back and bangs it against the plastic wall. 'Stop doing that,' I say. 'Are you nuts? You're going to hurt yourself!'

His arm moves to cover his balls for some reason, maybe he's weird about their size, as his knee protrudes into my stomach. Both of us are trying to maneuver around the pee on the seat and the walls, which forces us to engage in a sort of awkward squat. Finally, I feel his thighs tremble with the emotion I was talking about earlier.

'Charley Horse!' he shouts, moving urgently to the left to free his locked calf. His other knee is still digging into me, but it's gone from erotic to quite uncomfortable because it's now pushing into my bladder. His eyebrows are twisting around, seeking answers, but I just keep smiling so he knows this is supposed to be fun. I'm leaning so far forward at this point that my weight is completely on his and on the wall. The tension in the room has created so much heat, the walls have become slippery and my right hand falls down and accidentally hits the flush button. The violent sound of its vacuum frightens us both so much we jump in panic and twist into each other more deeply. There's a foot now close to my face, there's grunting and pee and sometimes one of our legs hits the sink faucet, but between the strain on our faces and the sweat there's this level of calm that's beautiful and untouched.

Now, instead of looking like two novices playing Twister, we look like Russian contortionists auditioning for a show.

'Isn't this nice?' I whisper, examining his beard for pieces of life, picking at it with my free hand like a monkey cleans her children. 'A final moment away from your sister and the chance to experience true love at an altitude disproportionate to ourselves.'

A supercilious grin appears on his face, like a shining sun through a blanket of dreary sky, and I see him smile. I didn't expect such a rash turnaround. He opens his mouth and he's got a tongue ring. Oh no. He's bad. Real bad. This couldn't be more fun if I imagined it.

'Have you just been eating a sandwich?' he asks me, sniffing the air.

I take his signal and rip his shirt open and see a tattoo of the band Nickelback on his chest. My heart sinks because now I know he loves terrible music and all of a sudden I can't see our future together anymore. I tear more and more of his clothes off as he stands there, bewildered, and find a plethora of unbecoming tattoos including, but not limited to, a lucky charm ('from when I was in Ireland') and a tribal tattoo, probably inspired by hitting rock bottom in the nineties. I don't like this. I don't like this at all.

He looks at me like he is going to hurt me and I start to panic. He lifts me up on the wall and bites my ear to escalate the romance but it's all going much more quickly than I had hoped. I wanted time to talk and get to know each other.

'What are you doing?' I ask.

'You want me to fuck you, don't you?' he says, crassly. Heartlessly.

'No!' I say. 'I want you to be knocked sideways with affection and adoration and think it's the most magical experience, us coming together in a plane bathroom. Love at first sight. Destiny. Fate. Whatever. You know, all the good stuff.'

'You expect romance by following me into a toilet?' he says.

This doesn't feel like my idea anymore. I feel gross now that he wants it.

'This isn't romantic!' I scream. 'One minute ago you were cupping your balls and now you're into it? I liked you more when you were shy and unaware of your charm.'

This unfortunately turns him on. How unusual.

'Stop!' I say as his willy waits before my cookie, hard from adrenaline but lingering as if waiting for the signal to land.

I fluff my hair and pull my skirt down.

'I want you to woo me,' I say. 'I want to feel wanted, needed. What happened to courting a woman?'

'You followed me in here!' he whispers again, quite loudly. A shot of hot breath hits me hard on the face. 'I was taking your cue.'

'Cues? No one in their right mind follows cues.'

'You're very confusing,' he says.

We are staring at each other with lost yet focused attention, the cabin air pressurizing our hearts so we probably can't tell what is real and what isn't. It feels like we could be dying, but we aren't sure.

'You can't have romance when there's no spark,' he says.

'I thought we had a spark,' I counter. 'You've been eyeing me up all flight long.' I stop. Think. 'Wait . . . Your name is Jimmy, right?'

'It's Tim. I thought I cleared that up before when I told you my name wasn't Jimmy.'

Well, that makes sense. Any man with a Nickelback tattoo is certainly not a spy. Right then, someone knocks at the door.

'The toilet is for single use only!' the flight attendant yells. She bangs again, making us jump. 'Out now or I'll write you up for illegal and indecent behavior.'

'I was just leaving!' I say to the woman but the idea of some sort of certificate to show my friends and mom sounds fun. Just before I open the door I turn to Tim and ask, 'Why Nickelback?'

'I was their guitar tech when I was twenty-five,' he says. The more I hear, the more I can't take. The more I thank the Universe for interfering before I lost my heart to the wrong guy.

I open and close the door behind me so people don't see us walk out together. When I take my seat again, I buckle up and let out a huge sigh. Insides falling out all over the place. I see

Tim sneak out and back to his seat next to his sister. But now that he's Tim, not Jim, for all I know, it could be his girlfriend. The flight attendant is throwing martial art weapons of disgust at me from the other side of the plane.

'You're a whole new brand of Cracker Jacks,' Tony leans in and whispers. 'Never seen anything quite like you before.'

'What are you talking about?' I ask. 'I just had to pee.'

'It sounded like someone was throwing a piano down a set of stairs in there,' he says, winking at me.

I can't help it but tears start to stream down my face. Embarrassed, I try to wipe them away before anyone sees. 'I just don't understand why it's so hard for me to find the person I'm supposed to be with.' It's amazing how you can cry to a stranger but not to your own mother.

'You're trying too hard. Let a man come to you.'

'But he was cute, he even tried to kiss me. He has tattoos and a sexy tongue ring and used to be a big band's guitar tech . . .'

'I love big band music,' he interrupts.

'No, a big band. A popular band. Doesn't matter. Anyway, he said we had no spark.'

'You're telling me you're crying because some douche bag with a tongue ring and a terrible band tattoo says you don't have "sparks"?' Tony says with a smile, patting me on the back to comfort me, slightly too hard. Too abrupt and awkward, but it's sweet.

'I have done everything under the sun, short of boning a a little person, and nothing is working. I can't figure out where I'm going wrong.'

'I'm a little person,' Tony says.

I gasp in fear at what I've said. The harm I've done. I cover my mouth. 'I'm so sorry. I'm sure you'd be great in bed!'

'I'm only kidding, kid,' he says. 'See what I mean? You're too uptight.'

So now Tony's a bit of a humorist.

'That's funny. You should save that for your standup routine,' I say, pulling the tuna fish out of my bag. I'm feeling peckish as you do after sexual activity, and start taking little bites here, little bites there, all the while looking at Tony properly. I'm taking all of him in. I wonder how big Tony's willy is but not in a weird way. Purely out of interest, a normal thought when you meet someone new. That's what women do. Like when you imagine what sex is like between odd couples. Not because it's a sexy thought but more of a complex logistical puzzle, to figure out how it works when one is too small, the other too big; one too short, the other too tall. Sure, it's strange, but you can't help but think about it. At least I don't imagine what their faces look like while orgasming. That would be really over the top!

'You're beautiful,' he says.

'Tony,' I say. 'You're blind! How do you know I'm beautiful?'

'I'm not that blind.'

'You're very cheeky. I'm sure with women, you always made the first move and it worked. Isn't that the same as what I'm doing by getting the ball rolling? Sometimes you have to make people like you. Or at least, steer them in the right direction . . . right?'

'No,' he says. 'Wrong.'

'Well then I officially don't understand,' I say, looking up towards the sky as if talking to any listening angels, but all I see is the ceiling of the plane. All I see is plastic, and it's killing me like it's destroying our seas and our planet.

'When I met my wife, she didn't like me because I was a cocky little son of a bitch and she wanted nothing to do with me,' he tells me. 'I was a bit of a wise ass. Girls loved me because I was a smooth talker and had an unjustifiable amount of confidence for a man of my class.'

He pauses. Blows his nose. Needs a pill.

'Well, don't stop now,' I say. 'I love a good love story.'

'I gathered that,' he says as he adjusts himself in his seat, excited to have a captive audience. 'I first saw Rosie when she was eighteen. I was nineteen, living in St. Louis. She worked as a receptionist at a doctor's office and I managed a diner directly across the street. I used to watch her through the blinds every day as she'd leave. I kept trying to get her to come in so I'd have an excuse to talk to her but she totally ignored me. Said I was a jerk all the time.'

'Why would she think that?' I ask.

'Because I was. I had already dated her friends and pretty much every woman in the town who didn't have a ring.'

'Look at Tony go,' I say.

'So anyway, one day she came in with her boss and I ignored her, well, more out of respect or hopelessness because I knew she didn't want to talk to me. I'd run after her down the street calling "Baby" so many times I figured I'd lost my chance. Once I stopped trying, she relaxed a little. Slowly but surely, she started making excuses to come in for a milkshake here, a milkshake there . . .'

'I bet she did!' I exclaim, laughing, to which he just shakes his head.

'You're missing the point,' he says. 'The point is that the minute I dropped the act, she turned around.'

It takes me a moment but I process this. I feel it going through my nose and into my brain, seeping down my temples.

'What's your biggest fear?' Tony asks me. He's got a piece of salad on his chin from the meal earlier and it's seriously distracting. I don't want to make him feel self-conscious by getting it off, and hope he'll just naturally brush his hand over his face and knock it down.

'Lovelessness.' It just slips out so quickly, like a knee-jerk reaction. I don't even know if it's a word but it feels like the best way to describe it.

Tony digests this silently. 'I think you're a catch, KK. Just focus on loving yourself and the rest will work itself out. Maybe you're going for these men because you know you'll never end up with them. They're safe.'

His words make me wonder if maybe I'm picking all the wrong men because subconsciously I want to keep our family just the way it is. To keep my mom close, needing me like she only does when she's alone. I hope that's not true.

'How would I know if they were right or not before we date?' I reply, but Tony's losing steam.

Finally, Tony scratches an itch on his chin and the lettuce leaf falls off. The flight map says we have two hours left until we reach Frankfurt. I close my eyes and try to take myself back to the place I last felt hopeful and confident, to the moment right before I went into the bathroom. I ruminate there, and let myself doze off to a world where chivalry and romance are as common as tying a shoelace.

When I arrive in Frankfurt, my daisy is itching so insanely I can barely see straight. I shouldn't have eaten the in-flight dessert because I just cannot process sugar. And you know, sugar aggravates candida and there you have it. I'm feeling an odd mix of emotions because I can't quite seem to get my head around the fact that Tim wasn't Jimmy, and Jimmy wasn't on the plane, and that Jimmy is still out there.

People aggressively push past me after we exit Customs as if they're all late for their lives. You're never supposed to make plans immediately after your scheduled flight arrival because everyone knows it could get delayed. This is how I live, without plans. This is how I avoid panic and confusion.

I see Tim and his sister in front of me in the Customs line. They go in the 'Nothing To Declare' line but you know they've got some secrets. He should be saying, 'I'm a dickhead! I'm bringing dickheadedness into your country!' By this time, I've lost Tony; no idea where he went. I tried to help him with his things but someone was waiting to scoot him away in a wheel-chair the minute we exited the plane, that sneaky bastard. He really has learned to live well.

The Frankfurt airport is huge. Everything is very clean. Very organized. Very German. I search frantically for a pharmacy and finally find one and walk straight up to the woman behind the counter.

'Hello,' I say, smiling through the pain. I lean in to whisper. 'Do you have any yeast infection cream?'

'What?!' she says very, very loudly, with a very German accent.

'I think I have a yeast infection,' I whisper again, trying to signal with my hand to lower her voice. I start looking around to make sure no one can hear.

'Okay,' she says. Thank goodness, she gets it. I wait as she tries to get the attention of her co-worker in the back of the shop. But instead of waiting for her to come over, she does the unthinkable.

'Hilda? This lady has fungus of the vag-ina,' she screams as everyone, of course, turns to look at me. 'Inside fungus or outside fungus?' she adds, for confirmation. The word *vagina* sounds so vulgar when she says it like that, as if it were a disease itself. Something you wouldn't want to be caught dead with.

'No!' I yell out. 'No, no. A misunderstanding!' I throw my body over the counter with what's left of my pride and say, again in a whisper, 'Please, I don't want people to hear.'

'So you do have a fungus in your vagina or not?' she says, too loudly again, too matter-of-factly. I look around at the faces of customers and come, to my horror, to Tim and his companion, sister, whatever, who have surfaced from behind one of the aisles.

'Okay,' Hilda shouts. 'I'm coming. We have something for you.'

Tim looks at me in a way I've never been looked at, and all I can do is run out as quickly as I can as the German pharmacists call out after me, the girl with the itchy daisy.

I need to find a phone because I need to get all this disappointment off my chest so I walk into a telephone booth at the airport and pick up the receiver. I don't know who to talk to. I know I want to talk, I just don't know whom to call. I can't call Brenda because she doesn't entertain my meandering questions and I think my mom said she'd be away with Gary, her new boyfriend, this weekend and wouldn't be available.

So I call Bridget.

Bridget and I haven't spoken in years, probably since high school, but she's always been someone I can turn to. It's like we can have years go by without seeing each other but it doesn't change how close we are. She's still my best friend.

'Hello?' she says.

'Bridge!' I delight. 'Hey, it's me.'

'Who?'

'Tabitha,' I say. There's so much silence I am not sure entirely what to do.

'How did you get my number?' she asks. 'How are you?'

'I'm great,' I lie. 'On holiday in Germany right now. Just wanted to see how you were. Needed a friend to talk—'

Kids are screaming in the background, shouting variations of 'Mom!'

'I'm so sorry, Tabitha,' Bridget cuts me off. 'One of my kids has a temperature and I'm trying to cook everyone dinner before my husband gets home. Is there anything you need? It's just not the best time to catch up.'

The room feels colder and I put my jacket on. I look down at my feet. The way they turn out from all those years of ballet as a kid. Then I look at the cuticles I need to cut on my fingernails. The polish I need to reapply. How my hands are starting to look a lot like my mother's.

'Oh,' I say. 'Of course. I'm fine. Let's talk soon then. Hope your kid feels better.'

'Thanks,' she says as a pan clinks in the background. 'Okay, thanks for calling. Bye.'

I hang up the phone and stand in the middle of the busy airport. All alone in Frankfurt, wishing I'd met Jimmy already. I circle around a few times, looking at the German headlines on celebrity magazines. I don't recognize anyone except for Princess Kate and Prince William, who just had their first baby son. I think about going outside for a while but instead wait inside as it's so cold. I'm not itching anymore so maybe it was just nerves. I am nervous after all. Sometimes that happens. False alarms! I'm plagued with them!

I find a bar in the area, sit down at the counter, and order a beer because I know that's very German and when in Frankfurt, etc. I'm starting to think that this whole search for love is making me look crazy. I know I'm a good person; I don't know why it's taking me so long to find someone. Maybe I am being desperate. Being in a foreign country really puts things in perspective.

I'm chugging my beer down as I hear someone calling out my name.

'Tabitha?' a woman yells. 'Tabitha, is that you?'

I turn around and find Joyce Devons, one of my mother's friends, running towards me. 'I can't believe I'm seeing you in GERMANY!'

She laughs too loudly and has a tight-fitting black outfit on with pearls and high heels. When she walks, she looks like she's about to fall, ankles unsure, like a drunk gazelle on ice skates. We give each other a hug and kiss on the cheek, more of an air-kiss it turns out.

'What are you doing here?' I ask.

'I have a convention to attend. Musikmesse. A music convention. One of the biggest in the world. Absolutely exhausting but it's great in the evenings when we can all go out for drinks and pretend we're strategizing. Why are you here?'

I think about how I'm going to respond without perpetuating my heart-breaking story so I say, 'I just needed to get out.'

'To Frankfurt?' she says. 'I didn't know people came here who didn't have to, but that's great news. I bet you're following in your mother's footsteps, getting up to wild things, aren't you? Speaking of, I need to call her. How is she?'

'She's the same as always,' I say, wondering if it's true. 'Busy.'

'Good. Busy is good. I'm still livid with your father for leaving you all like that.'

I don't really have anything to say so I just stand there. Quiet for a minute. 'That was a long time ago. We're over it. The Grays are pros at moving on.'

'I have to run, but have fun on your adventures!' she says, blowing me a kiss.

'Joyce?' I say as she turns to leave. 'Are you okay?'

'Didn't your mother tell you?' she says. 'Michael ran off with a nineteen-year-old stripper about six months ago. Thirty-two

years of marriage down the drain because some Eastern European with displaced daddy issues enchanted my husband's
dick.'

I went over and hugged her with both arms. 'Well,' I say, 'I
think it's exciting because it means that you can now meet the
one you're supposed to be with. He's still out there!'

'I'm not so sure about that. At my age, it's hard pickings.'

'You can get it wrong a gazillion times but it doesn't matter
because you only need to get it right once. You only have to
meet one good one. The rest is practice.'

At this point I'm not even sure what I'm talking about
because it's been one fail after another but for some reason
I'm fired up about the future. I'm still on the rollercoaster
Chrissie Hynde was telling me about. And when it's down, it
means it's about to go up.

'Thanks, Tabitha,' she says. 'You're absolutely right.' She
takes me all in and adds, 'Boy, you're really growing up, aren't
you? I think these adventures are doing you good.'

I'm so happy someone's noticed.

The Bartender

The phone rings and it's Milk. Being my neighbor, he's hard to escape. I'm hungover from my long flight back from Germany, binging on too much emotion, up in the air, and we all know altitude magnifies things. It took a lot out of me; the comedown is hard on the nerves.

'Hey,' he says. 'What are you doing right now?'

'Oh,' I jump. 'I'm busy.' I'm lying on my bed but start to hit pillows and ruffle things up so it sounds like there's a lot going on.

'I know you're lying. I'm watching you.' When I glance over, I see him on the phone staring at me from his kitchen window. He points at me with an '*I got you.*'

'Goddammit, Milk!' I shout. 'Stop spying on me!'

'I saw you get back last night. I thought for a minute you'd be away a little longer, hunting down European men usually takes at least a few days, right? Even for you, Queen of Haste.'

'Yeah, yeah, very funny.' I pause. 'I'm picking up Mary soon and have some things to do at home. Some very important things.'

'Like what?'

'Like finishing *Lolita*.'

'You've read that at least fifty times.'

'Well, I've been a little confused lately, and Jeremy Irons' voice on audiotape makes me feel less alone, okay?' I'm hoping he'll think I'm bananas, I'm weird, but he doesn't even flinch. That's probably why he's so good at martial arts.

'I have a place I want to take you,' he says, suspiciously.

'Like an adventure?' I ask, excited at the thought but also dubious because, well, it's Milk. He nods but I'm still unsure. 'What kind of adventure?' I add. 'Give me a hint.'

'You're always talking about wanting spontaneity. Here it is.'

I can feel my face contort, lips purse, the lines in between my eyebrows scrunching up into squiggly shapes.

'Aren't you the one who's always saying you have to be proactive and make things happen rather than waiting for things to come to you?' he continues, pushing. Pushing!

Next thing I know, I'm driving in my car with him to get Mary. He scratches his nose in my peripheral vision.

'I can't believe I'm being blindly led by a guy who lives at home,' I say.

'Oh, and you don't?'

I shrug, unable to source a comeback.

'We're both doing the same thing,' he adds. 'We're taking care of our parents.'

'Is that really why you're home again? To take care of your dad?'

'He started leaving the gas on,' he begins, softly spoken, slowly, 'and wandering around the streets in his robe in the middle of the night. I didn't want to hire anyone because no one would take care of him like I would. So I rented out my place and moved back in.'

'I'm sorry,' I say, feeling guilty that he's probably my closest friend and I never have really taken the time to find out. I've always thought of him as just being across the street, but when I really think about it, I remember a big block of time when he wasn't there. He hasn't always been across the street, after all. 'I should have known that he was sick.'

I can't look at him properly anymore. My eyes start to itch, my vision blurring out of focus with each blink. I guess I've never let him grow up. If he was an adult, getting on with things, then I was the adult who wasn't. His family had been the refuge for my father when he couldn't stay in our house, which I felt divided us. As if being close to them meant not siding with my mother. Maybe that's what had always obscured my view of him.

'Mary's like a little alien, right?' I jest, trying to change the subject.

'She's got the whole thing in control,' Milk says.

'It's like someone is whispering all the answers into her ear.'

'I'm pretty sure we both know who that person is, and I wouldn't call them answers.'

'Truths are subjective!'

'Good point.'

I park the car and the two of us head towards the steps Mary will soon be bouncing down, belly first, hair jumping, giggles abounding. Principal Chandler walks towards us, her smile fixed like a slice of summer melon.

'Tabitha!' she says with a plastic wave. 'Is this your new boyfriend?'

Milk and I exchange an awkward look and at once say, 'No.'

'Oh,' she says. Her hair is dyed red and too long for her age. It's wrapped tightly in a low bun. I worry about how headache inducing it is; I want her to loosen the pieces pulling the skin around her temples, straining her eyes. She looks surprised, botoxed, stressed. A gray suit mirrors the color of her skin and the shade her hair would be under that masking red. 'Mary mentioned there was someone special in your life. I just assumed.'

'Really?' Milk says, turning to me. 'Who?'

'I've got a lot of admirers,' I tell the two of them.

'I just have one thing to ask you, Tabitha,' the principal says as I lean in, naturally. 'Mary's been getting bullied at school for telling preposterous stories that I must admit are pretty absurd. And I'm concerned.'

'Oh really?' I light up. 'Like what?'

'Well, she told one of her classmates the other day that her television only turns on when it detects enough food in her stomach.'

'So?'

'Well that's a lie,' she says defensively, feathers tangled. 'All I'm saying is that these kinds of things will just get her into trouble. Kids love to make fun of other kids and these stories, well they're just ammunition for ridicule and . . .'

'Lies are a part of life,' I counter. 'I'm teaching her survival techniques. And it's how I get her to eat enough. It's actually quite smart. How does she take it? Does it upset her?'

'The other kids laugh at her but she just sits there and smiles as if the joke's on them.'

'Sounds like Mary,' Milk says, chest out.

'Thanks for letting us know,' I say, extending my hand.

'There's more,' she starts. 'I overheard her telling a group of girls during playtime that you're her mother. She came up with this elaborate story about how her mom was arrested by the, and I quote, "boring police"?'

'She used that phrase?' A feeling of warmth and gratification sweeps through me, that I am maternal, that my stories are being heard, that I'm influencing another human being in a way that I think will make her happy, that it's all paying off. 'I'm so proud!' But then, of course, it is quickly intercepted by a wave of guilt and sadness for my sister.

'Tabitha, this is serious,' she says. 'She also told her classmates that a boy's penis is in his heart and that's why it gets bigger when he's in front of a woman he's in love with.'

Milk bursts out laughing as my hands cup my face with excitement.

'That's the greatest thing I've ever heard! So romantic, right, Milk?' I exclaim.

'You're insane all right,' he chuckles.

The principal looks very concerned. She is aching to say something at this point, I can tell from the way her hands press up against her hips and the faltering start and stop of her lips, how they open and shut. Open and shut. 'I'm afraid I think it's extremely inappropriate and, frankly, unacceptable. If the other kids go home telling their parents they heard these things . . .'

'Thanks for letting us know,' I eventually say. 'Her mom is going to be really pleased.'

'But, but . . .' she stammers until Milk interrupts her.

'We'll let her mom know. It was nice to meet you, Principal Chandler,' he says. 'Thanks again for looking out for Mary.'

The school bell rings and Milk looks over to me and pats

me on the back with a 'let's go.' Mary's little legs do as they always do and bicycle through the air towards us. She's hand in hand with Randall.

I grab her softly as soon as she's close, bending down to meet her on eye level. 'I need you to know something,' I say.

'What?' she asks.

'You're magic. You're filled with magic. All of you. Got it?'

'Yeah,' she says. I've been telling her this for so long it's like I'm telling her the same knock knock joke over and over again but she never tells me she's heard it before because her wisdom beyond her years reminds her it's something she needs to hear. I want it ingrained in her, and that happens through repetition.

I look over and see Randall's eyes pop with interest as he's listening to me as some kids their age walk by.

'Frog eyes!' one kid says to Randall. He just stares back, emotionless, like he's an extra in *Children of the Corn,* but I'm sure deep down it's upset him.

'Hey, kid!' I yell, all riled up. 'First of all, he has beautiful eyes. And even if they were frog eyes, frog eyes are awesome! You wish you had frog eyes!'

'Okay, okay,' Milk says before I morph into a salivating pit bull. 'Take it easy.' He turns to Randall and shakes the hair once settled on his head into a verifiable mess.

'Hey,' Randall says.

'Kids used to make fun of me all the time . . .' Milk starts.

'Me too!' I say, overly excited I fit into the conversation organically.

'But you're a tough kid. I can tell just from looking at you. They got nothing on you.'

'You're not just tough,' I interrupt again. 'You're a little king, okay? You're mighty. Don't even listen to that mumbo jumbo. I certainly don't and look where it's gotten me!'

Mary, Randall and Milk all share a worried glance, but I know they're just kidding. I look at the four of us, standing in the middle of the swell, and feel for the first time what it would be like to have a family. I imagine Milk as my husband (of course, that would be weird because I would never marry Milk) and Mary and Randall our children. Just as the moment glistens, Mary burps.

'Aw gross,' Randall says. 'What did you have for lunch? Farts?'

Mary lets out a yelp of excitement, her hubris bigger than herself.

'A little lady,' Milk adds. He turns to me. 'We ready?'

Ten minutes later we're driving down the highway listening to Steely Dan and singing with pitch so astoundingly awful it could be used in a Guatemalan torture chamber to expel traitorous words from an innocent captive. It's three in the afternoon and the rays of sun set the world on fire; we have to squint to see through the dashboard. West Hills never looked so good. It must be the light and the way we move around it because otherwise it's just flatland with rows of pre-fabricated homes you could buy from a catalog. But right now, in this car, with these people, under this fulgent sun, it's perfect.

'I don't understand,' Mary says, detecting a different route. 'Where are we going?'

'We're just taking a little detour,' Milk says as he instructs me to make a left at the next light.

'I'm so happy Milk is here!' Mary screams out. 'But why?' she adds, unable to subdue her insatiable curiosity.

'Tabby came to take a ju-jitsu class at my studio the other day,' Milk says.

'Why?' Randall interrupts.

'Because,' Milk says but stops, looks over at me for a moment. 'Well, I guess because she's looking for someone as tough as her.'

'So why is Milk here now?' Mary asks again as she squirms around in the back seat. 'And I thought fighting was bad?'

'Depends on what you're fighting for,' I say.

Milk directs me into a side alley and I park the car in a nondescript parking lot off of Ventura Boulevard. The metal belt buckle is still hot from the sun burning its way through the window. It's hot, this perennial desert weather, and nobody will tell you but this stagnant heat is tiring. The sun, it plays tricks on you. Sure, it's warm, it brightens you, but too much of it slows you down. Especially in the summer. Especially in the valley, where we're listless.

'I don't understand,' I say, my stare bolting from Milk to the sign in front of us for Monroe's Restaurant and Bar, and then back to Milk. Then back to the bar. 'This doesn't look like fun.'

'Follow me,' he says, holding my hand for some reason. Like it's some dramatic movie moment! Like I need to be led! I hate to admit it, but having my hand held feels quite nice. The four of us enter through dark wooden doors that reek of spray-painted cedar.

'I'll take Mary and Randall to the frozen yogurt place next door, okay?' Milk says, his smile remarkably tender, concerned. 'That way we'll be out of your way. We'll be ready whenever you are.'

'Ready for what?' I say until I turn around and see, to my amazement, my shock, my horror: my dad, serving drinks and laughing behind the bar with a couple of customers. As if my legs were attached to a different human, they buckle under me but Milk gingerly nudges me forward. Like a dad teaching his kid to ride a bike, it forces me to regain my center as I wobble towards the middle of the bar.

It's mid-afternoon so the place is quite empty, quite dismal, depressing, even more so because there's hardly any light. I can't get my balance and feel like a dog walking for the first time in shoes, awkward and unsteady. I'm hot and tingling, slightly paralyzed. I'd seen my dad a few times over the years since he left, but the token visits only made us all feel worse. Eventually, they just stopped. He didn't want to see me so why, how, could I put myself in front of him over and over again, torturing myself by trying to understand a man who didn't understand us? I start to panic and turn around, but Milk, Mary and Randall aren't there anymore.

I could kill Milk. I could leave right now before my dad spots me and I try, making baby steps. I don't like this. Not one bit. I want to run. I want to scream at Milk for taking me here, for this miserable surprise, for forcing me to confront someone I was prepared to never see again. I want to run not just out of the restaurant but out of town, out of this world. And just as I'm about to, as I'm waving my hands around in defiance and anger, I subconsciously stomp the floor like a kid having a tantrum, making noise, and when I look up, my dad's caught me.

'Tabby?' he says, putting the glass he's wiping down. A tea towel is draped over his shoulder. He looks older than the man I remember crawling into bed with when I was little. My eyes are doing that itchy thing again, causing them to twitch and blink incessantly. It keeps happening. I can't stop it. As I feel them throb, I'm speechless.

I take the closest seat to me at the bar because I can barely keep myself up.

'Gary!' a waitress calls out from the other side of the restaurant. 'Two gin and tonics for table four.'

His unfaltering stare sticks to me as he calls out to her, 'Just give me a minute, Francie.' He walks slowly, stiffly, towards me, bending his neck and squinting as if to make sure I'm real.

I'm trying to remember the shape of his face when I knew it and if I could make sense of this new one, but I can't. He was supposed to be depressed. He was supposed to be fat and dripping in alcoholic sweat with dirty clothes. But this man, he's doing just fine. I liked my memory of him before, the idea he had gone downhill. This, this is unsettling. It's downright unfair.

'It wasn't my idea to come here,' I declare, protecting myself, my disappearing heart. Trying to prove I don't care. 'Milk brought me. I didn't know you were working h ere.'

'I'm so sorry, Tabby,' he says. 'I thought your mom told you. I wanted her to know where you could find me in case you asked.'

'Well, she didn't.'

We both just look at each other. I can feel my lip quiver, my eyes start to water, but I won't let him see me cry.

'Tabby, God, I've missed you. Wow, you're so grown up. You look great.'

It's all too casual, too easy. I wanted plates thrown. I wanted drama, but this felt like a normal afternoon chat with an uncle I hadn't seen in a few months.

'I thought you were supposed to be a loser,' I say, still flabbergasted he is so well intact. 'Well, you're still a loser because you lost me and Brenda. And worst of all, you lost my mom, and ever since you left her, she's been lost. Do you know that? She's lost!' The volume of my speech jumps from level to loud. It all starts coming out of me so fast, exploding like a bottle of Veuve. And damn, how I'd love a bottle of Veuve right now.

'I know I was a shit dad,' he admits, now in front of me, voice down. 'And I don't expect you to get that right now, although I hope you will one day, when . . . if . . . you give me a chance to explain.'

'Is this how it happens?' I ask. 'I just waltz in here to quickly repair our nonexistent father-daughter relationship? I've tried to understand how a dad could leave his kids, his wife, on a flip, but sorry. I can't.'

'Look,' he says, wiping his face with his hand, rubbing his chin in reflection. 'Maybe we should talk about this somewhere else.'

'No,' I say. 'I want to hear it now. This is your chance.'

'It would have been worse if I stuck around. It would have been worse for all of us. I was doing it for us.'

'That's the stupidest thing I've ever heard. I'm an adult, you know. I can recognize bullshit.'

He looks around the room, as if the answers were in the cracks, the wood, the floor. Why do people keep doing this?

'Your mom exhausted me,' he finally says.

'Exhausted *you*?' I am so mad, I'm trembling. How dare he blame it on her. She was the one who was left. She was the one who tried.

'She literally took everything out of me. All my fight, my strength. No matter what I did, it was never enough, and after so many years, it broke me down.' There's this pain now in my chest as his words bury themselves into me like a tick in Woodstock.

'But, you loved her at one point, didn't you?'

'Of course I did. Who wouldn't have fallen for your mother? She was this insanely beautiful, creative creature, like a bird, flying all over. She made you want to fly too. And I did, and it was amazing, but I got tired. You have to rest if you want to do long distance but she'd get sad when we weren't up in the air, if that makes sense. She wanted fun and adventure not just every day but every second. When we were on the ground, it was my fault.'

He can see me wincing as I try to block the tears from falling. Memories flood through me from that morning when everything changed, when he stood up after breakfast, fetched his bag from the closet, and walked out. I hadn't even finished my cereal. I don't recall much except for my mother screaming as he walked through her, through the door and through us, and that when I returned to my breakfast it had wilted. Soggy and lifeless. I looked at those flakes of wheat drowning in milk now soured and wondered who would die first, the flakes or me. Twenty-something years later and I'm still not sure which of us suffocated but I try to perk up so I don't give him the idea that he was somehow responsible for the way I turned out. I am not here for me, I tell myself; I'm here for my mom. I'm here so I can look at her and tell her she was right and he was wrong, so she could finally stop all her frantic digging, shuffling, replacing. So she could just relax.

'But you could have just brought her flowers, or written Post-it notes and hidden them all around to make her happy because you knew that's what she wanted!' I plead too loudly. People are staring. 'That doesn't seem so hard to me! It would have been so easy to make her feel like she was always flying!'

'Gary!' the waitress screams. 'People are waiting!'

'Goddammit, Francie! I said hold on a minute!' he hollers, banging the bar counter with a fist. He turns back to me quickly. He's talking like he's running out of time.

'Don't you see? It wasn't something that could be fixed with flowers. The minute someone tells you they want flowers, there's no fucking way you want to give them flowers. If it wasn't flowers, it would be something else. I could never get ahead of her expectations. How can you be spontaneous when someone has already mapped it all out for you?'

'This sucks, you know!' I yell back. 'This is just the worst news of my fucking life!'

'I know it's hard to hear, because you're so much like her, but the way she was made it impossible for me to make her happy. Her needs were relentless, and our reality could never live up to the fantasy of what she thought her life should be like. I tried, of course I tried, Tabby, but it wore me down. It made me feel useless because I knew no matter what I did, it wouldn't be enough.'

'But she was just fighting because you weren't and someone had to.'

'What are you talking about? I did fight, Tabby. I fought for years. I fought to keep it all together but it was like two roosters in a cage, tearing each other apart. We both were trying to make it work so badly that we lost sight of what we were trying to keep together.'

My memory flicks back to just before I went to the ju-jitsu school, when my mother told me that I needed a fighter because she was proof of what happened when you married someone who wasn't, someone like my dad. I see now that maybe he did try, but it just wasn't enough of the right kind of fight. They confused passion and zest with anger and frustration, intertwined and contorted until they couldn't tell them apart. But then it makes me wonder: if my dad wasn't so lazy after all, if in fact he did fight and my mother just never could see it, then what would that mean for me? If she was loved by my dad and fought for but was impossible to please, then what hope did I have of finding someone who would stick around? I had to hold on to the sliver of hope that maybe my dad wasn't telling me the truth. I knew that what he said made sense to some part of me, deep down, but I wasn't quite ready to acknowledge it because its consequences would be too great.

'She fought so hard all the time but love is supposed to be effortless. Life is hard enough. I don't want to see you end up like her.'

All of a sudden I realize that's why he told me to tell Heralda to go away all those years ago: he knew first hand the effects of someone who couldn't make herself happy, who wore you down. He thought Heralda was doing to me what my mother did to him. Yet no matter how much I understand it now, I'm still so angry he told me to tell her to leave me.

My dad picks up a glass to start making the drinks, and stares for a moment at it in the light, inspecting it for fingerprints and marks he might have missed, something he should have done with his wife when he was married before the relationship became too dirtied with fault and blame.

'Sometimes love just isn't enough,' he concludes, ending the discussion.

The light flickers above us, casting an intermittent orange glow in an otherwise dimly lit cave. It's a place where people go to pretend to be other people, a place they go to hide. When he smiles, the lines around his eyes pronounce themselves and for a moment he looks happy. We all do in certain light.

'Will you come in again?' my dad asks. 'So we can get to know each other? Or I can meet you somewhere, anywhere you want.'

'You can't just repair twenty years with a drink,' I say, grasping for a line that measures up against my frustration, but I can't. I don't want to know if he has another family. I don't want to know how happy he is and how much energy his new wife gives him, but he is still my father. 'I'll think about it.' I am not even sure I mean it. In fact, I probably don't. I just hate the idea of leaving things without hope. That's the worst thing I could do to a person.

He walks to the other end of the bar to place the gin and tonics down for the waitress to collect. I turn to leave but stop mid-way.

I can't take thinking my mother had hoped in vain all this time. It makes me want to fight for her even more, to vehemently prove she wasn't impossible.

'By the way,' I yell out to my dad. 'Someone is going to buy me flowers one day. I still believe in the fight.'

I walk out the door and head straight to the car in silence as Mary, Milk and Randall spot me from the shop next door and follow a few steps behind. I shut the car door as hard as I can as if it cements the closing of a moment. I don't understand why Milk cares about me seeing my dad. He never asked about how I felt about it. If I'd recovered.

'Why did you tell the principal that I was your mom?' I ask Mary, turning around to look at her in the face.

'Because you're more fun.'

'Do I exhaust you?'

'What's that mean?'

I sigh and turn around, folding into the crevasses of the seat. 'That's why I love you, Mary. Because you get it and you don't even know what it means. Why did you bring me to him?' I ask Milk.

'Because I've lost my dad, and you still have yours.'

The two of us just look at each other in silence. The layers of Milk began to show themselves, not for lack of being there but because I had just missed them all this time.

'And because you're like your mom,' Randall says. 'Milk told me he doesn't want you to be exhausted, either.'

'History repeats itself,' Mary adds. 'Like mother, like daughter.'

'Who are you guys?' I say. 'Where do you learn this stuff?'

Milk stares out the window quietly, fidgeting, again not knowing where to put his hands. I can't figure out why he's so restless but I'm too confused and tired to try. I understand why he took me here, why he thought it was so important I find out the other side of the story. I guess I never wanted to even entertain the thought that my mother's solitude, her depression, her gaps, might be from her own doing. If my dad left my mom because of who she was, and I am like her because that's who I am, then I, too, will one day be left.

Maybe Milk was right . . . I need to change my tactics. I am pushing too hard, I need to relax but I can't give up now. There is that saying that when you're not looking for it, it shows up. I somehow have to keep trying but, at the same time, not look for it. This is all just too complicated, it's making me sleepy.

As we drive off and out of the valley, towards the hills, the mountains, I see how it could have been depleting for both my parents. Of course it looked like she was exhausting because they were so mismatched. Trying to be people they weren't, on both sides, was probably what made it so difficult to endure. The difference was that my mother was making the same mistake over and over again, while my dad knew when to call it quits. Despite what I learned today, I

300

cling to the belief that with the right person, you don't end up hassling the other because it just works. You're just you, and you're not a nag because you never even had to ask in the first place.

The Librarian

Seeing my dad really threw me. I've been crying for the past hour in the bathroom, sitting on the top of the toilet, begging for a sign I'm on the right track. I wish I could cry harder but I can't so I just hold my hands together and pray. And when I pray, I pray angry. I'm pissed. Infuriated. Confused. *Come on,* I say to the sky like those kids do, looking for answers in the blue. *I'm ready. I'm trying. Please, please.* I'm sort of punching the sky now, looking like I'm practicing some tribal dance. A dance to worship the sun. I'm going to have to start imagining what life is going to look like alone, but then a bird flies into the window and scares the self-pity out of me, reminding me of how pathetic it all sounds. I wash my face and give myself a pep talk in the mirror as I dry every bead of water, one by one, telling myself I'm still a lion even though I feel like a fucking house cat.

Then I tell myself to cut it out. Grow some balls. I do know something's definitely shifted in me, though, because I don't even want to listen to Jeremy Irons. It's gotten *that* bad! I'm walking around doing a little baby tantrum, stomping the ground and growling, furious that it's come to this, but also looking around to make sure no one can see me doing it because I know how ridiculous I'm being. I hate that I'm so aware of myself! My anger fuels something inside, energizing me in a delirious, manic way – like when I have too much coffee. And then I shake my mood off, bored with myself, knowing I probably just need to get out of the house and hang out with Mary and I'll feel better.

'What are we going to do today?' she asks me when I get to her place. She's wild, clearly having been up for hours and it's only 8:00 in the morning. Both of us wired: dangerous combo.

'I'm thinking we should be clever and go to the library,' I reply.

'Is that because you have a boyfriend there?'

'No, it's because I'm trying to educate you. Show you the ways of the world.'

Mary rolls her eyes.

I came across a quote the other day when I was reading up about 'being a genius' and this quote from Einstein blew me out of the water: 'There are only two ways to live your life. One is as though nothing is a miracle. The other is as though everything is a miracle.' The best thing about this quote is that it made me realize that if Einstein thought this, and I already live like this (for the most part, disregarding my current state. Although Mary's almost snapped me out of it), it means I'm a genius. Very exciting news, although there are questions I often have that I haven't been able to answer, like why people don't say bless you to strangers and why anorexics don't get the same belly bloat that the starving Ethiopian children get when I see them in the ads. Faced with all these unwanted questions, I figure taking Mary and myself on a date to the Santa Monica library is a great idea.

When we walk in, I am surprised to see so many homeless people. Who knew homeless people were so literate!

'It smells in here,' Mary says.

'Keep your voice down,' I say. 'You have no idea who is and who isn't a prophet.' Sometimes I slip a ring on my ring finger so I feel like I'm married to my dream man. I'm wearing a gold band now with a costume piece (cubic zirconia) as the engagement ring. It twinkles as I walk, and I periodically look down, move my fingers like I'm playing air piano, just to see how it looks. This is what it will feel like one day, when I'm married and taking my kid to the library. I'm getting really good at visualizing my affirmations.

'Okay,' she says, nodding but not entirely understanding.

We walk together up and down the aisles of books. Every now and then I stop to peer through the gaps in case my dream man is waiting for me on the other aisle, like in the movies.

'What are you doing?' Mary asks.

'These gaps in the books are like openings to love,' I explain. 'You could look through one and at the same time the man you've been waiting for could also be peering back from the other side, waiting for you.'

Mary starts to look through some of the holes, reaching up onto her tippy toes to get a straight angle.

'Can I help you find something?' we hear someone say and we both turn around to find a very cute, eligible bachelor. He's wearing a Hawaiian shirt.

'That's a terrible shirt,' I say, delicately and covertly slipping my rings off my finger and onto my right hand. 'But I like that you have the balls to wear it.'

'She doesn't mean that,' Mary adds. 'I like it.'

'Well, thank you, miss,' he says to her.

Mary looks over to me and then back to the librarian. 'My mom is looking for books to make her more smart.'

I can't believe it but she's role-playing. I've never felt so proud. She knows she's good too, based on her grin.

He's still staring at me so I say, 'What's your name?'

'Hans,' he says.

'Oh, great, I'm Solo, too!' As it comes out of my mouth, I cringe at my awkwardness. It's apparently impossible for me to communicate naturally. I mean, how would you even respond to that?

'Something classic then? Or current?' he says, moving on.

'I'm not sure,' I say, wondering if this is a pickup line. 'What do you recommend?'

He takes us through to another section under the header,

'Historical Fiction.' Mary asks what it means and we both attempt to explain it to her, settling on, 'Based on true events.'

'Like your life!' she screams. I look over, blushing, to Hans and he smiles through closed lips.

'Historical fiction isn't my favorite,' I say, eventually. 'I prefer surreal, fantasy, and of course, the odd romantic comedy. I don't think my stomach can handle tragedy or anything resembling an outcome less than savory. I mean, that's why we read, right?'

'Unless you escape in your own life,' Hans estimates.

'Is he a pro-pheet?' Mary says, trying to recall the word I used earlier. 'A homeless pro-pheet?'

'Well, I'm not homeless,' he says. Hans has short blond hair with curls that twirl around his ears and down the back of his neck. I can spot some scraggly bits trying to make their escape from his Hawaiian shirt and find myself quite transfixed by them. A desperate plea for help; although, I must admit, I abhor a shaved chest on a man. I want wild and unruly. Grizzly-bear style, so I feel more like a woman.

Mary kicks my leg to awaken me from my chest hair trance and I see Hans staring at me. At once, as if coordinated, we both smile. A rush of emotion floods through my body; swarms of bubbling, vivacious energy itching to jump out of my skin, all because of this guy with the smile and the Hawaiian shirt. I've never felt this way before but I can only imagine it's a good thing.

We wander together down the aisles and I learn, through carefully executed interrogation, that he lives in Venice Beach. 'Speedway,' to be specific.

'I can see that,' I say. 'I bet you ride your skateboard to work, too?'

He nods and I have visions of me on his back while he rides his board. The sun's halo dancing around our figures, crossing through our faces, blocking out our noses but it doesn't matter because we're free and happy as we glide along the bike path; the ocean breaking just to our left. It's around sunset time, and the surfers are backlit. All I see when I look at the ocean spread are bobbing black wetsuits, submerging and re-emerging, sparkling. It feels good to be alive again. I wonder, as I'm standing at the library in front of him, if that vision was imagined or if it came to me from my future . . . a gift from historical fiction.

I look around and see people passing by our row and secretly want them to think we are all together: Mary our little girl; we've been in love for years; we met in a library. He led me to the Historical Fiction aisle but really he led me through Fantasy into Memoir and Autobiography. I try to imagine what we look like from someone else's point of view. I think we look cute. I think we look fucking adorable.

I'm trying not to be too forward because I've been told that's not the best way to get a man, but I can feel my eyes are too big as I'm looking at him, taking him in, gobbling him up.

They open too wide and they show too much of me. You can't *be* the alpha female if you *want* the alpha man, but then I've grown up thinking I needed to be a lion. All these lessons, they're so confusing! Let him be a male, my grandma says. 'Let a man be a man; stop controlling the whole goddamn thing.' So here I am, waiting. I'm waiting for Hans to look at the three of us and see the future I see. After a few awkward moments, wherein I pretend to rummage through things in my bag to look busy, a sinking feeling dissolves my stomach and begins to convince me that maybe the dude in the Hawaiian shirt is never going to ask me out. Why would I ever think this beefcake would want to go out with me, anyway?

Feelings of self-consciousness swarm through my insides like ducks over scraps of bread and there's no way to thwart their mission. I keep telling myself that it's never going to happen, then the optimist in me counters with: it's going to happen. *I am loving. I am loved*, I tell myself. *I am worthy of a date with this librarian.* I feel hot, as in sweaty and sticky. Uncomfortable with this mixed bag of emotions, this influx of juxtaposing thoughts. That's it, I think. I'm done with romance. I'm done being a hopeless romantic because look where it gets me. I'm going to freeze my eggs and run away to the Amazon where I will be devoid of human contact and all that plagues me so.

I look down, mid-fake-rifle, and see exactly where it's gotten me: appearing not so fit in ugly brown corduroy pants I should have thrown away last summer that, despite their comfort, really just look awful. I'm over putting myself out there only to be humiliated when it turns out everyone was right: I'm unlovable. In college, I lived with a Spanish guy who'd always ask me to imagine the worst-case scenario. Really *imagine* it, get comfortable with it, sit in it. Once you know how it feels, it's not so scary. Once the fear is taken away, there's nothing to worry about. This all worked well when I was trying to date the magician I met freshman year, but now, faced with years of disappointment, this is a whole different story. What's the worst that could happen, I ask myself, if I never find love? I'd die a million deaths, that's what would happen. I have so much love in me to give, so many scenes out of romantic comedies to live out in real life. What an absolute shame it would be to never dance in the rain with the one you love.

'When's your birthday?' I say eventually, determined not to give up. Because I can't, I'm too romantic.

'The end of July,' he says.

'A Leo! Oh that's perfect.'

'Ha,' he says, laughing but confused. 'Perfect for what?'

Oh fucking shit, I've done it again. Let the cat out of this suitcase-sized bag and ruined it. Now he's going to know I'm into astrological sign matching, which apparently scares men off. They think it's a sign for crazy. One of his co-workers walks by us and stops.

310

'Oh, is this your girlfriend?' she asks.

Hans laughs it off and adds, 'Well not yet. We've only just met. Give us a second.' He winks at me and at once, my faith is restored. This flip-flopping is so exhausting; I don't know how my mother has done it for so long.

'Suzy,' he says. 'This is . . . wait, what's your name?'

'Tabitha,' I say. 'And this is Mary.'

'Hi,' Mary says. We all cross hands in a shake meant for two people that somehow gets much more complicated with three hands.

There's a moment of silence until Mary says, 'Are we going now? I'm hungry.'

'It was nice to meet you, Tabitha and Mary,' Hans says as Suzy waddles off. His stare lingers a moment too long and I wonder if I'm doing what I always do and take everything as a sign or if, in fact, it is a sign. But if we didn't have chemistry, then why would Suzy think I was his girlfriend?

'Let me know if you need anything else,' he says in his closing credits. 'See you around.'

And that's the end of it. I knew I should have never worn these stupid corduroy pants and I'm set to light them on fire the minute I get home and burn every last trace of my old self. Mindful not to rush out of there too quickly as it would look suspicious if I didn't flick through some other books, I take Mary's hand and lead us to the poetry section where one experimental section grabs my eye. There's a book that looks like it was just recently skimmed through as it's not been re-shelved properly. Its binding is worn with marks of ink on the spine. It reads: *When I Was You* by Marie Kulip. I pick it up. It looks like it's not supposed to be in a library. It looks self-published.

I open it to a page with a small poem, entitled, 'RIP New Self.' This is definitely a sign.

'Read it to me!' Mary says as she sees my eyes bulge open and drop like waves, and so I begin:

'RIP New Self

'I made my way to the man who bought
My old self from me.
He had it, my fermented self, pickled in a glass jar,
Behind him, labeled: YOUR OLD SELF.

'He said if I didn't have a receipt, I couldn't get it back.
I said I'd give him my new self in exchange, but he said,
   No.
Old selves to this salesman seemed to carry some weight.
Why? I asked.
Because it's got all the soul, he told me.
I went to leave but then he stopped me and said
I could get store credit, if I wanted, for someone else's self
   but not for my own.

'But I gave up my old self so long ago, I've lost the receipt,
   surely.
He shrugged and so I faked to look for it in my bag,
Jingling the keys in my pocket, stalling.
Then another girl came in and in that moment of her
   asking
The shopkeeper, my self-keeper, a question, I jumped over
   the counter.
He looked at me, startled, so instinctually, I punched him
   in the face
And grabbed the glass jar with my old self in it,
   cradling it.
I started to run, leaving only the particles of dust I kicked
   up behind me.
And I ran really fast.'

Mary's mouth is open, she's looking at me like I just told
her Santa Claus doesn't exist.

'What do you think?' I ask.

'I love it!'

'Good,' I say. 'Me too.'

I take it with me and wait in line to check it out. I wonder
if I've lost my old self already. If all this misguided, seemingly
hopeless quest for love has unfairly warped the person I was.
A girl without hope is not the girl I was. I look down at Mary

and see her little sparkling eyes look back at me, knowingly, and it makes me so sad I have an overwhelming desire to make s'mores and drink Brandy Alexanders. I want to cry in the aisle as I wait to check out the book but that would be crazy. Crying is for sheep, I tell myself.

Just as we pass through the exit I hear Hans calling after me, 'Hey!'

When I turn around he's slightly shifty and out of breath, which concerns me because we're only a foot from the exit. He didn't have to run far.

'Sorry, I'm a bit nervous,' he says.

I feel hot again.

'Haha,' I say. 'Don't be silly. We're all nervous!' Once I say it, I wish I never did. It doesn't even make sense.

'I wanted to give you my cell,' he says, holding out a torn piece of paper with his cell scribbled on it. 'If you want to get a coffee sometime, give me a call.'

I must look really shocked because his face searches mine for a response but I'm expressionless. I can't remember the last time I was asked out. Then I remember that I've never been asked out. I look around me, checking over my right shoulder, then my left. Peering up at the security cameras.

'Am I on *Candid Camera*?' I say. 'Am I being punk'd?'

Mary kicks my ankle, and starts shaking her head, No.

Hans is smiling, hopeful, thank God.

'Oh,' I say, finally. 'I'd love to!' I pause. Waiting. Wondering if I've said enough before I add, 'You mean, like, for a date?'

'I guess so, yeah.'

Mary's smile is so wide it looks like it's going to rip her face open. Mine is mixed, unbelieving that this is really happening.

'Yay!' Mary creaks. 'A date!!!'

'Talk to you soon, then,' he says. 'Are you free tomorrow night?'

'Yeah, okay,' I say. 'Saturday night! It's a date!'

When he walks back into the library, I turn to Mary and she's as happy as I am. We cover our mouths with intoxicating excitement. It feels like I'm hovering. Maybe that's why my mom always looks like she's an inch from the floor. At last, my future is looking as bright as I'd always imagined it would be. On our walk back to the car, I panic, reciting the words he uttered and entertain the thought that maybe I just made them up. Then doubt and skepticism creep in; I wonder why he'd be free on Saturday night (overlooking, of course, the fact that I was, too). I worry with each step I take towards the car if I'll be interesting enough on our date, if I'll have enough to say. And then, as if she knew what I was thinking, Mary comes out with, 'You're going to have so much fun!'

As we pull into our driveway – an adventure in itself quite nerve-wracking as we have too small a space to park two cars as well as it being on a hill, doubling its precariousness – I see Milk coming out of his house. 'Hey!' I scream, trying to get his attention as I frantically roll down the window. 'Hey! Hey! Hey!'

He looks over and smiles. 'I hear you,' he says as he walks over. 'I'm coming.' I try to get out too fast and forget to unfasten my seatbelt so it whips me back a few times. I finally unbuckle it and struggle out through a tight space, mindful not to bang the side of my door on our mailbox. All of a sudden I'm dancing and head banging and screaming, 'Wahoo!!! I got asked out on a date! I got asked out on a real, real, real date! I didn't even have to make him ask me or do anything too tricky to make him feel he had to! He just did it! On his own accord! Isn't that exciting?'

'So who's this lucky guy?' he asks. His smile is returning in slow measure. He drops his head to the left while keeping his eyes on me.

'This amazing guy who works at the library. He's smart, charming, handsome, handsome, handsome! I think he could be the one. Like, the one, the one.'

'See?' he says, looking down, kicking the pebbles in the concrete around. 'I've always told you you'd be fine.'

Mary starts yelling from inside the back seat.

'You forgot me!' she says. 'You always forget me!'

'That's not true,' I say defensively, unbuckling her. 'Absolutely not true.'

She rolls her eyes in habit and runs over to Milk, who embraces her as if he's shielding her from harm. She spears my heart with devil eyes but then smiles to relieve me. I see an extra car parked on the street outside our house. It's a pale blue Honda Civic, and I know what it means: Delina and Julia are over visiting Mom.

'When is this big date?' he asks.

'Tomorrow night!'

'Can Milk look after me while you go on your date?' Mary asks.

'I think your mom will want to,' I say. 'She never gets to see you.'

'Please?' Mary begs Milk, clinging on to his leg. 'We can dress up as fairies!'

'I can't, Mary,' he says. 'I've got plans.'

'With who?' I question.

'I'm going to see The Pixies with this girl.'

'Is she pretty?' Mary asks.

'Yeah, she is.'

All of a sudden, I'm feeling very jealous but I don't know why. I mean, it's Milk for Christ's sake.

'Oh, cool,' I lie.

'Mary, come on. Let's go in.' I give Milk a hug goodbye and I release before he does because I hate to be the one who's let go of first; I'm changing. His sweater is so soft I lift my hand up to rub his sleeve but then realize it's weird, this rubbing, so I stop.

'Bye, Milk!' Mary yells even though he's right in front of her.

When we approach the front door, I can hear the pop of a champagne bottle. Party time. I love when Delina and Julia come over. The lights are on downstairs and Frank Sinatra is playing, which means my mom is in a great mood. This day keeps getting better.

'I hear the footsteps of a darling!' Delina yells as she throws her head out of the kitchen doorway.

'What a beautiful child you are,' she says. 'And you know what they say?' She looks me up and down and pats my ass. 'A girl can never be too rich or too thin.'

'Amen!' Julia and my mom yell out from the kitchen.

'Aren't you hot?' Mary asks Delina because she's in a coat despite this LA weather.

'I'm always hot, darling! But I'm fat right now so can't bear to take off this jacket.'

'Oh,' Mary says.

'I have the absolute best news to tell you!' I scream, colorful by osmosis.

'Well stop being such a pussy tease, darling, and tell us!' Delina says.

My mother is making a roast with a cigarette hanging from her lips. 'It's like Shabbat without the headache,' she says. Even when her hair is messy, there's something mysterious about her. She's like a dark-haired Brigitte Bardot, chopping potatoes with a knife that looks too big for her.

'I have been asked out on a date,' I say.

'A *real* one!' Mary highlights.

'*Mamacita*'s gonna get some dick!' Julia says, clapping her hands together. She's got lipstick on her teeth but I don't want to make her feel self-conscious by telling her.

'Positively delicious!' Delina adds.

I want my mom to ask me about him. I want her to put the knife down and ask me about this date, but she doesn't.

'His name is Hans Tuckerman,' I tell them, and then it turns into what it always does when you come home to spill yourself over a new potential love: you google him, find everything you can, and ask them all what they think. Julia has a habit of taking the image on the phone and putting it up next to you, so she can imagine what it's going to be like when you're together.

'There's a vibe, you know, between faces,' she says. 'You have to look like you could go together and you know,' she stops to wave her hand between the picture and me, squinting her eyes as if to laser her focus, 'this is cute. I really think this could be something.'

'Yeah, I know,' I say. 'It was just so serendipitous, our meeting today. Had I not gone looking for smart guys at the library, I never would have met him. It's a sign.'

Mary scrunches the space between her nose and forehead. 'That doesn't sound like a sign to me.' I hold my finger up to her and purse my lips, implying to zip it quick, to which she responds by sticking out her tongue.

'Mom?' I ask. 'Did you hear any of that?'

'Yeah,' she says distractedly. 'He seems great, just play it cool. Don't fuck it up!'

The problem is that I don't know anyone who plays it cool. My mother does when she's in her Dorothy Parker mode, despite my knowing that she secretly wants to be eaten alive by romance, and then fails miserably when she slips back into her neurosis. I guess Julia and Delina play it cool, but then again, they don't date anyone.

'Darling!' Delina says, pawing at the air to keep my attention. 'This new date sounds fabulous and I have a good feeling about it, but you know—' she stops to look at Julia '—we want to know why you've never dated Milk? He's really quite a catch, don't you think?'

'They had a bit of an incident a while ago,' my mother interrupts.

'It was just something that was embarrassing that happened and it made it pretty clear we wouldn't be able to be together. Case closed,' I say before anyone else has a chance to chime in.

'All right, then! I just had to ask. Anyway, there's a book,' Delina says, 'called *The Rules,* and it says, in a nutcase – I know, I know, it's "in a nutshell" but isn't *nutcase* so much better? – that you can't let the first date last more than five hours, that you have to end the date first, and that you are never, ever, ever allowed to call a man first. Oh, and be busy. Always be busy.'

'Busy I agree with!' my mother shouts between puffs as she stirs and prongs juicy chicken. When she opens the oven to test if it's done cooking, the gust of heat fogs up her glasses. Each time, she's exasperated by it, as if she didn't anticipate it despite it happening every time. She huffs, temporarily blind, wipes her lenses with her T-shirt – flashing those around her – all the while never letting anything drop except for the ash from her cigarette. She's the perfect woman.

'But Delina,' I argue. 'You know how I hate rules.' I start dragging my heels along the floor and pout my lower lip in emphasis and throw my body to the wall in a dramatic display of emotion: think drag-queen impression of a diva. I'm clawing the wall now and freeze mid-climb. I'm frozen but turn my head out just enough to see if anyone notices but no one does, so I drop it.

'And look where not following the rules has gotten you!' Julia and Delina say smugly, almost in unison.

'But what about you both?' I counter, testy. 'You live life the way you feel you want to live it. It's definitely not by the rules.'

'The rules of dating are the same for everyone. You have to know them to break them,' Julia says. 'You have to understand why they work so you can also understand when they don't. It's the same for a modern artist. It's not all just splish splash, you know. They're trained painters, can paint the shit out a realistic portrait, but only go off the edge because they know where the lines are supposed to be. Do you get me?'

I nod because what else can I do?

'Just don't be too available,' my mother pipes in, ironically. 'Men get turned off when you're too available.' To this Mary gasps, amused, with a 'get a load of this' gesture.

'You know,' I start, unable to let it go. 'All this advice is so confusing! I just want it to work out . . .'

'Men can sense desperation,' Delina interjects, sniffing the air. 'Don't act like you want it too much.'

'Are you both dating now?' I ask Delina and Julia. 'It's been a while since . . .'

'Honey, I don't need a man to keep myself open,' Julia says. 'I'm still in the "care" stage since my operation.'

'What does that mean?' Mary says.

Julia looks to us adults as if to exclude Mary, talking in whisper but still loud enough for her to hear. 'Three times a day, I use my vibrator, just to keep the hole open.'

'Oh yes,' Delina chips in. 'I had to do that for three years.'

'You masturbated every day for three years?' I ask, realizing I'm doing it way less than other women. I can't tell if that makes me feel better or worse. 'Or else what would happen?'

'We'd close up, darling!' Delina says as Julia laughs, as if it's an inside joke, literally.

'What will close up?' Mary asks.

'Don't worry, *mamacita*. You will understand one day,' Julia says. A nod emanates from my mother in the corner as she cools and tastes a hot potato. 'You just have to do whatever you need to in order to keep yourself open.'

And that's when it hits me: we're just trying to keep ourselves open. We're trying to survive, to keep our faith in the idea that everything works out the way it's supposed to despite the mountain of setbacks and disappointments we face.

When we sit down to eat, we do an obscure version of a prayer. Delina, Julia and my mother link hands and Mary and I follow. Delina leads.

'Thank you, Mother Nature, for this glorious food. This pesky roast and sumptuous feast to fill our bellies as well as our hearts. Salute!'

'Salute!' we all say in unison.

'So tell us a little more about this Romeo,' Julia inquires with beady eyes, smiling devilishly.

'He's a Leo,' I say first, because I'm in front of two astrologers and I know it will tell them ninety-nine per cent of what they need to know. Given I'm a Sagittarian, he's a good match for me. Our love is pretty much written in the stars. Well, Aries are the best fit for me, but beggars can't be choosers. I'm naturally this capricious. As expected, they ohh and they ahh until my mother says that my dad was a Leo.

They're liking the sound of this guy, I can tell by the way they chew their food and look at each other in between gulps.

I tell them about the swagger in his walk, the way his shirt was halfway out of his pants, his unruly hair. Oh, and that moment when he asked me out, how he literally ran after me just like they do in the movies! And how he had little beads of sweat around his temples, which was an obvious sign that he liked me and was nervous.

Delina, at one point – while my mother is giving Mary an angel halo made out of her napkin and Julia paints lipstick on her – leans over to me and says, 'Just keep telling yourself that whatever you need to know will be revealed to you when you need to know it. Just show up on your date with that pretty smiley face of yours. The rest isn't up to you.'

'Thanks, Delina,' I say. 'You always know what to say.' I stop, meddle absentmindedly with my plate of food, bringing green beans and peas to the left and the meat separated to the right. Compartmentalizing. 'I just want it to make sense, all this blind chasing. I'm sick of being crazy.'

'Why be sane?' she whispers. 'It's a mad, mad world.'

*

When I wake up on Saturday morning, I have the world's largest pimple on my chin. It's not just a normal, coverable, concealable pimple. It's the kind that could be given its own name. In fact, when Brenda eventually sees it, she names it Alice. Alice, my almost twin. Alice, the biggest pimple in the world on the day of my big date. Alice, the cunt.

I'm in the bathroom for probably an hour examining it.

'Don't touch it!' my mother says as she walks by. 'You'll make it worse.' When she comes over to take a look, she bursts out laughing.

'Hey!' I pout. 'Oh God, now you're making me feel worse. This is just terrible.' I cup my head in my hands and fake cry, but each time I look back in the mirror, my eyes are dry. Not even a tear to reflect this aching, breaking heart!

'Oh stop being so dramatic,' my mother says. 'It's just the biggest blemish I've ever seen!' She slaps her thigh mid laugh this time, really getting a kick out of the misery I've settled into on this dreary Californian morning. All day I pace. I touch every strand of carpet and every pane of wood throughout the house, hoping that by the end of it, by the time I get back to my room and my mirror, it will have only been just a horrible nightmare. I pray to all sorts of gods in the hopes that one will have pity on my unfortunate situation, but alas, no gods do. It's just this fucking pimple and me.

I get a text from Hans around three in the afternoon telling me to meet him at PF Changs in Santa Monica at 8 o'clock. 'We can have a bite,' he says, 'and just take it from there.' It seems promising, leaving the rest of the evening open to love is always a great start.

I look at myself in the mirror again, pimple still present, and try to see myself clearly. I tell myself all the reasons why I'm a catch. But now that I have a real date approaching, I can't shake this kernel of fear that something is going to go wrong, like it always does. I know that deep down, I like myself; I know what I've got. But ever since seeing my dad at the bar, realizing it was my mother who ran him down, who pushed him away with her wild expectations of love and fantasy, I don't trust myself. I'm trying to believe my mom and I are doing it right, though. I have to hang on to the idea that we're going to be okay without having to change who we are. I just have to keep being the vivacious me, my optimistic self, difficult as it is at times, and trust that Hans is going to see this bright light that my mother gave me.

I'm all dressed up but I'm thinking my vibe looks casual, with high wedges and a skirt to look feminine and light and open. I'm dressed in a summer orange too, as black signals baggage. As I'm leaving the house, I scream out to Milk to come over, that I need him just for a second. Finally, he opens the door and I rush over to him.

'I have the worst pimple!' I can't help but blurt out. 'All he's going to be able to look at is Alice.'

'Who's Alice?'

'The pimple! It's so big my sister named it.'

He laughs and draws in his breath. On the exhale, he puts his thumb gently between my furrowed brows to soften them out, massaging the space like his thumb could erase the lines my anxiety creates. 'Don't you worry,' he says. 'He won't be looking at Alice with that smile of yours.'

All at once, I feel as if he's lifted me back to my usual plane of confidence. He's always been able to do that, to get me back on track. Get me back to me.

'Thanks, Milky,' I say calmly. 'Have fun on *your* date tonight.' I give him a hug and scruff his hair up, and touch his newly grown beard for good measure.

'I need to shave,' he says.

'No!' I yell. It comes out too quickly. 'Messy beards are great. She's gonna think you're a real man!' He grunts at me, in sarcastic acceptance, and ends our little driveway rendez-vous with, 'Don't do anything that gets you in trouble. I've got a pretty date and don't want to have to explain that I have to cut it short to rescue you from the police station.' He winks more casually than he usually does, or at least how I remember. When I think of Milk winking, he's usually quite awkward: one lip always turning up, an exaggerated tilt of the head. He might as well give me a thumbs-up at the same time. This time, though, with his body relaxed, he owns it. That girl's going to fall in love with him.

I reminded myself the entire way to the restaurant to play it cool this time, just as an experiment to see if it works out better. I must have repeated 'Keep it cool' so many times it started to blend into 'Keepitcool' until it eventually sounded like a completely different word in another language and by the time I parked in the dismal parking lot, I caught myself saying, 'Kepitcol.' The hostess asks me for how many and I beam when I say, 'A table for two, please!' She jumps at my enthusiasm. People are on dates all around; I can't believe she's not used to this level of happiness. I'm taken to my table and perch next to a couple eating in silence. I order a dirty gin martini because it sends the right signals, and after a few sips I get a tap on my shoulder. It's Hans!

'You came!' I say, unable to hold myself. When he smiles, I see a dimple surface that must have been hiding in his double chin. He's not fat, but his youth still clings to his face, revealing his softness. He's got a little stubble, too, and I want to bury myself in it. Make him read to me while I'm in there, nestled and warm and at home. He sits down and, despite having told myself to not talk too much, I can't keep my mouth closed. As I'm talking, I'm hearing my voice and it just sounds so embarrassing. It's too high pitched; I'm boring myself already. Surely, I'm exhausting him. As I ramble on about everything I can think of to avoid a silent gap, I witness his eyes widen and close, jaw dropped open.

'So are you from LA?' I ask him, trying not to sound too much like an interviewer.

'I'm from Milwaukee. Moved here ten years ago after college. It's a seductive lifestyle here. Hard to let it go in exchange for the Midwest.' I'm not used to this sort of chit-chat. Is this what most dates are like? I'm usually moving so fast, I'm uncomfortable with sitting still and letting it unfold naturally. I blame my impatience.

'Fair enough,' I say as our waitress comes over. Hans orders a Heineken and I get my second martini. 'With olives, please!'

'I could eat olives every day, forever,' I tell him. 'I'd never get bored. I think my biggest fear in life is being bored; equally, being boring. But for some reason, daily olives are an exception.'

'Maybe it's the salt,' he guesses.

Exactly. Exactly. Exactly. I learn what his last meal would be (steak and fries, then a Big Mac and an Oreo milkshake). Whenever I see people eat fast food, I imagine their insides rotting and how that would make their breath stink. I have to shake my head to erase the image. He's got great breath, I repeat to myself.

Laughing and giggling and flirtation fuels our conversation, letting it flow delicately like a game of badminton.

I lean in towards him across the table, hair accidentally dangling into bok choy and oyster sauce and spicy prawns.

'Do you think it's weird that people around us are just having dinner but not talking to each other?' I ask him. 'Have they run out of things to say? Is that what happens when you've known someone too long? It would be the death of me.'

He looks over to observe those around us. 'I think it's just that they're comfortable with each other. You don't have to talk all the time to prove you have something to say.'

Oh great. I've clearly already messed this up. He's obviously referring to my inability to revel in silence. Or am I taking this too personally? It's not always about me, I remind myself, and then I keep talking. With each martini, my heart warms and I become a loopier and more swishy version of my sober self. I reach out and touch his arm when emphasizing a punch line, and he reciprocates. It's all going so well; and I haven't had to even manhandle him to get him here. He's sitting here by his own free will. Every now and then he twists a lock of hair out of his eyes and smoothes it back to meet the other waves. He looks like he could have been the South African doctor in my dreams; you know, the one who I always thought Simon was? It's so obvious now, in retrospect, that it's Hans. He even looks like a doctor, off duty and on vacation.

'What happened to your Hawaiian shirt today?' I ask. 'I thought it might have been some signature look for you?'

'Nah,' he says, smiling, bashful. 'I'm a bit more spontaneous than that.' Oh God, he's also spontaneous! He just keeps getting better and better. We order Mongolian beef next, grinding the gristly meat between our teeth, imagining what sex is going to be like. I imagine baby names and how many baseball bats I'm going to have to keep in my trunk for our six children together. I just can't wait. The bill comes and it's that awkward moment of who is going to pay.

'Here,' I say quickly, jumpy. 'Let me put down half.' I want him to pay for the whole thing, not because of the money, but just so he can be the man. The gentleman who wouldn't have it any other way. I'm sure feminists would gasp at this, but I can assure you I'm all for equality and having things even out on date two. I don't need anyone to take care of me: it's just old-fashioned chivalry on the first date, because it sets the tone for the rest of the relationship. I slide my card across the table, my gaze on him steady, but before I lift my fingers off it he grabs my hand and pushes it back towards me.

'Let me get this,' he says as I'm dying from jubilation. He's looking at me like he's in love. I really think he's in love with me already! When we get up, we're both a bit wobbly. I say I have to go to the bathroom and so does he, so he follows me from close behind through the restaurant towards the toilets. There's a darkly lit hallway, with UB40's 'Red Red Wine' playing on the speakers, with signs for the boys to the right and the girls ahead.

'See you in a minute!' I say, far too zealously for the situation. I'm thinking to myself, *What's wrong with you, you moron!* I put my head down to hide my enthusiasm but then he grabs my shoulder and turns me around, pushing me against the wall and without missing a beat he kisses me. It's everything I've been waiting for, storybook romance, culminating into this moment in a bathroom hallway at PF Changs. My purse drops out of my hands; for the first time in my life I'm being pursued and it leaves me weak at the knees . . . that or the martinis. His lips are wet, not slobbery but more slippery, as I navigate around them, moving where he tells me. It's not really in rhythm; I can't keep up with his tongue; it's like a washing-machine cycle, but I'm not worried because this awkwardness will subside when we aren't so nervous. His hands are soft around me, twirling atop my bare skin until they reach my palms, ending in a surge of butterflies when they land there. We're holding each other's hands tightly now, gripping them as hard as we want ourselves to latch on to each other in this cold, scary world! His hands are giant paws, borderline paddles. He stops for a moment and tilts his head back, his eyes cross ever so slightly as he stumbles to keep straight. Oh shit, I hope he's not just kissing me because he's drunk. I rationalize he's just dropped his inhibitions, doing what he really, truly wants to do. Our relationship being nascent, I choose to ignore these pesky signs of insecurity and rationalize that everyone gets drunk on a first date. We're nervous! It's how we cope. I haven't actually *had* sex with another person in a long, long time. Years, I'd say, because it always gets ruined just before the good stuff. I blame bad timing.

Without saying anything he kisses the lids of my eyes, then my forehead, and leaves me in the hallway to go to the men's toilet. I gather myself slowly, consciously, and go into the girls'. When I look at myself in the mirror, I don't notice Alice. I feel slightly light-headed but I think it's just elation, giving me a buzz on. I knew it would pan out if I just waited long enough to find someone who really got me. I go into the toilet stall and do a small thank you prayer and stamp my feet and wave my hands in circles in a sort of victory dance. The alcohol is really kicking in now; I can tell because I miss the door handle on the way out a few times.

I see Hans in the hallway, waiting for me patiently (what a doll!) and I wink at him. It just comes out of me, unplanned, and it elicits a smile. I can't believe this is going so well. I keep thanking all the angels I've prayed to all my life under my breath; every now and then he says, 'What?' and I realize I've been muttering too loudly. I tell him it's nothing and we move on.

'Thank you for the lovely dinner,' I say. I'm not sure what to do next. It's never really gotten this far.

'Want to go for a stroll and find somewhere for a nightcap?' Ladies and Gentlemen, it's *his* idea to keep our date going. He reaches for my arm; we're walking hand in goddamn hand and it's electrifying. I can't stop smiling. Light collects around us like we're spotlighted on a stage and I finally understand why my mom looks like she's half her body weight when she's in love. It literally makes you feel light; I'm skating on a moonlit street on a date that will surely change my whole life's trajectory. The full moon's inciting my sexuality; I'm heightened, through my senses, to an apex I've never met before. I'm crossing the Rubicon. I can relate to Julius Caesar. But I'm so full on food and life and love that I'm not looking down and so I trip over a large crack in the cement and totally eat shit. In one move, on my big date night, I land on the floor like a dead person. I've had way too many martinis. Goddammit, I should have never worn heels. I can't walk in heels!

He quickly grabs my arm, bends down and helps me up. He stops and looks at me. Pulls his head back, tightens up. I'm praying that he just totally missed my face-planting.

'I'm sorry I just fell,' I say, eyes big. Wide. Beaming. Embarrassed. 'I can't walk in these shoes.'

'Eh, it's nothing,' he says. 'Everyone falls. I'll probably even fall before the night's over.'

As if I hadn't just tripped horrifically, I continue on. After passing a certain uncountable number of lines in the cement, we turn in to a sports bar. It's the only one open as it's just turned 11 p.m. and the chairs are upside down on tables in all the restaurants save for this sports bar, Yankee Doodles. It's offensively unromantic but I'm so happy that I almost don't even notice the inconsiderate beer bellies, belches and stares. I learn about his nomadic adventures through Brazil, wandering around to find himself through the Amazonian jungle, getting his toes nibbled by the piranhas in the swampy waters with the locals who coaxed him to jump in with them, his time volunteering as a humanitarian aid in Cuzco, Peru, his first sips of an authentic Pisco Sour and how he found what he was looking for through an ayahuascan revelation.

'I saw everything, laid out before me. A map,' he tells me.

'A map of your life?'

'Of where I was going,' he says.

'And where's that?'

'I'm not sure yet. All I know is that I want to keep moving. I'm going somewhere.'

I'm hoping he's meaning somewhere with me. I picture us moving to South America to return to the work he's done, work we can finish together, as a team.

'I've always wanted to go to Peru!' I say, accepting the invitation early.

'You should go, for sure. It's a great place.'

He didn't say 'go with me to Peru' and it sets me into panic, imagining that I might be making this all up. Insistent upon not letting this shit get to me, I gather all of my better judgment and imbibe every ounce of confidence in myself. For all I know, he was probably just being polite and trying not to look too eager and presumptuous. Oh goody, that's it! I have to work on not jumping to conclusions before I fuck this all up big time.

I don't look at my watch and completely ignore the rule Delina gave me about not letting my first date last more than five hours because, let's face it, I'm dating more than her!

Another kiss leads us to his car, which leads us to his apartment. Once we are back at his house, we drink copious amounts of wine (a 'special' bottle he was saving) until we can barely walk to the bedroom and, when we do, it gets all sorts of silly. Our rolling and tumbling is exciting but awkward because neither of us have the wherewithal to know where to put what (of course, I blame the alcohol). He's not grabbing me in the right ways, the ways I've always dreamed he would, but I tell myself he's probably a bit shy. I notice under the covers I have a colossal bruise on my left leg from the fall. It's literally the size of a football and for a moment I wonder if a blood clot will be the inciting incident to my death. I don't die, though. I just keep trying to roll around, hoping his booziness won't impede his ability to get a hard-on for the entire night, but indeed it does. I try to arouse him but, with a floppy penis, it just looks like I'm driving stick shift with an uncooked hot dog. Before long, the engine stops.

The next morning I wake up with a hangover so bad it sets me into the sweats and I can hardly distinguish what I'm saying out loud and what I'm thinking. I catch myself a few times unintelligibly uttering my thoughts, pushing him further and further away from me to the sides of the bed. I wonder why he's not trying to have morning sex, why he's able to keep his hands off me. Why aren't we cuddling? This isn't how I pictured it, but maybe I'm expecting too much.

'I have the worst headache I think I've ever had,' I explain. 'I never drink that much!'

'Yeah, yeah,' he chuckles and smiles. 'That's what they all say.' He looks at me from the opposite side of the bed, his hands behind his head on the pillow as he looks up to the ceiling.

'Do you want me to run you a bath?' he asks.

A slow smile emerges from my face. 'Are you kidding? I'd love that. That would be so divine.' There's a shadow behind his irises, casting a darkness in him, but I can't tell if it's just his old soul or if it's something deeper. I want to kiss his darkness away and let my lips climb around the smile lines cupping his eyes but before I have the chance he gets up to run me the bath.

'I'll make you some coffee, too,' he adds. 'You want it with milk and sugar?' I must have just been worried for no reason, scared from my past. I lay there waiting for the tub to fill, telling myself he's the man I am going to be with. I just have to let it happen naturally.

Over the next few days, we speak with relentless enthusiasm. He is crazy about me. Finally, some reciprocity! He tells me about how he hates his job, how he hates the people he works with, how he doesn't understand the meaning of everything and how he feels bad bringing kids into such a fucked-up world. How he distrusts people even though he tries not to. How he doesn't think he'd like to be a dad. Of course, I ignore this because all I can think about is his dreamy mention of kids! It's okay that he's sad, because I'm happy, I tell myself over and over. I could pump him up and make him see there was something real that made it all worth it.

Four days later, though (FOUR. PAINSTAKING. SEEM-INGLY MONTH-LONG DAYS!), I'm sitting in my living room with my legs on the wall, letting the blood circle back to my diseased and miserable heart, with no word from Hans. I feel like a flaming cheese plate at a Greek restaurant: I look great and delicious from afar but when anyone's tongue gets near for a taste, I burn it. I miss the days when I felt I was better up close.

'Have you called him?' my mom asks as she whizzes by, fresh off a date with a senior citizen she's convinced doesn't need Viagra because he's chock-a-block full of man, which of course makes me envious because all thirty years of youth in Hans couldn't stand up against the limp-inducing effects of alcohol on our night of passion. My successful date with Hans reinvigorated her, as I imagined all this time it would, although now that it's not working out I panic, hoping it doesn't affect her newfound giddy with the old guy. I'm also overwhelmed with embarrassment that I told everyone, including Michael, the owner of the local Canyon Gourmet Foods grocery store while ordering spicy tofu slices, that I found the man I was going to marry and that this time, it was for real. Now I'm going to have to explain it wasn't. Goddammit, I should have kept my mouth shut.

'Yes,' I reply to my mother, but the breath barely slips out of me, I'm so tired. 'I've emailed him and texted him.' No response. Not a wink or an emoticon or even a friend request on Facebook. I've replayed everything from that night, wondering where it went wrong. Wondering how my playing it cool brought the demise of what could have been everything. I decide I'm going to work out everyday from now on.

After a painstaking waiting period, he texts me back explaining why we can't be together. *I'm a pessimist. You just make me feel worse about myself because you're an optimist,* he wrote. I pleaded and attempted persuasion but nothing worked. I was dumped for being too positive. Talk about a catch-22. Maybe it's my mom's fault for never telling me, 'No.' Everything's always been within reach, or at least it seemed that way until I fell off the ladder.

That, or maybe it was because I drank so much that I face-planted. That's usually a no-no on a first date. No wonder he ran.

'You didn't even know him,' Brenda says as she puts on the last of her makeup. She always looks at herself in a certain way when she's putting on makeup. The squinty, bird-like makeup face afflicting women worldwide.

'Send him cupcakes at work,' my mother poorly suggests. 'Dessert always works.'

'Mom, that's a terrible idea,' Brenda interjects before I let the option sink in. 'That's insane, psycho behavior. Your best option is to just do nothing. If he's interested, he'll call. Otherwise, move on. This is why I don't date. It's the fucking worst.'

'Oh lighten up, you two sour birds!' my mom says in a voice on par with her level of reverie. 'It's just a date. What's the worst that can happen? You might as well try; you've got nothing to lose!'

My mom's only like this because she's back on the dates. Love is her drug but she never buys enough to give us our fix, too. She just gets high and overdoses. Dorothy Parker is hidden under the bed but will surely be taken out to join her bedside table once she's taken off the drip and goes into withdrawal. If she were in that state now, she'd be telling me that cupcakes are for pussies and that I should never, ever call him.

'Well,' my mom adds. 'He didn't look smart in his picture. I didn't like him anyway. You can do sooooo much better. Sadness is infectious, you're better off sticking with us.'

This is the kind of shifting she'd always done that's confused me since I was old enough to understand logic and why I vacillate so often between mindsets. It's screwed up my paradigm for dating. I've attempted to dissuade myself from using logic (or at least, my mother's logic) to the best of my ability; it just doesn't make sense. This upsets me though, because if Hans and I do work out, then I don't want to know this shit. I want to know she liked him. That she thought he was smart. It's like when you break up with someone and everyone says he was an asshole but then, when you get back together, everyone who said something negative doesn't know what to say, because now you know they don't like him. It's doomed; how could you ever get married to the person you know everyone thought was a dipshit?

'But he works in a library!' I say, defending him, just in case.

'Did you tell him you were fertile this time?' Brenda asks with a monkey's smirk.

'You know what? No. I didn't. You know why? Because I knew it would mess it up. I followed the rules, well, not all of them. But I didn't make any first moves, I played it cool, whatever that means, and it's fallen flat and I have no idea why!' It's hard to breathe all of a sudden. My chest hurts. I hate dating.

'Welcome to the real world,' Brenda says.

'Well, I hate the real world!' I counter. It's the best comeback I have at the moment, in this kind of heart-crushing heat. The day after the date, you couldn't have wiped the smile off my face. The birds chirped sweeter, the sky was so magnificently blue I almost had to shut my eyes before the beauty and sunshine brought me up so much it ended up withering me. He had told me that I was 'sexy' and how he loved my tongue, how it presumably circled. He asked, as we were parting, where I'd been all his life. 'I'll see you soon, babe,' he said as he gave me a wink. I wanted him to ask me how my heart was, but even though he didn't, I ignored it. I brushed it off, convincing myself it didn't matter. The worst thing is that (besides my fall) I did everything right, and it still didn't work. I want to have a real answer to why he didn't like me; the vague optimism comment and lack of communication out of nowhere is just disheartening. I can't imagine how upset I'd be if we had actually been able to have great sex; his limp whisky dick saved whatever is left of my heart. Maybe Brenda is right; maybe this is how people behave now. Maybe this is why dating is so confusing.

Just like my mother, I hear my thoughts fluctuating. *It's all going to shit* one second to *I'm going to be fine* the next. The reality of someone not wanting me after I didn't do anything wrong, after I played the game the 'normal' way, has my psyche spasming in the way I wish his dick did. My head throbs and like a dirty rat a migraine slithers in and attacks me. As I'm bracing my head, pressing my fingers firmly against my temples, I see myself stuck in my aura. I don't know much but what I do know is that I'm as lost as I could be. My optimism is shivering and I have no blanket for it. I want to tell it that it's going to get warmer and not to worry, but I just don't know. I can't lie when I know the forecast is so dismal.

The not knowing why he never called is worse than an unflattering truth being revealed because you're left in the dark, with no closure, and there's nothing you can argue because you weren't even privy to the fight.

'But he did give you an answer, darling. Some people just can't be around too much sunshine. There's nothing more to explain. Closure is for the very lucky,' Delina tells me over the phone when she calls the house to check on me and see how the date went. 'You can never count on it. It's a luxury for even the fortunate. I'm afraid, my darling, that we aren't necessarily one of those lucky few.'

I try to steady my legs on what feels like quicksand. 'Delina?' I start, trying to order my thoughts into some coherent state. 'Does it get any easier, or does it always feel this way?'

'Oh darling,' she starts. 'I don't think it ever ends. We're all just little girls, waiting for someone to love us.' And that's what did it. That's what drove the dagger through my already wobbly chest. Maybe Chrissie Hynde was right, too, just like Delina. If they all thought so, there must be something to it. We're all just exactly the same. Lions, sheep: we all just want to be liked. But then the idea that I need someone to love me angers me. I don't need anyone to justify my worth. Yet I spend the next week writing down on paper my affirmations that he'll call me. He never does. I hope he calls to tell me he lost his phone, that it was all a big mistake. He never does. Two weeks, three weeks, they all blend together. All without a word.

I realize all I have now, instead of a string of adventures, is just a pile of shitty stories with bad endings. One big face-plant, and the fighting doesn't even matter because there's nothing to fight for. I just keep getting kicked. The next morning, I hear this woman talk to me. She says, 'Don't be scared, toots. Don't be scared. You're a babe. You're going to be better than fine. I promise.' I wonder if it's Heralda but the voice is different. She could have aged since I last heard from her; she's probably more wise. Oh man, I miss her. It's 10 a.m. and I wonder if it's too early for wine. I tell myself that drinking early is okay because I can't shake this sadness, this relentless cycling of negative thoughts. This is why I've always been an optimist; I can't take life's lurid reality; prefer to be delusional.

My eye keeps catching the phone. It's like a bag of heroin a sober man finds in an old pant pocket. I want to talk to someone but I have no one to talk to. I pace for a few minutes with my hands on my temples like actors do when they look like they're thinking, and surprisingly, it works. A thought appears like doves under a magician's hat: boom. I start dialing numbers randomly, letting my fingers move wildly around the pad just to see what happens, like I did in the old days, but then I realize what I'm doing and hang up. It feels wrong now. Fake. The phone rings again. Maybe it's star 69 and he's called me back, thinking I'm someone important trying to reach them, but when I answer, the reception is bad. I can't hear him.

I am running around my living room screaming into the phone, 'Hello?' and 'Speak up!' I am jumping over couches, saying, 'I can't hear you!' I panic and jump off the couch but trip on my way down and I fall, smack, on the ground so hard it's like I jumped from the apartment above me. And the phone is now sliding across the room with momentum from the crash and I can hear his voice but it's getting more and more faint until all I can hear is the sound of the line going dead.

I lay there limply for a while, a dead fish in a room with harsh lighting, under inspection like a mental patient. I can't even lift my hands or face off the ground, so I let my cheeks rest fully, feeling the wooden panels. They are cooler than my feet have relayed in the past. I am embarrassed I called a stranger, embarrassed I'm not growing up. I really just wanted to call Hans.

My mother comes into the room and rushes over to me in horror. 'Tabby!' she screams, thinking I'm dead. 'Tabby, what's wrong, baby? Tabby!!!!!'

'I'm okay, Mom,' I say, surprised she had such a violent reaction. It takes me a moment to process her interest and response, as usually she'd just pass by and say, 'Stop feeling sorry for yourself and get off the floor.'

Instead of pulling me up, she gets down with me. Both of us on the floor, side by side, and for the first time she doesn't give me advice, or tell me an anecdote of her time as a Playboy bunny or a whale watcher, or someone who shagged Tom Jones in the sixties. She just lays with me in silence. The sounds of our chests rising with hope and falling with loss.

'Mom,' I say, unable to look at her. 'Are you happy?'

'Happy?' she says. 'I don't know how to define that word anymore but I'm damn well trying.' I turn over so we are both looking up at the ceiling together, silent and pensive and sur-rendered.

'I thought lions were happy but sometimes they just got lost, so they made friends with a bunch of sheep until one day, they were so used to being around sheep that they forgot who they were. I thought after Dad left that you forgot you were a lion.'

She laughs and reaches out to grab my hand, to let me know we're fraught with this disease of incurable romanticism together. Together, fucked by genetics.

'I saw Dad the other day,' I tell her. 'It was hard to see him, but harder to hear what he said. That you were too much to handle. Maybe we're both too much to take on because we want it all. We want fun and romance all the time. Maybe that's impossible.'

'He's probably right,' she tells me. I'm shocked, because she says it like she's known this whole time. 'It might be impos-sible, but I am what I am. He was who he was. Square peg, round hole.'

'But did you learn from it?' I ask. 'Didn't it change you?'

'I learned that it's not easy. That you have to be accomo-dating but also find someone who gets you. You can't be with someone who wants you to change. We all have things to work on, to improve upon, but we are who we are. I might be crazy. I might be impossible, but if I dampen what keeps me going, then I've lost who I am. If I get someone being another person, then that's not what I'm looking for. Eventually, it won't work. You have to just think of what you've learned from each thing and be grateful for it,' she says, 'even when it's hurt you. Anytime you get sad, just remember you're a piece of stardust. You're nothing and you're everything.'

'What do you mean?'

'If you listen to the good stuff, then it means you have to also listen to the bad stuff. You just keep living, knowing there's good and bad but you pick up neither. I heard Maya Angelou say that once when she was asked about being an idol and receiving praise. And if you realize we're just vessels through which breath comes in and comes out, we're no different from this wood here,' she stops to knock on the floor, lets the ring reverberate through us. 'That wood used to be alive once. It used to breathe like us, so look how lucky we are. You can't take all these rejections personally. You and I, we're not your average woman. Men are just big babies. They can't handle us.'

'But that's also kind of unfair to them, don't you think? I mean, it's impossible to expect that life is going to be as good as our dreams. To live a lackluster life, to be married to someone who you think is just okay, to have a career your whole life that resembles nothing of your personality, that's reality. Expecting it not to be is just a slow death.'

'I raised you to be an independent thinker, to "be the one who loves the less" so you stay in control but I also let you be

free because I can't imagine anything worse than being con-
strained.'

'That's so confusing, Mom!' I scream. 'They're polar oppo-
sites!'

'I just didn't want to quiet your spirit. My mother did that
to me and it made me even more wild than I already was. As
far as dating is concerned, of course, you have to put in the
effort yourself, as I've always told you, because *you're* the
fighter. You have to make yourself happy. But you also need to
find someone who wants to jump in the car for the ride. And
when it doesn't work out, you have to keep your head up high.
What's one good thing you learned from this . . . what's his
name . . . Hans?'

'That a man will run me a bath and bring me coffee without
me having to ask for it.'

'Good! You see? He did what you'd want without even
asking for it. So use that in the future. Be in control but also
surrender enough to trust the universe to let the magic
happen!' There she goes again, being confusing. 'You learn
from them, you find something they taught you, you grow and
stop doing the stupid shit that ruined the last one and just
remind yourself that the best stuff is still coming.'

This is all getting a bit too earthy even for me, but her
words, like Dorothy Parker's all those years ago, sink in and
get comfy, creating a bed, a home, and for the first time
maybe I think Parker was right. Maybe you have to protect

yourself. It makes me sick because I know it's true; I know where I get it from and for the first time I realize there might not be a cure for it, this insatiable need to love and be loved in the way you know it should be, it can be. And just as there's no cure for curiosity, there's no cure for optimism. I realize in that moment my mom and I are just a couple of Heraldas, trying to fit into a place we don't know how to be a part of, lost spirits in a physical world. But just as I think she's getting soft, opening up, she starts looking around the room in panic.

'I can't find my socks,' she says. At first it's always quite calm, then as the rush of losing something rises, her eyes bolt around the room. And that's when it hits me, here on the ground, as I lie depressed and hopeless, unable to feel the outline of that lion I've been hanging on to. As my mom searches for her socks that surely are just in her coat pocket, I realize I too have been searching for something that's probably not lost. I move my head around on the ground, just to feel where I am, to feel the wooden boards under me, to locate some spine or splinter of a foundation. The same floor on which I once felt I know everything was now reminding me I know nothing. Not understanding my mother, my world, myself was like having a wound I couldn't see. I wanted to believe it was superficial because then I could heal it, I would know where to put the bandage. But the deeper it is, the more impossible it is to know how to fix. I want to ask her why she's always given me terrible advice, but how can I? I did the same to Mary. Not because I was trying to trick her, feed her intangibles, make her believe in unicorns, but because I wanted to believe it too. My mom and I, we were living the life we wanted to believe existed, despite knowing deep down it probably wasn't real.

My mother was flipping from paralytically romantic and hopeful to jaded and indifferent, like a beached whale. She still had life in her, she still had fight, but with each breath she was dying. I had always assumed her sadness was because she'd been around men who didn't get her. That's why I'd fought so hard to prove to her that a man who'd love her the way she was loved in her dreams was out there, just around the corner. But now that I know it's because it was us, being unrealistic, impossible, unlovable, I can see that being cynical wasn't just a protective measure against being hurt, it was the whale knowing it can't un-beach itself.

We must have fallen asleep on the floor because I woke up frantic, knowing I should be somewhere but having no idea not only where I was, but where I was meant to be. This happens to me pretty much every day.

My mom and I jump up off the floor, both in equally confused and unsubstantiated distress, puff our hair and squeeze our cheeks to get the life back in them.

'Oh, track and field!' I scream, feeling terrible I might be late for no other reason than my self-pity.

'Is that a new swear word?' my mother asks.

'Mary and Randall have their track and field day today! Shit! I can't believe I'm late. I promised I'd be there to cheer them on,' I say as I move in circles, looking for my bag and jacket. 'I'll see you back at the house in a little bit. Love you, Mom. That was good before.'

'I'm coming with you,' she declares. 'You're in no state to be alone!'

By the time we reach the school, I realize we're not late at all. Well, it's just about to start but we haven't missed it. There are lots of makeshift referees (a.k.a. parents) and whistles and bright colors and flags and busy bodies and orange cones. Dragging my mom across the field is near impossible, so I eventually have to grab her arm so she doesn't get too distracted by literally anything she walks past or spots in the distance. She needs a leash.

'Why are we here?' my mom asks for the fourth time.

'To support Mary and Randall,' I say, shaking my head. 'And even if Mary weren't here, I'd want to come for Randall. I doubt his foster parents are coming so I wanted to be here for him.'

I see Mary on the field next to the principal and hope she isn't telling her anything about the Rastafarian that may jeopardize my freedom. As we walk towards her, a few kids stop to look at us like we're a couple of intruding zebras. I'm so riled up with the track and field spirit it's hard not to want to chest bump Mary when she runs over to us.

'Auntie Tabby! Grammy!' Mary screams, hugging my leg with one hand while the other grasps my mother's frailer limb.

'Hey, you adorable little athlete!' I say as she blushes, exercising that fake coy technique I showed her ages ago. 'You're going to kick some serious ass out there.'

'Yeah!' she yells out.

'Where's Randall?' I ask.

'Oh I see him,' my mother says. 'He's over there.' She points to the other side of the field and I see Randall just as he spots me. His eyes light up as he waves.

Their teachers start to call for them to get ready in line. All the kids are haphazardly organized into teams based on age and grade. It's an elementary school track and field so the kindergarteners are segregated to a smaller, more controlled area so five- and six-year-olds don't start running rampant into other lanes.

Randall organizes himself behind the start line as the referees try to align the other kids and Mary shuffles her feet next to him. I don't know if she even understands that this is a race because she keeps looking around, distracted.

'Come on, Mary and Randall!' I call out, hands around my mouth like a speaker. 'Beat the system! Give it all you got!' Then as I look across the field I see a kid staring at me. He's probably sixteen years old or so, chubby, rough looking, shaved head. He's sending me a look of utter disgust. When I look back to the kids, upon their imminent start, I see Randall's face drop at the sight of the kid across from me. The boy's look is sullen, jowls too droopy for his age.

'Randall, there's that whore you're always talking about,' the boy yells out, audible for everyone to hear. Parents gasp and some kids chuckle and point towards me.

'Excuse me?' I ask, flustered.

'You're just some crazy-ass bitch.'

Randall's face goes beat red, nostrils flaring.

The referee shoots the start gun as everyone around me stands frozen, shocked. Confused. Kids start running down their lanes but Randall takes off diagonally across the field, dodging others as he charges towards the boy and in one supremely elegant and seamless movement he kicks him right in the balls.

Everyone along the sidelines is silent as we wait for a reaction. Then, as expected, the screaming pours out.

'Ahhhhh!!!!!!' the kid shrieks as Randall just stands in front of him. The boy falls in incremental measures, like an accordion, to the ground; at first quite slowly and then all at once, hands cupping his groin.

The principal marches furiously towards Randall, who's staring over the boy he just flattened, surprised by his own strength. She grabs him by the skin on the back of his neck as if he is a disobedient puppy and drags him off silently as mouths remain agape. I run over to Randall, screaming after him.

353

The principal shoots me a stare. 'He's on a time out.'

'But he was just standing up for me!' I beg as I race over to them. I grab Randall and hug him and hug him and hug him until I fear I've cut off his circulation. When I pull back I see he's looking down, those long gorgeous eyelashes rimming his view of the floor. I lift his face up with my hand and look him in his cowering eyes because I need him to know he's done nothing to be ashamed of. He stood up for me; the one thing I didn't know I've always wanted someone to do. My little fighter.

'Thank you, Randall,' I whisper. I ruffle the hair on his head affectionately and hug him again because I've never felt so loved in all my life. 'Who was that kid, anyway? Do you know him?'

'He's my foster brother.'

'And you told him about me?'

'I told him you have funny stories.'

'How did you learn to kick like that?'

'Milk. He told me to look out for you.'

'Really? Why would he tell you to do that?'

'Don't you get it, you moron?' he says, an adult in a little body. 'Milk loves you.' And it hits me. Milk's been the one behind the scenes the whole time, standing up for me both in front of me and without me seeing it for all these years. I've just been too stupid to realize it until now. 'He taught me when you went to that party with your mom and sister. He wanted me to know how to fight for someone I loved.'

The boy, who apparently is named Kyle, whimpers off to the nurse's office as the principal warns Randall about the repercussions of violence. We wait for Mary to finish the race – she came fifteenth out of twenty, sweet thing, but she doesn't seem to care – and pile out of there as fast as we can. The games are still going on but Mary seems content with any excuse to leave. On our way home, we're all silent. We drop Randall off at his house and I give him one more hug until his hands lose their grip. I walk him in while my mom and Mary stay sat in the car.

'He did so well today!' I say as his dad opens the door, completely omitting his disqualification, but I get no interest in return. It's hard to leave Randall here but I know I have no other choice. He pats him on the shoulder and says, 'Good job, buddy. Go wash your hands before dinner.' I stop him just before he closes the door.

'So . . . Kyle?'

'What about him? Did he start some shit again?'

I want to ask him so many questions but know it isn't my place. There's so many stories behind these doors I can't even begin to try to unravel and I might do more damage than good if I do. All I can do is make sure Randall's okay and be here for him.

'I don't know where he is now and I'm sure he's fine, but he wasn't feeling too well so he went to the nurse's office at their school. I just didn't want you to worry if he's late coming home.' I look at Randall and send him a wink. He catches it without a blink, smiles and waves goodbye.

Doors close; engine's on; seatbelts buckle.

Milk! I can't wait to get back; each second, each block too long. I look at my mom in the car and see that she will never change, and even if she doesn't, she'll be just fine. We both will.

The minute we pull into the driveway, I jump out of the car and run to Milk's house, hoping he's home. I see him in his living room on the treadmill, running with headphones on. I start yelling his name to get his attention but he can't hear me so I bolt into the house and charge towards him.

I run up behind the treadmill and reach my hand out to grab him, anxious to talk now that I've woken up from this thirty-year slumber. When I touch him he freaks out and jumps, flicking his iPod headphones out of his ears as if a swarm of bees is attacking him. His wild movements throw him off the machine. He falls back onto me and we both start screaming.

'Ahhh!' he's screaming.

'Ahhh!' I'm still screaming as he rolls off of me. Still frightened.

'What the hell, Tabby?' he yells. 'You freaked me out!'

'I'm so sorry!' I scream as I, subconsciously, pounce on top of him. I'm straddling him now as he lies frazzled on the floor, iPod thrown somewhere off in the distance. 'You love me!' I yell, because we are both yelling and the release of all this warranted tension feels amazing.

He puts his head back down on the floor and laughs, reaching his arms behind his head.

I'm smiling and hugging him, still on top. 'But can you move over?' he asks. 'You're on my ribs. I can't breathe.' K-Ci and Jojo's 'All My Life' is playing loudly from his headphones, setting the scene.

'Who works out to K-Ci and Jojo?' I ask.

'I do, apparently.' He touches my hair. 'You look great,' he says, smiling at me in the way he's always done. 'I love it when your hair is all messed up like that. I don't know why but it makes me happy.'

It's a strange feeling when you can feel yourself, when you can feel every cell in your body.

'What you did for Randall, teaching him how to stand up for someone,' I start, unable to really get the words out.

He doesn't have to say anything so he doesn't. All he does is reach out for me. I thought he'd be more awkward but he hugs me so softly, my face resting perfectly on his chest. I didn't feel I had to make up stories, or imagine a best-case scenario, I just let us be there. All this time, Milk's been right in front of me but I was too close to see him clearly. A level of calm, not feeling a need to fill the gaps, blankets us.

357

'But you think I'm crazy,' I say as I pull back. 'You must, I mean, you've seen me do the most ridiculous things, you've seen me have food poisoning, seduce blind men, and embarrass myself. You've seen too much in all these years, I figured you'd be grossed out. And, even though I just kept doing the stupidest things, you never told me not to.'

'It's what makes you so fascinating. I wouldn't want you to change.'

'You know, for so long I ruled you out because of that prom moment and because I thought the reason my dad left was because he was having an affair with your mom. I thought that was why he kept going over here. I didn't realize that their friendship, the fact that your family was his safe haven, was what you were trying to tell me, you know, when I came to your ju-jitsu school. That it wasn't about taking sides, or being against my mother. It wasn't about any of that. I couldn't get it then. I couldn't see it.'

He keeps his stare on me. Quiet.

'Say something! You're so quiet,' I say.

'I'm taking it all in.'

'Okay,' I say, returning the smile. Realizing silence can be okay sometimes. 'And the reason why you took me to my dad, it was because you wanted me to see for myself what really happened so it wouldn't happen to me?'

He nodded.

'But what about your date?' I ask, the machine still running in the background.

'Well, hey, she wasn't you.'

If I were standing up, my knees would buckle like Delina's do when she stands in heels too long. Good thing I'm sitting down.

'So you knew all this time we were going to end up together?'

'I've been hoping,' he says. 'But you're a hard one to wrangle.'

My eyes light up. 'Like a slippery, elusive salmon trying to swim upstream?' I ask him, because I know all too well what it's like to swim against the current. Hopeful.

'Um . . .' He laughs. 'Sure. Yeah, I guess you could say that.'

All I can do is ogle at him. Every now and then I forget to breathe and take in a deep breath. When I look over to my house, the lights are all on, and I see Mary and my mother looking at us from the window, smiling. I can finally see my mother clearly.

'Are you going to kiss me now or what?' I ask. Wondering how this works.

'Well, give me a second to find a less contrived moment,' he says, kidding; the fact we are still on the floor is evidence enough of spontaneity. You'd never plan a fall!

'Good!' I yelp. 'I hate contrived!' I pause. Wait. 'Well, I mean, we could—'

'I kind of always thought of kissing you in a supermarket, around the fresh fruit section when you were picking out cantaloupes or watermelons,' he indulges me. 'I'd stop you while you were telling me a story and turn you around and kiss you. The fruit would dislodge and we'd be making out while those bowling balls of fruit would fall, one at a time until the stand fell over, melons rolling out in all directions.'

'And do we fall over? Do we trip?'

'Yeah,' he says.

'You'd think we'd see it coming, maybe move to another section or something, but we don't because we're so happy. It's our spot?'

'Yeah. But sometimes we go to the freezer section to mix things up.'

'Does this happen every time we go shopping?'

'Yeah,' he smiles. 'Every time.'

Acknowledgements

Had *The Optimist* not ended up in the hands of a long list of incredibly kind and supportive people, I fear it would have become a very different book. In particular, had I not serendipitously walked into The Society Club – a place that would soon become a world of inspiration to me on every level – my story and the characters in it would have had another evolution. The Society Club taught me, through the people who filled the room and the beautiful books that lined its shelves, how to live richly and curiously no matter how broke I felt.

Thank you to the ever-magnetic Babette Kulik, for her magic, wisdom and guidance. I am forever grateful to my agent Carrie Kania, who I first met on that fateful night at the club, for encouraging me to write this novel and for steering me every step of the way with her experience, and for talking me off the ledge every now and then with her confidence, steadiness and practicality.

John Mitchinson, the greatest, thank you for being an unshakable champion of this book from the very beginning. To Rachael Kerr, the best editor I could ever imagine working with, for your expertise, your insight, your incredible skill. This novel is entirely better because of you. To the miraculous patience and attention to detail of Anna Simpson, who kept me sane (almost) and comforted me throughout the production process, and to Amy Winchester for her enthusiasm and belief in Tabitha and what this book is about. And a huge thank you to the entire team at Unbound who helped to bring *The Optimist* to life in the most effortless way.

I must also thank Stephen Cooper and David Holub, who saw the potential in Tabitha in her first outing in *The Gymnast*, which was published in *Kugelmass: A Journal of Literary Humor* in 2013. As well as the amazing Amy Ephron for her early read of the book, and Chris Keith-Wright, for his constant reassurance, help and kindness.

Everyone who pledged their support via Unbound, including the unbelievable generosity of Steve and Leslie Carlson, Olivia and John Easterling, Danny O'Donoghue, Lene Bausager and Joanna Dudderidge.

Lastly, of course, to all my cherished friends and family. My brother, my nana, and my mum and dad. Thank you for pushing me to remain optimistic even when I wavered.

Supporters

Unbound is a new kind of publishing house. Our books are funded directly by readers. This was a very popular idea during the late eighteenth and early nineteenth centuries. Now we have revived it for the internet age. It allows authors to write the books they really want to write and readers to support the books they would most like to see published.

The names listed below are of readers who have pledged their support and made this book happen. If you'd like to join them, visit www.unbound.com.

Kristen Alpaugh

Shannon Alton

Kaye Wilson Andrews

Lail Arad

William Austen

Michelle Bakva

Nicole Bakva

Lynn Barrie

Doug Beatty

Gabriel Benjamin

Olivia Benson

Robert Bentley

Bob & Addie Berman

Florence Bertinotti

Jean Pierre & Sabine
    Bertinotti

Donna Blake

Aaron Bleyaert

Anne Bliss

Hannah Bliss

Janet Bortoli

Maggie Britton

Priscilla Camelo

Will Caradoc-Hodgkins

Kristen Carlson

Steve and Leslie Carlson

Craig Carroll

Teresa Carter

Heather Case

Nicole Chabre

In-Sook Chappell

Nick Chetwynd-Talbot

Lisen Ydse Christiansen

Giovanni Cianci

Patty Colora

Cristina Covblic

Paul Daignault

Natalie De Luna

Gillian Deck

Ariana Dedianko

The DiFonzos

Slater Dixon

Simon Douglas

Joanna Dudderidge

Ilan Eshkeri

Andrew Faris

Stephanie Farrar

Andrew Fingret

Kali Fontecchio

Margaret Frame

Val Frampton

Zoe Frampton

David Frank

Douglas Freund

Kate freund

Zoe Gillis

Joan Golden

Solomon Golding

Andrew Gould

Benjamin Greenspan

Deb Groves

CiCi Hankey

Anna Harari

Stella Harding

Alicia Harris

Tops Henderson

Cassidy Hughes

KD Hughes

Linda Ilsley

Alexandria Jackson

Andrew Janss

Danny Jelinek

Judy Jones

Erin Karr

Chris Keith-Wright

Jen Kelly

Autumn Kerr

Dan Kieran

Michael Killeen

Alma Kipner

Harrison Kipner

Hayley Knapp

Babette Kulik

Bénédicte Lack-Jacquet

Jonathan Laird

Sarah Lambert

Colin Landis

James Landry

Max Levy

Paul Lisberg

Alec Lytle

Terrie Marroquin

Brenda Mcarthur

Alden McDaniel

Stephanie McIntosh

Lauren Merage

Violeta Meyners

John Mitchinson

Charles Morgan

Amy Murray

Carlo Navato

Olivia Newton-John

Catherine Nieves

Andy O'Neil

Siboney O'Neil

George Packe-Drury-Lowe

Andrew & Charlene
   Papastephanou

Mick Patterson

Elizabeth Pelly

Jennifer Pierce

Maya Pizzati

Jaclyn Pollack

Justin Pollard

Donna Prizgintas

Mande Raiher

Damien Read

Lisa Reiling

Alexandra Rembac

Paul Rice

Michelle Rosato

Kate Rothwell

Danny Rowley
Shannon Schnurr
Jeremy Shawn
Lisa Sheldon
Elliot Shiel
Lisa, Andy, Elliot and
   Annabel Shiel
Samantha Shiener
Tamara Shiener
Angad Singh
William Skeaping
Rhiannon Skyrme
Sheila Smyth
Rick Sorkin
Daniel Stein
Evan Stein
Nina Stein
Tracy Stent
Jordan Stephens
Meredith Swanson
Harumi Takata
Jen Tank
Scottie Thompson
Paul Tompsett
Laura Toolan
James Tovell

Laura Tovell
Zoe Tyrrell
Cara Usher
Thomas van Straubenzee
Mariana Saori Wall
Amanda Weir
Debra Weir
Steve Weir
Zachary Weiss
Emma Wilkins
Julie Williams
Jacky Winter
Alexandre Xavier
John Zambetti